MW01099065

NORTHERN LIGHTS

Finding love in the heart of Alaska.

When New York CEO Renzo Gallini shows up with papers saying he owns the waystation Jess lives and breathes for, she laughs in his face. But things get tense when he's got the paperwork to prove it...and her father, who apparently signed her home away, is nowhere to be found.

Alaskan native Jess Jenkins has lived most of her life at Last Chance Camp, a man's world where femininity is relegated to wisps of time behind closed doors. Yet she's proud of what they've built here. Last Chance is all she needs to be happy and no amber-eyed city-boy will convince her otherwise.

Ren left New York on his mother's foolish errand, to turn an Alaskan truck stop into a vacation destination. He finds little of merit in the wide spot in the road until the small community, led by a fiercely loyal tomboy, shows him there's more to Alaska than just ruts in the road. That survival depends not just on good planning, but on each other. And love can be found in places where you least expect it.

NORTHERN LIGHTS

By Laurie Ryan

This book is a work of fiction. Names, characters, places, opinions, and incidents are either the product of the author's imagination or are used fictionally. Any resemblance to actual persons, living or dead, or to actual events is entirely coincidental.

www.laurieryanauthor.com

DEDICATION

To Alaska, for making me fall in love.

Prologue

Owen Jenkins was torn like he'd never been before. In the Fairbanks airport, waiting for his plane, he clutched the new cell phone tight in his hand. He wanted desperately to make the call, to tell his daughter what he'd done.

He'd set things in motion that would turn her life upside down. Granted, it was for a very good reason, but she wouldn't see it that way. He loved his daughter more than life and only wanted her to be happy. But she was stubborn. Got that from him. Which was why he'd come up with this idea. Why he was forcing her hand.

He had to hold onto the hope that she'd eventually forgive him.

Owen scrubbed at his clean shaven jaw, still wondering if he should call and tell her. He'd never lied to her before. Somewhere in her life, she'd come to hate lies and he'd honored that.

Technically, he wasn't lying now. But she would probably not see it that way. He pulled up her number on the phone, staring at it as his flight was announced.

He wouldn't call her. He couldn't. He'd promised. Owen joined the throng waiting to board, still torn. Once in his seat, he fought his sense of right one more time before shutting the phone down and stuffing it in his backpack. He couldn't stop things now anyhow.

And she'd find out soon enough what he'd done.

Chapter One

Jess Jenkins dealt with complications on a regular basis. When home was a truck stop in Nowhere, Alaska, they came with the territory. Today, however, those complications seemed bent on finding the breaking point of her patience. It was as if the machinery had gone on strike. First, the coffeemaker sprang a leak, then the commercial dryer conked out. With a busload of tourists due in—she glanced at her watch—less than an hour, she had no time left for fixing broken equipment. And her computer seemed to sense her mood. It wouldn't bring up the latest weather forecast. The satellite must be in cantankerous mode...again.

She smacked the side of the monitor and leaned her elbows on a desk overrun with paperwork and equipment manuals and rubbed her forehead. Just one more problem. That's all it would take for her to scream.

"Uh, boss?"

Jess's straight, dark hair, a gift from her Alaskan mother, swung as she turned to glare at the young man standing in the doorway of her office. Rocky Thompson was her junior by only a couple years. Being lanky and long-limbed, coupled with sandy blond hair cut in some eye-covering modern style, made him appear much younger than twenty-two. He'd been working for them for a couple years now and had quickly become a pseudo-brother to her.

"What?" She recognized the terseness in her voice and made an effort to regroup. "Sorry. Bad day. What's up?"

"Well, uh, I kind of hate to mention this, but..."

An urge to pummel something grew until Jess hid her clenched hands under the desk. "Spit it out, Rocky."

"The plumbing's gone south again."

"Over at the inn?"

"Yep."

He looked as if he would split and run if she so much as twitched. Did she really appear that menacing? Forcing herself to relax, Jess tried to smile at the absurdity of her day. The change in her attitude worked on Rocky. He relaxed against the door jam, shoving his hands into the pockets of jeans with more holes than the current trends allowed as acceptable. Jess reached for her to-do list and wrote down *order jeans-Rocky*, rolling her eyes. He wouldn't think to buy them on his own.

"Did you shut the water off?" she asked.

"Yep."

"Has John taken a look at it?" Now that they'd let the seasonal help go, John and Mary Martin, along with Rocky, helped maintain the place, although John was getting up in years, as his wife reminded everyone on a regular basis.

Rocky nodded. "Said it was beyond him and needed the boss's talents, since you designed the system."

"Okay. I'll be over there in a bit. Is everything else done? Are the rooms ready?"

"Close. Another load out of the dryer and the last of the beds will be made up."

Jess sent a quick prayer skyward that her jury-rigged fix would keep the dryer working. They were so close to the end of the adventuring-tourist season. If they could just make it through a few more days, she'd have time to fix things properly over the long, dark winter.

"Okay," she answered Rocky. "Thanks. Tell John I'll check on the plumbing, then you can go see if Mary needs help with food prep."

The salute he tossed her way as he left made her smile. Offering Rocky a job and bringing him to Last Chance Camp had been a good idea. A spontaneous one, but he'd proven himself a hard worker again and again, and was an integral part of their Last Chance family.

A family missing it's patriarch. Jess glanced over at the photo close to being shoved off her desk by paperwork. She steadied it, and her fingers lingered on the image of her father. A tourist had emailed it to her last year. Owen Jenkins stood on the restaurant's porch, greeting a new batch of guests. That was the part of owning the camp he loved...socializing. It showed in the wide smile and sea-blue eyes that sparkled with pleasure.

Where are you, Dad? He had picked the worst possible time to go on one of his walkabouts. This place, both their livelihood and their home, needed him. Jess pushed off the desk and headed in search of her plumbing supplies.

She needed him.

Jess sighed, trying to slough off of the sixth sense that told her ill winds were about to blow in. If they were, there was nothing she could do about it until it happened. She settled her tool belt around her waist and glanced at her nails, rubbing the cuticles. They were in dire need of a manicure, which, as usual, would have to wait.

She paused on her way across the gravel lot to frown as a sleek black SUV with tinted windows drove into the camp. No rigs were due in today other than the tour bus.

Last Chance was pretty much the only way station between Fairbanks and the oil fields, and no one drove here without a plan. Not this time of year. She looked up at a sky that had the smell of snow. The first of the season would be here soon, and she still had a lot to do before it hit. With another glance at the parking area, Jess headed for the inn. If the folks in that SUV had driven up here on a whim, they didn't have much sense, and she had no time to knock it into them.

"My mother must be out of her mind." Standing outside his car, Renzo Gallini turned a full three-hundred-and-sixty degrees. "What the devil could she possibly see in a place like this?"

Last Chance Camp, the newest property his mother seemed bent on acquiring, lay spread out around him. A few buildings plunked down in the middle of nowhere, surrounded by the color of dull with a splash of yellow.

He turned again, a critical eye scanning the wide stretch of gravel that served as both an informal parking lot and building access. One structure stood out on the opposite side. As near as he could tell, it was a building. It looked like five or six generic white cargo containers had been laid end-to-end, with a porch added to the front for effect. A sign hung from the railing that indicated it was an inn of some sort.

Someone marched across the compound wearing a tool belt. The jeans, work boots, flannel shirt, and ball cap all said male. Hips that swayed in a distinctly un-masculine way said something quite different, and Ren paused a moment to appreciate the movement. Whoever the woman was, she walked with an assurance and grace that, even from this distance, stirred a long-suppressed need inside him.

She disappeared inside the inn and Ren wondered for a moment what she looked like. Shaking his head, he refocused on his mother's foolish errand. He had firsthand knowledge of the aggravation involved when business got mixed up with pleasure. Hence the lengthy, self-imposed celibacy.

Turning away, Ren leaned a hand on his rented GMC Yukon, then brushed his hand off. Over two hundred miles of dirt and grit covered the SUV. His mother insisted this backwater camp was salvageable. Since he was in charge of acquisitions for the family business, she'd tasked him with personally checking it out.

He should have flown. He'd intended to, if only to gain some distance from the women in his life. Between his mother's pointed remarks about wanting grandchildren and Kathryn, his company's human resource director and sometimes date, indicating her willingness to fulfill his mother's desire, Ren spent most of his time dodging the decision they were both bent on pushing him into. So Ren had hopped a plane from New York with more speed than normal. In Fairbanks, where he'd intended to charter a plane to get to Last Chance Camp. Instead, he'd given into an unusual restlessness and headed north by car. Six hours and a whole lot of dirt later, he was well inside the Arctic Circle and wondering what the hell he'd signed up for.

Pulling his leather jacket closed to ward off the cold, Ren glanced around again. This had to be some sort of colossal joke, but he didn't feel much like laughing.

Nothing he saw seemed worth salvaging. He cocked his head from side to side, stretching neck muscles tight from too many hours behind the wheel. Tomorrow, he'd call and give Mother his assessment and she'd see the error of her ways. For tonight, he needed a stiff drink and a comfortable bed, something he doubted he could find in a truck stop in the middle of nowhere.

Ren headed for the nearest building, pulling up short as he passed a truck well beyond its prime with what appeared to be a dead caribou casually laid across the hood. He stared at the lifeless eyes and wondered what episode of *The Twilight Zone* his mother had thrust him into. Shaking his head, he climbed the few steps to a porch that, like everything else here, had seen better days, and opened the door.

Inside the restaurant, mouth-watering aromas assailed him, and his stomach did a very un-gentlemanly grumble. Ren sniffed and realized it wasn't just food he smelled. There was coffee. Even if it was drip-brewed, the caffeine would be the jolt his body needed to dispel the nightmare he'd driven into.

A portly woman walked by with a tray of dirty dishes, her salt and pepper braid trailing all the way down her back. She glanced his way, curiosity peeking out from behind warm eyes, but didn't stop.

"Excuse me," Ren said.

Without breaking stride, she spoke over her shoulder. "Grab whatever grub you want, then pay on the way out."

"I'd like a cup—"

He was too late. She'd disappeared into what must be the kitchen. Ren investigated and found the commercial coffeemaker. He picked up an ivory mug that had a network of cracks covering its surface and was gratified to find the inside clean, at least in appearance. The coffee he poured was dark and aromatic. With an appreciative sniff, Ren smiled. He could tell this brew packed a caffeine punch he would appreciate. He sniffed again. Nothing beat the strong scent of good coffee.

Cradling the cup in both hands, he searched out the woman he'd seen earlier. He found her in the kitchen, brandishing a spatula like some sort of weapon.

"Employees only back here. Food's out that way." She waved at the doorway he'd just come through. Ren imagined the gravel in her voice and that brusque manner fit in well with life here.

"I'm looking for the proprietor."

"The...what?" She stared at him.

He sighed. "The owner?"

"I know what a proprietor is, mister." She waved the spatula again. "Don't get smart with me. I just haven't heard that word around these parts in, well—" She shrugged. "Heck, I don't think I've ever heard that word used here."

Starting to lose patience, Ren drew a breath and tried the smile that usually got him what he wanted. Only it didn't disarm the woman. In fact, she raised the spatula even higher.

The absurdity of Ren's day caught up with him, and he chuckled. When the cook's lips quirked up, his chuckle turned into a full-on, long, hard laugh. He damn near had to wipe his eyes dry.

"My apologies, ma'am," he said. "I can only claim that

it's been a very long day. I'd dearly love to complete my business and be done with it, but I'm looking for the owner of this camp. Would you know where I can find him?"

She set the spatula down, and he could see the effort she made to keep the grin off her face. "That would be Owen Jenkins."

Ren waited for more information, but none was forthcoming. Apparently, no one here liked to talk. He shook his head. "And I can find him where?"

She shrugged. "He's not in camp at the moment."

As his humor faded, Ren vowed to have a long talk with his mother about wild goose chases. "All right. Who takes charge in his absence?"

The woman stared him down for a long moment. "That would be Jess."

"Fine. And where might I find him?"

"Since a busload of sky-watchers are about to show up, I'm guessing Jess will be makin' sure everything's ready over at the inn."

"The inn, which is...on the other side of the lot?" Ren could hold eye contact longer than anyone he knew. He refused to flinch first.

Finally, she looked down briefly, then waved the spatula, indicating the door behind him. "Yes."

"Thank you—" Ren let the question intentionally hang until the woman responded.

"Mary."

He grinned. "Thank you, Mary. That wasn't so hard, was it?"

When the spatula in her hand started tapping on the counter, Ren decided retreat was the best option. With a stop to refill his coffee, he headed outside. The blast of cold momentarily stripped the breath from his lungs. Leather clearly was not warm enough for this climate. He pulled the jacket tighter in a futile effort to ward off the chill.

The walk across to the "inn" seemed to take forever. It was probably only a couple hundred yards, but felt like a mile in the mid-October weather. White puffs of breath led the way as he clutched both jacket and mug in an effort to hoard as much warmth as possible.

He tromped up stairs that didn't budge or creak. Once inside, he shut the door against the cold, looked around, and saw little in the way of welcoming. Things looked no better than on the outside. Indoor-outdoor carpet, in a shade he expected was called something akin to beaver-skin brown, looked a little threadbare. Paneling straight out of the seventies covered the walls. There were no tables or chairs, just a small mantle along one side that sported a steno notebook with "Lights/Wake Up" written at the top. Underneath were a few names and what he surmised were room numbers. Good grief. Was this their wake-up call system?

Ren shook his head and set his mug on the mantle, after one last sip. So far, the only thing he'd found of any merit here was the coffee. He needed to find this guy, Jess, say what he'd come to say, and get the hell out of here.

"Damn it all to hell. Budge, you crotchety old bucket of bolts!"

He couldn't quite tell if the voice was male or female, but since it was the only sound he'd heard since entering, Ren followed it down one of the long corridors. Used to upscale hotels with expansive hallways, this one made him feel almost claustrophobic.

At the end, he turned to an open doorway and froze. The first thing he saw were the hips he'd admired earlier. They were encased in jeans molding a backside that teased his imagination more than any had in quite a while. When he saw the wisp of material that could only be a thong, he started to sweat as a long-denied libido struggled for dominance. A will not entirely his own nudged him forward for a better look. If the strap he saw was any indication, the thong was hot pink...and almost hidden underneath lumberjack's clothing.

Would her bra match?

That was the moment the pipe burst, spewing water in every direction. The perfectly shaped ass in front of him backed out of what appeared to be a plumbing room in a hurry, and straight into his arms. He grabbed hold as they were both propelled backward.

"Oof!"

His arms tightened around her midsection as the momentum slammed them into the wall and the breath whooshed out of him. Before he had a chance to regain his equilibrium, the woman was squirming.

"Let go of me!"

Ren released her and she yanked off the flannel shirt, then crawled back into the spray. He couldn't tell what she was doing, but it couldn't be easy, the way she was grunting and groaning.

"Hand me a wrench," she yelled.

He grabbed the wrench from the tool belt sitting on the floor and thrust it into the disembodied hand that snaked out from the spray of water.

After some more indistinguishable sounds, the spray lessened and then, finally, stopped. Ren swiped water off his face as she backed out of the room shaking her head and mumbling. "What a messed up day." She threw the wrench at the tool belt and glanced up.

Cocoa-brown eyes stared at Ren. She looked young, mid-twenties at the most. With skin that hinted at some native Alaskan heritage, a heart-shaped face, and hair the color of gleaming wet obsidian, she gave off wholesome beauty in waves.

When she sank down to sit with her back against the wall, Ren's mouth went dry. Years of honing skills for boardroom negotiations threatened to desert him as his jaw went slack. Her white t-shirt, soaked through, clung to curves that were only outdone by perfect round breasts encased in that hot pink bra he'd been thinking about. Nipples protesting the wet-cold held him spellbound. It took everything he had to yank his forgotten manners out of his back pocket and stop staring.

When he looked up, fire had replaced the warm cocoa in her eyes. She clutched her arms in front of her, and her face took on the contortions of a storm cloud as she gnashed her teeth.

Even her obvious anger couldn't completely quell the spark of need inside him. What the hell was happening that some wisp of a girl could affect him like this? More off-kilter than he'd ever been before, he cleared his throat, trying to dig up some saliva—and some intelligence—so he could speak.

He failed at both.

Jess Jenkins glared at the stranger in front of her and felt a cold permeate her that had nothing to do with being soaked. She'd seen that hungry look in men's eyes before and all it meant was trouble. She didn't care how handsome the guy was...and he was smokin' hot, with those hypnotic amber eyes, the neatly-styled dark hair, and a day's stubble.

She steeled herself to go beyond the physical, because the expression on his face told her everything she needed to know. Even that last glimpse—confusion, maybe—had to be contrived. She'd lived in this camp her entire life and had seen a lot of comings and goings. Most of the regulars were good folk. It was the transients, some single, some not so much, that tried to push the limits. Those were the ones who would say anything to get what they wanted. This guy was no different. Ever since she'd grown boobs, she'd been hit on. Her frown deepened.

Well, she had no need for any guy ruled by his junk.

Jess struggled to get up using one arm. There was no way she'd pull the one that covered her chest. Where was her flannel? When she saw it, piled in a sodden heap on the floor, she swore. Now what was she going to do? Her trailer was back behind the restaurant and she couldn't cross the camp wet. She'd freeze before she reached it.

Sensing movement, she jerked back from the man who now stood with a leather jacket held out in front of him.

"If you live across the way, you'll never make it to dry clothes."

Jess eyed the jacket. "It's wet."

He shrugged. "It's better than nothing."

Searching for the ulterior motive in his gesture, she

couldn't find one. So Jess reached for the jacket. "What about you? How will you get across the way?"

He spread his arms. "I'm open to suggestions."

Jess found herself momentarily speechless as the wet Henley-style shirt clung to pecs that screamed regular workouts. When he smiled, any remaining chill switched to instant heat. Damn. Even the man's teeth were perfect. That smile could melt glaciers, and Jess tightened her arms over her chest. No matter how good looking he was, or how warm her body had begun to feel, she knew nothing about him. She needed to remember that.

His grin took on a bit of a cockeyed lift to it and she realized she'd been caught staring, so she yanked the jacket around her shoulders with one hand, feeling his lingering warmth.

"Have a little care with my coat, beautiful." His voice, low and inviting, warmed her further, damn it.

"I'll try to find you something to wear," she mumbled.

"No need. You can bring my jacket back to me or grab the duffle out of that filthy Yukon. I've got a change of clothes in there."

Good thing. She didn't think anyone who worked here wore a size that would cover those shoulders. He reached for her hand and a tingle slid up her arm and wound its way around her spinal column. He turned her palm up, placed keys in it, then folded her fingers over the keys. Was it her imagination or did it seem like he took his time at the task? She looked up and saw the smoldering smile still on his face. Her own face flamed red in response, and Jess did the only thing she could think of.

She ran.

Chapter Two

Even at a fast jog, Jess's teeth were chattering by the time she reached her trailer. The ground sparkled, already covered with the sheen of early frost. Alaska, especially inside the Arctic Circle, was known for frigid winters, but this year, the season seemed anxious to settle in before its time. Jess made a mental note to send for their winter food supply earlier than usual. The Dalton Highway, which ran between Fairbanks and Prudhoe Bay, closed rarely and never for long. But in Alaska, survival was still defined by how well one prepared.

She wanted to take her time changing so City Boy, whoever he was, could just sit and stew in his ardor, but the bus due in at any moment made delays problematic. With a muffled curse, Jess dried and bundled up in clean clothes. She stopped by the supply shed to grab pipe and anything else she'd need to fix the leak. That incoming bus had been on the road since early morning, and she knew folks would be coming in hungry and road weary. Things would deteriorate quickly if Last Chance Camp couldn't provide hot water for showers.

Halfway back to the inn, Jess stopped in her tracks, scowling as she thought about the soaked stranger waiting for her to return with dry clothes. Yanking his keys out of her pocket, she marched back to the SUV. Sticking her head inside, she paused at the whiff of cologne that was both earthy and sophisticated. She'd caught the same scent earlier, when she'd backed into him in the hallway. Jess grabbed the duffle, taking a moment to appreciate how clean and organized the man's SUV was. His map, paperwork, coffee mug, everything was neatly stacked and in its place. Perfect. Just like his smile. A shiver coursed through her, one she couldn't completely blame on the cold. Shaking it loose, she headed back to the inn and found him just inside the door.

He leaned casually against the wall, as if having a conversation while standing on carpet made damp by his own wet clothing was normal. In fact, he made the look sexy. As quickly as the thought popped into her head, Jess forced it to the back of her mind.

Tossing a towel, his still-wet leather coat, and his duffle at him, she crooked her head to the side. "All the rooms are booked, but there's a bath next to the pipe room you can change in. It's labeled. Just don't use the sinks until I get things fixed." She turned to go.

"Are you always this abrupt?"

A smoothness in his voice, one she was certain was meant to influence her, instead set her on edge. "Only when strangers try to cop a feel."

He held up his hands. "Incidental contact only." But the laughter in his eyes told her he'd enjoyed it altogether too much.

Just the memory of how he felt, all hard and...male, was enough to make her tingle. Worse, the hint of...vulnerability she'd seen in his face earlier threatened to undermine her belief that he was just like most men. His current smile belied the fact that he was anything other than a vulture, though. A smile meant to disarm, to drawn her in. Jess unbuttoned her coat. Was it warm in here?

Then she frowned. "Who are you, anyhow? I don't have any single travelers scheduled for arrival today, so you didn't make a reservation."

"You're right. I did not make a reservation." Now it was his turn to frown as he looked around. "Actually, I'm looking for the person in charge while the owner's away. Somebody named Jess."

"Why?"

"I have business with him."

"Well, if it's a him you're looking for, you're going to be searching for a long time." She stuck her thumbs in her waistband and stared up at him. "I'm Jess. What can I do for you?"

She had to give him credit. He registered only the barest hint of surprise and regrouped quickly, with only one raised eyebrow as any indication she'd caught him off guard. She enjoyed his fleeting shock. It almost made up for the man's arrogance.

"You can speak legally in relation to Last Chance Camp?"

She straightened. Who *was* this guy? "If you need something, I'm your person. You can either deal with me or wait until Owen gets back," she answered.

"When will that be?"

Jess shrugged her shoulders. "Don't know," she said.

"Don't know or won't tell?"

"He takes off once in a while. Sometimes he's back in a couple days, sometimes it's a week or two."

"How long has he been gone?"

"A couple days. Who are you, anyhow? And what do you want with Owen?"

He paused for a moment, then, as if making a decision, he held out his hand. "My name is Renzo Gallini. Ren, if you prefer. I have paperwork that shows Owen Jenkin's intent to sell Last Chance. My company will soon be the new owner of this," he looked around the entry they stood in, "inn."

Jess Jenkins stood still as stone for three breaths, then erupted in laughter. And she kept on laughing. It spilled out like a happy song and even threatened to infect him. He could feel the edges of his mouth trying to lift.

Ren wasn't sure what he'd expected in the way of reaction from this little spitfire, but this was definitely not it. He got the distinct impression that she held a very proprietary interest in this backwater facility and wouldn't see any humor in a change of ownership.

Several times she opened her mouth to speak, but the laughter bubbled into a frenzy again. When she finally regained control, she surprised him yet again by walking away. Jess headed down the hall, still chuckling. He heard the words "new owner" and renewed laughter followed it.

He watched her duck into the plumbing room. Picking up his duffle bag, he followed more slowly, trying to puzzle out her reaction. It was obvious she didn't believe him. But why? When he'd tried to talk his mother out of this folly, she had led him to believe it was pretty much a completed transaction. Yet Jess seemed to think the sale of Last Chance Camp was about as impossible as snow falling anywhere near the equatorial line. What stake did his mother have in this, anyhow? Ren shook his head. Something did not feel right here.

The bang of the main doors as the wind threw them open kept Ren from getting his answers. Jess stuck her head back through the doorway and they both watched a group of forty or so people crowd into the small entryway that served as the inn's main foyer. The time it took for them to all squeeze through the main doors mixed enough outdoor chill with indoor warmth that no one took their coats off right away.

She muttered something under her breath about unanswered prayers, wiped her hands on her jeans, and headed to greet the busload of tourists.

"Hi, everyone! Congratulations on making it through to Last Chance. How's the adventure gone so far?"

A young boy around the age of seven stepped forward. "We saw a bear. A big one." He held his arms open wide and growled, trying to mimic a bear's noise, and the crowd chuckled.

Jess squatted down in front of him. "Well, now, that's an excellent start to your trip. Not very many people get to see bears, so you must be very special."

"We're gonna see the lights," he said, pointing to his chest.

"Seeing the Northern Lights is never a sure thing, you know."

The boy's smile wavered as Jess's brightened.

"But things look favorable for tonight. I think—" she leaned toward the boy, "that the spirits want to come out and play."

Ren almost laughed out loud at the wide-eyed stare of the boy.

"Spirits?"

"Sure. My people believe that the Northern Lights are the spirits of our ancestors come out to play ball."

"Neat!" Ren watched as the boy pulled back and eyed her. "Hey, are you a Eskimo?"

When Jess Jenkins laughed, her long, straight ponytail swayed from side to side. Would it feel as silky threaded through his fingers? The idea enticed him. *She* enticed him like no woman had in quite some time. Not even Kathryn, who'd made it very clear she'd like to be more than just his friend and an employee of his mother's corporation.

Ren smiled at Jess's easy way with the boy as she answered, waving a young man forward who'd just entered with a clipboard in his hand.

"Not exactly," Jess said to the boy. "I'm a Native Alaskan, but there are a lot of different groups of us. I'm part of a tribe that is Athapaskan. Another group, the Inuit people, used to be called Eskimo. But they prefer Inuit because it means 'the people'."

"What's Eskimo mean?" the boy asked.

"Ah, you see—" she made a face. "Eskimo means 'eater of raw meat'."

"Ewwwwwww," the boy's face scrunched up. "That's gross!"

"Now you know why they changed the name." Jess's laughter rolled off in magical waves and the little boy grinned in response.

In fact, as Ren watched the group, he could see them all falling under her spell. They listened quietly while she continued with information about their stay.

She kept her tone light and pleasant as she lowered the boom. "We've had a small issue with the plumbing."

"We have bathrooms, don't we?" The question came from a nervous little man standing off to the side of the group.

Jess smiled at him. "You've all got working bathrooms in your rooms, yes. And I'm off to fix the water pipe so you'll have hot water for showers soon."

"No showers?" A woman in front asked the question and Ren could see tired written in the drooping lines on her face. The other guests were starting to shuffle in place.

Jess clasped her hands behind her back. "I know you'd all like showers, and we will accommodate you."

When Ren saw the crossed fingers on both hands, he recognized just how good she was at her job. And how much trouble she'd be in if she couldn't get that plumbing fixed.

She gestured to the young man beside her. "Rocky here will give you your room assignments. I suggest you settle in and then pop across the way to the restaurant. I'm sure some hot food, and a cup of coffee—"

"Or a stiff drink," a man in the back inserted.

Jess laughed. "We were a dry camp until a few years ago. You'll have to settle for a cold beer or glass of wine if it's spirits you're after. We've got a great cook, though. I think you'll find the food to your liking. And I'll be over to let you know when everything's back on track."

She motioned Rocky to take over and passed Ren on her way back to the plumbing. Her mood had turned decidedly foul again, judging by the glare she sent his way. Ren opted to shelve any further discussion for the moment and went to change. He could feel the wet cold seeping into already tired muscles. He needed dry clothes.

Later, in dry jeans and turtleneck, Ren hung the only jacket he'd brought to dry in the plumbing room. The leather was most likely beyond repair. His trek across to the restaurant was swift by necessity. Had the temperature dropped? He stopped at his SUV to grab the paperwork about the sale, then hustled indoors. Marathon sessions in the boardroom hadn't tired him as much as this day's drive had. He needed coffee, or something stronger, and more to eat than the power bar he'd had on the drive up.

The room, with its long cafeteria-style tables, was filled almost to capacity due to the busload of tourists. Add in the big rigs parked outside, and the station seemed near capacity.

He saw a sign over a doorway that said "Bar" and headed that direction. The room was nondescript, with more of the same tables and chairs. The bar itself, though, looked like something out of an old time saloon, and Ren took a moment to appreciate the carved wood and mirrors. He settled on a stool, then noticed small screw-cap bottles of wine lined up on the bar. Jess hadn't been kidding about the absence of liquor. This didn't bode well. The kid he'd seen earlier sauntered in. With an innocence in his face that said he shouldn't be old enough to drink, it surprised Ren that he was serving. Rocky, Jess had called him.

"What can I getcha?"

"Are you the bartender?"

The kid laughed. "Bartender, muscle, dishwasher, maid. I'm a little bit of everything around here. Whatever the need, I fill it." His chest puffed out with obvious pride.

"Did I hear right that you don't carry whiskey?"

"Sorry, mister. No hard liquor here. Only beer and wine."

"Not much of a bar."

"Hell, wasn't long ago they didn't have any alcohol here, so this is a step up. Want a beer? We've got Coors Light, Bud, and MGD."

Ren stood. "No, thank you. I think I'll get some dinner instead."

"Enjoy, then. The grub's good here."

Not expecting much from the "grub," Ren picked up a food tray and looked around the buffet. At least they offered a wide variety of food, from salmon and steaks to pasta, along with vegetables, fruit, and salad. He opted for steak, vegetables, and a salad. And another cup of wonderfully aromatic coffee.

He set his tray down at the end of a long table occupied by a few men who looked like they didn't want to talk, if their scowls were any indication. That was fine by him, so he sank down onto the bench.

"That table's for the long haulers only." He turned as Mary, the cook, sauntered by.

The cloud over Ren's head darkened at this new inconvenience as he stood back up. The only other spot was at one of the filled tables. He grabbed an empty seat at the end and stabbed uncharacteristically at his steak. This place seemed to bring out the worst in him.

As he chewed the tender meat, the flavor started to seep in and mellow him. It was good. In fact, it was very good. It had a flavor he couldn't quite place, and he considered himself a bit of a gourmet. Good food was a definite bonus. Maybe this place was salvageable after all.

At that moment, Jess walked in, well bundled in coat, gloves, and hat. As she pulled the layers off, their eyes met. The lines on her face deepened for a moment, then the innkeeper in her took over.

"Hey, everyone," she said to the diners. Ren saw relief in the grin she planted on her face. "Water's fixed. Should be heated and ready in, oh, half hour, tops."

A general cheer went up and happy noise followed her as she wandered through the crowd. She plopped down in a chair next to one of the truckers. Ren could see she knew them. He'd done a quick bit of homework before heading north. With Last Chance pretty much the only place with gas and re-stocking facilities between Fairbanks and Prudhoe Bay, working truckers stopped here regularly.

When one of them leaned an arm over her chair to whisper something in her ear, an uncharacteristic vise tightened around Ren's chest. He turned back to his food, then wondered why his mood lightened when she walked past him and into the kitchen moments later.

Jess saw him. Ren Gallini. Who could miss him? That man would stand out in any crowd with that chiseled face and those light brown eyes that were in no way diminished by the commanding eyebrows over them. Hell, even if his clothes didn't give him away as an outsider, that look would. Who did he think he was, coming in here and saying he would soon own her home? Her father would get a good laugh out of that when he got back. Her frown deepened. Whenever that would be.

Owen Jenkins had lit out like an eagle with prey sighted several days earlier, leaving no indication where he was going or when he'd be back. Her dad had been doing this walkabout thing for a couple years now. He always came home and always seemed happier for the break, so she'd never worried. Until now. Something felt off. And this new guy...well, she wished her dad were here to deal with him.

As for Jess, she didn't care if she ever left this place. Memories shadowed her vision. This was home and home was where she planned to stay.

She wandered into the kitchen. "Hey, Auntie," she said to the cook. "Hi, Uncle John," she added as he came through the back door, pulling off his cap and running hands through his shoulder length dark hair.

"Hey, yourself," he said. You get that plumbing fixed?"

"You mean the leak that turned into an all out gusher? Yep. It's fixed." She pointed a thumb over her shoulder. "Lots of happy campers out there, thanks to hot water and another great meal."

"We aim to please, eh?" he said. "You see that fancy-schmancy SUV sitting outside?

Jess picked up a piece of celery and took a bite. "Yep."

John peeked through the kitchen door window into the restaurant. "That belong to the guy sitting solo I see in the restaurant?"

Jess sighed. "Have you met him?"

"Nope."

Mary peeked at the tables. "I have. He didn't come in with the bus?"

"No. He drove himself."

"What's he here for?"

"He says he's about to be the new owner of Last Chance Camp."

Mary's eyes widened as John pulled his coat back on and mumbled something about having to help with luggage.

Jess watched him leave as Mary commented.

"If that isn't the most ridiculous thing I've ever heard. Your father would never sell this place."

"I know," Jess said. "Problem is, why'd the guy say that?"

"You're gonna have to ask him, honey."

Jess shook her head. "I don't care to have anything to do with him." Her body disputed the statement as visions of falling back into him, feeling the hardness of his chest, warmed her more than the hot kitchen.

Mary eyed her closely, making Jess squirm. "Girl, you can't just hide out in here. That's never been your style. Plus, you're going to have to mingle at some point. And you need to figure out what that man's really after."

"I've *been* mingling, and I've had the day from hell. Even management gets a break sometimes, you know." She crossed her arms over her chest and leaned back against the counter.

Mary's silent nod and raised eyebrows said it all. As the owner of a place like this, the work never ended.

Sighing, Jess agreed. "Probably better get it over with."

She went out and shook her head at the emptiness of the restaurant, at least of women and the little boy she'd spoken to upon their arrival. Her announcement that there would soon be hot water had just about cleared the building. Only a few men remained, watching TV or unwinding in the bar. She grabbed a tray of food and dropped into the chair opposite City Boy, wishing she could wipe that slightly cockeyed grin off his face. She didn't much like that she noticed the hint of a dimple in his smile.

"Why'd you come here?"

"Nice manners for someone whose livelihood depends on customers."

"You aren't a customer. Now, why did you come to Last Chance?"

"I told you—"

"I know what you told me, but that can't be the real reason. Owen would never sell this place." She tried not to raise her voice, but it was hard, especially when City Boy didn't do the things that people normally did when they lied. He didn't look down, or shift in his seat or anything. Instead, he held her gaze.

"That's not what these papers say."

She glanced at the folded pile. "Well, there's no way you'll get me to believe that until Da—until Owen gets back, so why don't you just go home and we'll call you after we've sorted this out."

"Would you recognize his signature if you saw it?"

Jess shrugged, not wanting to give him the opportunity to prove anything before she could talk to her father.

Ren reached for the folded packet of papers on the table. He opened to the last page and showed it to her. "That's his signature."

She had to lean forward to get a clear look and caught another whiff of expensive cologne. It almost lured her in further. Trying not to breath, she stared at the signature for a long moment. "Looks like a forgery to me," she said. Ren pulled the papers back and covered her hand with his when she went to grab the paperwork.

"Say please," he said.

She felt her face warm with a flush she had no control

over. Planting her best you've-got-to-be-kidding-me face on, she pulled her hand back, picked up her tray, and walked back into the kitchen. No way did she beg. Ever.

Slapping her plate on the counter, she yanked a stool over and plunked down on it.

Mary stopped cleaning and seemed to watch Jess closely. "Didn't go so well?"

"He's an arrogant jerk who thinks he can come in here and tell me—I mean, tell us—what to do. So, no. It didn't go so well." She rubbed her palm, more disgruntled by the fact that she could still feel the heat of his hand on hers than anything else.

Jess ate her dinner, then helped Mary in the kitchen until she was sure the man would be gone. When she finally walked out into the main restaurant, she peeked out the window and saw his SUV still sitting in front.

"Looking for me?"

She held her thumping heart in her hands as she whirled around. There, not five feet from her, stood Ren Gallini in all his polished glory. Damn him. Jess wanted more than anything to wipe that satisfied smile off his face.

"I—I thought you'd get tired and go home."

"Really? I've heard the Dalton Highway is not one to be traveled at night, except in extreme urgency."

She didn't have an answer. Her brain felt muddled, and she was having trouble putting coherent thoughts together. How could she have forgotten he wouldn't be able to leave?

"Is that not the case?"

"Yes," she said through clenched teeth. "It's not for the faint-hearted in the daytime. It can be downright treacherous this time of year, especially at night."

He leaned past her and pulled the red-checkered curtain aside. "Well, since twilight has descended, it looks like you're stuck with me, at least until first light."

"Fine. Just stay out of my way."

He stepped close enough that his cologne once again threatened to jumble her senses. Did she imagine the flare of heat in his eyes? He smelled like leather and Armani and...tantalizing male. How was she expected to think around this guy when he smelled so good?

"That's not possible," he said, his voice low. "We have business to discuss."

She walked past him. "I don't have a thing to discuss with you."

He pointed to the papers sitting on the table. "Take the papers. They're copies. Read them, then we can talk after that. In the meantime, I'll need a room for the night."

Her eyes widened. "But we're full up."

"Come on. Every hotel keeps a room or two available for drop-ins."

"We're eight hours to the nearest city. No one comes here unannounced this time of year, unless they've got a cab to sleep in. Even then, they usually call ahead and reserve a spot."

"Then something else must be available. Isn't there another town near here? I think I saw it on the map."

"There's only one small place anywhere close to here. I got off the phone with them less than an hour ago. They have a few cabins, but are full up, too. Even our tour group's bus driver is sleeping in worker housing."

"What's that like? Maybe it would be possible for me

to sleep there."

"It's bunkroom style."

"No," Ren said. "I'm sorry, but that won't do."

The bus driver had taken the last ready bunk, but some perverse side of her wanted to see the man squirm. She smiled. "What? Too good to bunk in crew quarters?"

Ren moved toward her again, getting way too close for comfort. Jess hated herself for the anticipation of his touch, even as she backed up until a table stopped her.

It didn't stop him, though. He leaned until their lips were mere inches apart. She could smell the coffee on his breath and, for one frozen moment, she wanted to lean in and taste.

"I've never slept in a bunk...anything. Ever. And I'm not about to start now, beautiful." He touched her chin, branding her with his fingers while his eyes dipped to her lips. "So unless you're inviting me to *bunk* at your place, I'd suggest you find an alternate arrangement."

His voice sounded like velvet, warm and inviting, and Jess felt heat well up in her like a fountain. She had to get out of here. Away from him. She pushed against him, not surprised when the well-honed muscles didn't budge.

"Fine. You can sleep in Owen's trailer."

When he stepped aside, she snatched the papers from the table and clenched them in her fist.

"Careful with those, beautiful. You need to be able to read them."

She raised the paperwork and shook it at him. "I'll prove this isn't valid," she ground out, then left before her father's Irish anger made her say something she'd regret.

Chapter Three

Ren watched her leave, trying to fathom his reaction to the woman. He'd barely touched her and he was breathing hard. Grateful there was no one else in the restaurant, he sat and finished his cup of coffee, waiting for the calmness he defined his life by to return. The woman rubbed him in all the wrong places. No, that wasn't right. More like all the right places. Except this loss of control never happened to him.

He'd intimidated her. He'd fallen back on the only thing he knew. It was the only thing he could do. It might not be fair, but maybe it would keep some distance between them. If he couldn't manage to do that, he was in real danger of getting lost in that angelic smile of hers. Of wanting to stir the chocolate depth in those eyes. To learn the nuances that made her the woman she was today. And, God save him, to run his hands along those curves that no lumberman's clothing could fully hide.

Damn it. Ren shook his head. He needed to dot the I's and cross the T's on this foolhardy plan of his mother's, make her see how wrong she was to want to buy it, and get the hell out of Alaska. Quick.

He took a quick gulp of coffee, yelped, then realized it had cooled to lukewarm and hadn't, in fact, scalded him.

Yes, most definitely time to get back to his normal life.

Several minutes later, it occurred to Ren that he had no idea where Owen Jenkins' trailer would be located, or what it even looked like. He glanced at the door, knowing that searching out Jess for an answer wouldn't do any good. He shook his head. She'd probably gone into hiding. No doubt she knew a lot of places to hide around here.

With a weary sigh, Ren headed for the only other place he might get an answer.

"What is it about this kitchen that you can't seem to stay away?" Mary asked.

Grimacing, he pasted a smile on his face and set his mug on the counter. "Why, it's your lovely countenance, dear lady. I find myself drawn to it."

"That's a load of caribou crap," she answered with a laugh.

"Maybe," he countered. "I need to know where Owen's place is. It appears I'll be staying there tonight."

Mary's eyebrows rose. "No one sleeps in Owen's quarters."

"According to Jess, it's the only option available. She wasn't exactly forthcoming with other options and I'm too tired to fight anymore, to be honest."

Mary's grin confirmed that he'd found a tentative ally in the cook. "I don't doubt that one bit." Chuckling, she picked up a walkie-talkie from the counter and called Jess.

"You letting this city-slicker stay at Owen's?"

"There's no other choice." Ren heard the strain in Jess's voice even through the crackle of the radio.

"Show him Owen's place. And tell him he buys anything he breaks."

After finishing preparations for tomorrow's breakfast, Mary dried her hands on the kitchen towel draped over her shoulder and moved through the darkened restaurant to the front windows.

Twilight had yielded to night hours ago, which, here inside the Arctic Circle, came early this time of year. Mary tried unsuccessfully to rub the chill out of her arms. Winter would be here soon. Her bones were always right.

She pulled her salt-and-pepper braid around and began to untwine it as she looked up. Splashes of green had already begun to illuminate the land. The northern lights rippled and pulsated their way to life, and she could feel the familiar tingle of a strong auroral showing raise the fine hairs on her arms. The spirits would play hard tonight.

Jess always took the night duty of notifying the tourists up to view the Aurora Borealis. Mary shook her head. The girl worked too hard. Her focus on this place was absolute.

Whispering so as not to provoke the spirits, Mary spoke to the sister who had been gone all these years. "Ah, Maggie. You should be so proud of the young woman your daughter has become. I know you watch over her. Continue to guide her as we have tried. She needs to let go of this place. To experience new things, see life from different perspectives. But she won't leave the camp. Says there's no place else she'd rather be."

She freed the last strands of her braid. "We're working to fix that. Only time will tell if we're doing the right thing. I don't much like it, but I think, eventually, you're going to approve. She placed a hand over her heart. "We miss you still, sister."

With one final glance heavenward, Mary left on a few small lights for any guests who might wander in search of food or beverage, then went out back to the cabin she shared with her husband, John. His quiet snore told her he slept. She joined him. Days started early in Last Chance, so early bedtimes were almost mandatory. It was past time for her to sleep.

"Our girl doing all right?" John said, his snores disappearing.

"I think so. I hate that we're not telling her everything," Mary said. It worried her, and also made her angry, being put in this position.

"You know I've never been happy about this," John said. "Have you spoken to Owen?"

"No. He gave me a new cell number to reach him at, though."

"Maybe you should call him, tell him how you feel."

Mary nodded. She yawned and snuggled deeper into her husband's side as he pulled the quilt closer around them both.

"Tomorrow is soon enough, wife. Get some sleep."

Marry drifted off, cocooned in a warmth that pushed the worry away and let sleep drift in.

Long before Mary turned in for the night, Jess sat and tried to make sense of her day. The trailer she called home was a study in opposites. Slatted blinds against the windows kept the outside world from seeing the stylish curtains that hung on the inside. Sofa cushions had been painstakingly recovered by hand in a sage green and ivory pattern that matched the drapes. In contrast, insulated rubber boots, cold weather gear, and a tool box sat by the front door, at the ready for any emergency.

The doors on the overhead kitchen cabinets had been removed, those spaces filled with books instead of dishes.

Repair manuals shared space with books about business administration. Her small table was littered with information about hotel management, the last segment of the online courses she needed to get her degree.

At the moment, Jess didn't see any of it. She read through the papers from Ren Gallini for the third time, staring at the last page. The signature sure looked like her father's handwriting. But there was no way he would sell this place. Not ever. Not out from under her feet. And not without telling her. This was her home. Their home.

He just wouldn't do it.

Sure, he'd been taking these little trips and telling no one, including her, where he went. He'd never seemed unhappy when he was here in camp, though. In fact, her father was just about the most cheerful guy she knew.

Could he have been coerced? Jess's head shot up. Her father had gambled a bit when he was younger. Had he relapsed? And gambled the place away? Dear God! She needed to talk to him, and fast.

Jess slipped toes painted a vibrant shade of red out of slippers meant only for a woman's foot and into boots meant for construction workers. Tossing her coat on, she lit out for her office in the back of the restaurant. With shaking hands, she dialed the cell phone each of them took whenever they were off the property.

It rang once. Please, Dad, pick up.

Twice. Please. Dear God. Answer the phone.

Midway through the third ring, a voice she recognized answered the phone. And it wasn't her father.

"Gallini?"

"Hey, beautiful. Miss me already?"

"What the hell are you doing with my father's phone?"

"It was sitting here on the table. When it rang, I answered it. I figured you might want to talk."

"Never." Jess ground the word out, slammed the phone down, and sprinted for her trailer. Once inside, she let loose with a rip-roaring scream. She slumped in her only comfortable chair, an ivory colored leather recliner she'd had made special to fit the space.

How could her father just disappear like this? How could he do this and not stick around to explain it to her? This was not like him at all.

Think, Jess. Think. You can figure a way out of this. Jess dug at her rough cuticles, then grabbed her manicure kit. She needed busy work while she tried to figure out how she would find answers to the overwhelming number of questions running races through her mind.

Ren smiled as he set the phone back down on the table. That had been a very productive conversation. First, he'd realized that Jess was none other than Owen Jenkins's daughter. Second, if that muffled scream was any indication, her trailer was right next door to the one he was staying in. Information always helped in negotiations. Always.

He rolled a glass of whiskey between his hands. It had taken very little time to find Owen's stash of liquor and Ren gave the man credit for good, and expensive, taste. He looked around the trailer the man lived in, which was serviceable, if not stylish. Jenkins was as much of a puzzle as his daughter.

At the moment, the real puzzle was why his mother

had such an interest in Last Chance. Buying this place made no sense. Granted, he'd only been here a few hours, but he saw nothing that could be turned into any sort of resort option. The best he could offer his mother in the way of a suggestion was some basic improvements. This place wasn't his cup of tea. He swirled the amber liquid around the glass. He could see how some might be drawn to the adventure of rustic Alaska. But not him. And not his mother.

Reaching for his own cell, he called his mother. Not only did he get no answer, the immediate voicemail cue meant her phone wasn't even turned on. Unusual behavior like this wasn't his mother's way. She was punctual, organized, and reserved. And always available.

Although not lately, he had to admit. He'd caught her day-dreaming on several occasions. And he was certain he'd heard her humming once when he entered her office.

His mother was up to something. The issue was how to determine what that was. And until he could do that, he'd have to play along.

His cell rang and he glanced at the display.

"William? It's got to be one a.m. in New York."

"The early bird catches the worm, you know."

"More like the late bird refusing to leave the nest. Are you still at work?"

He laughed. "If I said yes, would you believe me?"

Ren grimaced. William Vander, his company's lead attorney and also his friend, had two specialties—legal battles and women. "Not this time of night. I'm guessing you're on your way home from the house of...what is she this time? A blonde?"

"Redhead. Natural, too."

Ren rolled his eyes. William had tried more than once to drag Ren out to the clubs. That was one of Kathryn's many criticisms that he agreed with. Instead of telling her that, he thought with a twinge of guilt, he'd used her as an excuse to steer clear of William's ways, then gone home to his apartment alone. Kathryn. He'd have to deal with her sooner or later. She'd been making noises, assuming a relationship that just wasn't there. Kathryn was good at her job. She was also nice. But nice left you with a passable, dispassionate relationship, like his parent's marriage had been.

Ren wanted more. He just couldn't decide what more or how much more.

"You still there, buddy?" Several clicks followed William's question, as if he'd knocked on the phone three times.

"Sorry. Long day. What can I do for you?"

"Just wanted to remind you about that oil company we're working with. You know it's, um, sale, is heavily leveraged over options to drill for oil near you."

"I remember."

"I still think we should buy that company, not facilitate it's sale to someone else."

"We're not in the business of buying companies like this, William. We've been over this."

"Yes, but it could be pretty lucrative to change our practices in this instance."

Ren sighed. "We've been through this. The answer's still no. Did you call me to argue about this yet again?"

"No. I just thought you should maybe check into the whole oil drilling thing. See if there's any way to change people's minds. It might help with the sale."

Irritation replaced fatigue, and Ren smothered the instinct to lash out at his friend. "I just arrived, Will. I'm tired and I've barely had time to get a basic sense of the surroundings."

"Well?"

Ren ran his free hand through his hair. "Well, what?"

"What's it like? All rustic and hunter-camp like?"

"Something like that."

"Why'd your mom pick this place?"

"I don't know. But there must be something salvageable if she did."

"Well, get it figured out, try to put a positive spin on the drilling thing, and then get your ass back here."

"Last I checked, I was your boss, not the other way around."

William laughed. "That's what you think."

Ren had to admit that William had taken on a lot of power in the company. He'd wondered for some time if that was a good thing, but the man hadn't steered him wrong yet.

"Is there anything else you called for?"

"Nope. Just checking in."

"Then I'm hanging up now."

"Yeah. Just remember to work on those folks, okay?"

"I'm too tired to argue with you. Good night, William."

"Good nig—"

Ren set the phone down and wondered yet again if William was manipulating him. He'd started this trip with a solid idea of what he needed to accomplish. Now, he seemed to have more questions than answers. And he didn't much like that. Not at all.

He scrubbed his face with his hands, giving in to the exhaustion of the day. Ren headed toward the back of the trailer to see what condition the bed was in. He found it neatly made and a note lay on top.

Sheets are clean. Make yourself at home.

Ren frowned. Another puzzle. Owen Jenkins had known someone would be using his trailer. He looked around and wondered whom the man had been expecting.

Jenkins hadn't even told his own daughter he'd sold the place. What was the old man up to? And how did Ren's mother—and by default, himself—end up in the middle of it all?

Once in bed, he felt grateful for the plush mattress. Jess's father clearly believed in comfort, if not style. Still, visions of a dark-haired, wet T-shirt clad tomboy made it very hard to let exhaustion take over. Giving in to this— whatever it was—with Jess would only complicate matters. Ren knew that. Yet every time he forced her from his mind, she crept back in.

After an interminable attempt at trying to sleep, Ren gave up, got dressed, and headed over to the restaurant, praying they kept that delicious coffee going twenty-four-seven.

Chapter Four

At one a.m., when Jess's alarm went off a scant two hours after she'd crawled into bed, she slammed her hand down on the snooze button and felt pain shoot up her arm. Groaning, she knew she wouldn't be able to go back to sleep. It was time to wake their guests for the show. Any other day, she'd jump out of bed, ready for action, but today…

Screw it. Jess rolled over and pulled the blankets up over her head. She'd go back to sleep and let her camp take care of itself.

Except it might not be her camp anymore. She sat up. It might well be…his. Ugh. None of her problems had disappeared in the past couple hours. In fact, with a monster headache trying to dig in, they seemed worse than before.

Crawling out of bed, she searched through cabinets for aspirin and downed a couple. Next, she ran cold water over her face to wake up. It didn't help.

Struggling into the same clothes she'd peeled off too short a time ago, Jess ran a brush through her long hair and stared at herself in the mirror. Dark circles shadowed her eyes as she checked the mirror. With a shrug, she turned away. Who would notice in the middle of the night?

On her way over to the inn, Jess paused, letting the quiet night calm her. It was colder than it had been and her breath preceded her in the frigid air. This time of night appealed to Jess in a way she'd never been able to describe.

The silence was almost total, broken only by the quiet whine of the generators. She knew the grounds intimately and sidestepped the potholes without thought.

The sky was alive with Milky Way star clusters, constellations, and more. Ribbons of green pulsed, and Jess felt them tugging at her.

Come play with us.

The Aurora Borealis, also known as the Northern Lights. This was what people came by the busload to see. And part of her job was waking them up in time.

She stretched her arms out to the strengthening light as the magical presence grew and its tendrils wrapped her in a cocoon of wonder. Legend said these lights were the spirits come out to play. For these few precious moments, she played with them. Sometimes, she could hear them whistle, but not tonight so far. Tonight, they played in silence, and she honored that with her own still voice, except for one quietly whispered word.

"Mother."

Jess smiled as she watched the lights weave their way across the sky. This was her favorite part of living here and the reason she would never leave. She glanced at the inn and sighed. Past time to wake the tourists up.

She hurried inside, grabbed the pad with room numbers written on it, and began a hushed tapping on doors.

"The northern lights are out," she whispered as folks with sleep-filled eyes opened their doors. Eyes widened, and as she walked back down the hall, she heard the scurry of people dressing like the place was on quiet fire. They left their rooms in all different types of apparel. Some were dressed, bundled head to toe. Some obviously wore pajamas and wrapped blankets around themselves for warmth. The ones with no socks or shoes on, she knew, wouldn't last long in this chill before they'd have to retreat inside.

Outside, she watched them filter through the door, walk down the stairs, and look up. The "oohs" and "ahs" were better than any fireworks show, at least from what she heard on television. She'd never seen fireworks in real life, but couldn't imagine they held a candle to nature's display.

She saw the little boy from earlier, blanketed deep in his father's arms. He raised his head and looked up. "Hey, I don't see no balls," he said with a sleep-filled voice. A reverent chuckle moved through the group as the boy laid his head back on Dad's shoulders and closed his eyes.

Ren sipped coffee from the restaurant's porch and watched the tourist group outside dwindle until only Jess was left. She pulled her hair free of its band and gazed skyward. Then, to his surprise, she began to twirl in slow circles, her body swaying in time to a music he could not hear, her arms outstretched to the meandering ribbons in the sky. Her dark hair, unbound now that her day was done, swirled about her in soft waves.

Ren froze, caught in the hypnotic display of her almost spiritual union with the sky around her. She moved with a fluid grace Ren found more profound and sensual than anything he'd ever experienced. He swore he could feel the thrum of the spirits flowing through his own veins as a web of peace settled around his beating heart.

As he watched, Jess's soft sounds of delight were

joined by another quieter, more elusive sound, almost like a hushed whistle. He smiled, betting that Jess would say the spirits approved.

He waited and watched as Jess danced in their midst until the last light faded from the night sky. He watched until she wandered beyond his sight. Even then, he stood, his coffee forgotten. He felt...bereft with her disappearance. He wanted to call her back.

Somehow, Ren knew that, with tonight's events, his life had been forever changed. And right now, at this moment, he didn't mind one bit.

After another short couple hours of sleep, Jess woke feeling much better and headed for the main building, stopping briefly to glance up. Shades of gray had begun to infiltrate the star-spattered sky. She made a mental note to check the forecast. The air felt like it had some moisture to it.

Jess hurried inside the restaurant, cranked the heat higher, and poured herself a cup of coffee, starting a fresh pot brewing. Heading to the kitchen, she found Mary already working on breakfast.

"Good morning," Mary said.

"Morning, Auntie," Jess answered, pecking her on the cheek. "I smell oatmeal."

"Yep. All ready. Help yourself."

Jess did, adding a healthy spoonful of brown sugar. The hot cereal warmed her as she swallowed.

"Folks get a good show last night?"

"One of the better ones. Mother Nature was having fun."

"Good." Mary took a closer look at Jess, who stared down into her bowl. "You okay? You look a little under the weather."

"I'm fine." She gulped more oatmeal.

"You don't look fine. You sleep okay?"

"Honestly, I'm fine, thank you." Jess's teeth clenched as she said the last words.

"Okay. Just making sure there isn't something, or someone, on your mind and keeping you awake."

The bowl clattered on the counter, and Mary stopped kneading dough and stared at Jess.

Jess pushed the bowl away. "I'm fine," she said yet again, adding a tone of finality she prayed would end the conversation. She stared into her coffee cup for a while. "Mary?"

"Hmmm?"

"Have you got any idea where Dad's gone?"

Mary turned away from her, setting the dough to rise by the stove. "How would I know that?" she said.

"I don't know. It's just—well, he ought to tell someone where he is. What if there's an emergency?"

Mary continued to fuss with the bread, her back to Jess. "Is there one? An emergency, I mean."

"Not really. I could have used his help yesterday, though."

"Well, I wouldn't worry. He always comes back from these little vacations of his. He'll be back before you know it."

Jess nodded. "I tried to call him last night, but he left the cell phone here."

Mary looked up from washing her hands. "That's

unusual, but Owen's been a bit...secretive lately. Maybe he needs some privacy? Not everyone can handle the close quarters we live and work in."

"I know. But he's lived here for years. Why now? Have you got any idea at all where he's been going on these little jaunts of his?"

Drying her hands, Mary walked over to lean against the counter next to Jess. "He's been pretty tight-lipped about where he goes. The guys think he may have a lady friend. Are you okay with it if that's the case?"

"Oh, sure. I kind of thought that myself. I just—" Jess shook her head. "He hasn't said anything to John, either?"

Mary put a hand on Jess's shoulder. "Not that I'm aware of. What's wrong, honey?"

"It's that guy who showed up yesterday."

"Ah."

Jess scowled deeper at the "now I understand" smile on Mary's face.

"So you like this man, eh?"

"No! Not. At. All." Somewhere, low in her belly, Jess's body rebelled at the statement.

"Why not?"

"He's too smooth. Too sure of himself. And his teeth are too damn white."

"Ahhh."

"Don't even go there, Mary. Geesh, I thought you were on *my* side."

Jess headed for the walk-in refrigerator to cool her burning cheeks. She came out with trays of eggs and began breaking them into the mixer.

"Hey," Mary said. "He's not bothering you, is he?

Because if he is, I'll have my John speak to him."

"No, no. At least, not that way." She ignored the warmth that deepened inside, curling into a restive need she couldn't shrug off. "He's—he's got papers that say Dad intends to sell this place to him. And now I can't find Dad anywhere." She broke another egg. "I don't know what to think."

Mary chuckled. "That is some high-falutin' talk that boy's got if he thinks he's going to convince you, or any of us, that Owen would sell this place."

Another egg plopped into the bowl. "That's what I thought, too. But—" Her voice broke. "The papers he has seem to prove it. It sure looks like Dad's signature."

"Could be forgeries."

"I agree. But why would someone try to buy, or steal, Last Chance out from under us? What's here that they find so worth this trouble? We're just a wide spot in the road to most people." Jess rubbed her temples, hating the misnomer. *This is my home.*

"It seems like understanding his motive is the first thing we need to figure out."

"That makes sense. But how do we do that?" She looked at Mary as she picked up the unused eggs to return them to the cooler.

"There's only one way." Mary had that damn smirky smile back on her face. "Somebody has to stick to him like glue."

"Stick to who like glue?" Ren's voice sounded from behind Jess.

Chapter Five

When Ren spoke, Jess spooked. Big time. The tray of unused eggs in her hands started to fly. By her side within two steps, he steadied the eggs and Jess by pulling both into his arms. As she leaned in to his support, he felt the shock of contact run through him like a shiver. What was it about this girl that turned his groin into the thinking part of his body every time he touched her? A flash of Jess dancing last night softened his heart even further. Hell. She even affected him when he was nowhere near her.

Seconds passed before she found her footing and he could step away. Considering the turmoil in Jess's eyes, he backed up several feet. He wasn't so sure he wouldn't end up with egg dripping down his chest, and he was wearing his only change of clothes.

"Good morning, beautiful," he said with a smile as he opened the cooler door for her.

"Stop calling me that," she grumbled.

Ren's grin widened even further as he caught Mary watching them both closely. When Jess exited the cooler with a container of milk and a glower that would make a grizzly bear proud, Mary quickly busied herself with food preparation. Ren recognized a dodge when he saw one. The head cook didn't want to talk.

"Why are you wearing my Dad's coat?"

He glanced down at the worn parka, then shrugged. "Because somebody drenched my leather one in water yesterday. I believe it's beyond repair." He leaned a hand on the counter. "I borrowed your father's coat so I wouldn't freeze. Or," he continued, enjoying his proximity to her even while knowing he shouldn't, "would you prefer I succumb to the elements?"

Anger, indignation, and what he suspected was a natural caretaking instinct went to war in Jess's face, and he backed off to enjoy the show. She opened her mouth, then shut it. Eyes that he could get lost in widened, then closed as she gathered herself.

"Patrons aren't allowed in the kitchen," Jess said, glaring at him. "You'll need to wait in the restaurant."

"What? No cheerful greeting? No offer of coffee? If this is the demeanor you run the inn with, I can understand why your father is getting rid of it."

Her eyes darkened with edges of red. "My father is *not* selling this place."

She poured milk into the eggs and hit the mixer's switch. He watched her back rise and fall with several deep breaths, then she turned back to him, a feigned aloofness barely hiding her agitation.

"There's hot coffee in the buffet area, so please, help yourself." She glanced at her watch. "Breakfast will be ready in about half an hour. But we'll have pastries out soon, and there's hot oatmeal if you need something now."

"I can wait. But thank you for the information. Now see, being nice wasn't so hard, was it?"

He buried his smile deep as he watched her lips become thin lines. Jess held a hand out, indicating the door. Tipping his head, he let her have the last word. Ren smiled, thanked her and Mary, and turned to leave, only to find Rocky glaring at him from the doorway. It seemed, Ren thought, as he passed the boy with a quick nod of greeting, that Last Chance Camp had gotten up on the wrong side of the bed this morning.

Jess glared at Ren Gallini's back as he left. Why did that man always make her see red? She rubbed arms that defied her brain and still tingled at the memory of his touch.

When she saw Mary's watchful gaze, with avid interest clear in the brightness of her eyes, Jess turned her back on her auntie, just in time for Rocky to stomp to her side.

She almost laughed at the way his chest was puffed out like a penguin. Pointing a thumb over his shoulder, he spoke. "That guy bothering you? 'Cuz if he is, I'll make sure he doesn't do it a second time."

For a moment, Jess was tempted to let Rocky talk to Ren. Reality stopped her in the form of remembered moments held in muscled arms. Ren would obliterate Rocky.

Jess stared at the still swinging kitchen door. Except Ren wouldn't fight Rocky. She already knew the man preferred words over brawn to resolve an issue. The vision of Ren in some sort of primal fight for territory, getting the pulp beat out of him, restored her good mood considerably, though. She pictured him bloody, then his body glowing with sweat, his muscles bunching and flexing like a tiger as he circled his prey.

"Jess?" Rocky's voice dragged her back to the present, and Jess loosened the collar of her shirt. Had the kitchen warmed up about ten degrees?

"Um, yes?"

"I said, do you want me to have a talk with that guy who's bothering you?"

"No." She plastered a smile on her face, hoping the action would cover the flush of red she knew had crept up from her neck. She placed a hand on Rocky's arm. "I know you would protect me. That instinct is one of the reasons you're part of this family, Rocky. But don't worry about this one. I can handle Renzo Gallini."

Rocky didn't exactly take her request graciously, but he did back off and went to wash his hands. While he spent the next several minutes cutting up fruit and putting juices and food out, Jess got the eggs cooking, then took over bacon and sausage duty from Mary. Even in the normal, sub-arctic world, the sun had not yet risen, but they had several trucks outside that would be on the road within the hour. Mornings began early in Last Chance.

Cooking at the stove gave Jess time to think, although she wasn't sure she wanted to. Her mind seemed to be the only sensible part of her left, since her body betrayed her every time Ren Gallini got close. She had gone weak as a newborn babe when they collided. Her body had actually started to quiver.

Folks that came through their little station were generally nice and well meaning. Especially the regular long-haulers. Still, over the past few years, she'd been propositioned by everything from guys looking for a little action on the road to poets under the spell of the Auroral activity. Jess was a pro at turning them down. A relationship didn't interest her. Neither, she tried to tell her body, did Ren Gallini. Remembered heat smoothed her irritated nerve endings as she told herself again he was nothing but trouble.

The man was too arrogant.

But driven to succeed. She understood that.

He was too metro.

He could make anything look good, even Dad's old parka.

He was too perfect.

Jess sighed. He was too perfect.

"Hey, you going to cook that bacon or use it to burn the building down?" Mary turned the stove off. "We've got enough for now. Why don't you let Rocky and I finish breakfast."

Setting down the tongs, Jess nodded. "I need to check the forecast anyhow."

Mary frowned. "Weather's coming early, isn't it?"

"Feels like it to me. How ready are we? How are our supplies?"

"We just got a shipment in, but I'll take a look at the winter reserves and get together a list. Better to supply early than get caught unprepared, eh?"

"Definitely. Thanks. We'll get this busload on its way back to Fairbanks this morning, then we've got one smaller bus coming in late tomorrow and that'll be it for the season. If winter decides to make an early appearance, we might have to cancel that last bus."

Setting another bin of fruit aside for Rocky to add to the buffet, Mary pulled the ever-present towel off her shoulder and wiped her hands. "I'll admit to being glad when we'll be down to just the long-haulers. Seems like this season has lasted longer than most."

Jess nodded her head. "It hasn't helped that Dad's

been gone more lately. If this keeps up, we're going to have to hire additional help next year."

She thought of the papers she'd read over too many times to count last night and wondered if she'd be the one doing the hiring next year. Jess slumped onto a nearby stool. "Dad sure picked a bad time to take off." She slapped the counter. "Why didn't he take his damn phone?"

Concern wrinkling her face, Mary settled her arm around Jess's shoulders, and Jess tried to lean into the comfort but felt too keyed up.

"I'm sure your Dad's fine, honey. He's just gone off somewhere to get something out of his system."

"Why now?" Jess gulped. "If he was planning to sell the camp, it's not like him to leave with someone due in to look things over."

Mary patted her shoulder. "You're right. That's not how Owen usually operates. So he must have some powerful reason for not being here. And when I see him next, I'm going to make sure he knows how I feel about him worrying his baby girl like this."

Jess tried to hold it inside, but felt like her whole body was going to explode. She blew out a deep breath and stood up. "It doesn't do any good for me to whine over something I can't control. Holler if you need me. I'll be checking to see what old Mother Nature has in store for us."

In her office, Jess booted up her computer. While she waited, she wondered if she should talk to the authorities about her father's disappearance. The local contingent of State Troopers, which consisted of two people, lived just across the road. She could probably talk to Rod Willson about the situation. The problem lay in the fact that her father had a habit of disappearing, so they'd think it was just an old man's eccentricities.

Her desk phone rang and Jess, startled, yanked it off the cradle.

"Jess?"

"Rod," she said as she tried to put her heart back in its normal spot. "Hello."

"You sound out of breath. Everything okay?"

"Everything's fine. You just caught me...daydreaming."

She smiled as his deep baritone chuckle resounded over the phone lines. "About me, right?"

"Always," she said with a laugh. Rod's good humor always managed to lift her spirits. He was also one of the world's biggest, and most harmless, flirts. Jess frowned. It wasn't like him to call and miss a chance to stop over. The one thing Rod liked as much as flirting was food. And there was plenty about to be set out. Something must be going on. "What's up?"

"Just wanted to give you a heads up we'll be short-staffed for a couple days. Meg will be the only one here. Rumors are rumbling around that there's someone here surveying the mood about drilling for oil in the ANWR."

Jess felt the familiar sense of dread settle like a rock in the pit of her stomach. The Arctic National Wildlife Refuge was the United State's largest refuge, with somewhere around eight million acres designated as wilderness. It was also the center of an oil drilling controversy that would probably rage on until desperation, on one side or the other, tipped the angry balance.

Things had been quiet for a while, and Jess had hoped

the trend would continue. "Someone's snooping around?" she asked Rod.

"That's what I've heard. And I'm heading out to make sure things remain calm."

"Where to?"

"I thought I'd hit a few of the towns, including Fort Yukon."

Jess's other home. She'd been born in Fort Yukon and spent a good amount of time there while growing up. She quelled the pang of longing. She was long overdue for a visit. "Is there anything we can do?"

"No. We want to be a presence in case any issues arise. And I wanted to let you know Meg would be on her own. Everything quiet in camp?" Rod asked.

No. My father's missing, and there's some city slicker trying to take my home. "Everything's fine. Be safe, and we'll keep Meg company while you're away."

After saying goodbye, Jess sat deep in thought. Meg, the only female trooper stationed at the Last Chance station, was a good friend. The woman was also completely, over-the-top in love with Rod. Maybe he knew, maybe he didn't. Jess couldn't tell. Until he was ready to settle down, it was a moot point, and Meg knew it.

With elbows on her desk, Jess rested her chin in her hands. Love was complicated. Which was why she had no intention of ever falling into that trap. Better to remain in control of your own life than to entwine it with someone else's. There were just too many obstacles to hurdle when love was involved.

Jess forced her melancholy to the back of her mind and got to work. Several minutes later, she was immersed in

weather forecasts when a throat being cleared interrupted
her.

"Is this a bad time?"

Jess's head whipped around. There, leaning against her
door jam in all his finely honed glory, stood Ren Gallini.
Couldn't he have climbed back in the hole he came from
and hibernated some more? She turned back to her screen,
hoping that would be dismissal enough.

It wasn't. He stepped inside and settled comfortably
into the chair in front of her desk.

"There's nothing we need to talk about. And I'm
working." She glanced at her computer. "You know, I've
just been checking the forecast. Looks like a storm is
coming. You might want to get out of here before that
hits."

He chuckled. "Nice try. I think I'll stick around for a
bit. When?"

"Not for a couple days, I think. The forecasters think it
will be a slow build-up. Good thing, too."

"Why is that?"

"We've got one last bus coming in tomorrow. If
there's any chance weather will roll in sooner, we'll have to
cancel that tour."

Ren nodded. "Err on the side of safety?"

"Always."

"Are you ready for the weather?"

She shrugged. "We're always prepared, especially this
time of year. We get some snow in October, but the real
snow doesn't generally hit until next month. The bus here
now leaves in about two hours. That gives us today and
tomorrow to devote to preparations."

"Hmmm. I had hoped I could steal you away for a few hours this afternoon."

"I'm not prepared to talk about those papers. Not until my father comes home." Her heart tightened as she wondered yet again where her father was.

"How about we compromise, then?"

Unsure of his motives, Jess eyed him. "What type of compromise?"

"A moratorium," Ren said. "On discussions about the sale of this camp, for, oh, say, twenty-four hours?"

She sat back in her chair and crossed her arms. "I'm listening."

"I know there's an airstrip here, so I've chartered a small plane. I'd like to see a little more of this state you're so enamored with."

"The six or eight hour drive here didn't give you enough of a look?"

He laughed. "Almost. I'd like to get a broader view, though. I thought maybe you could act as tour guide."

Whatever Ren Gallini did for a living, Jess figured that disarming grin of his got him far. Not here, though. She was immune to it. "Sorry," she said and waved her to-do list in the air. "There's a lot to do around here before the weather changes."

"That last bus is due in tomorrow by dinner, right? Go with me today and I'll help you get ready tomorrow."

Jess looked him up and down. He had jeans on. Probably designer jeans, if that thigh-hugging fit was any indication. The gray, long-sleeve Henley-style T-shirt and her father's winter coat didn't look like work clothes on him. Plus, the man looked like he had never picked up a hammer in his life. "I don't think—"

Ren's smile broadened and her resolve began to crack. Damn it.

"Come on," he said, spreading his arms. "I'm not helpless, no matter what you think."

"I didn't think you were helpless."

His eyes told her he knew she was lying. "You said yourself you're short-handed. If weather's coming in sooner than expected, you'll need more than just John and Rocky to get that list done. Especially since we'll be gone this afternoon." He pointed to the pad in her hand. "I worked my way through college doing construction. My parents thought I needed the experience. I can help."

Jess chewed her lower lip. She *could* use the help. But did it have to be him? "It will take time to explain things to you. You'll probably slow me down."

He fixed her with a stare. "I'll try very hard not to."

She glanced at the computer screen, searching for anything she could use as an excuse. She didn't want to be bottled up in a plane with Ren Gallini, even with a pilot along as a third party.

"Where are you planning to go? Maybe I don't know much about the place."

"Since I've seen this central portion—"

"There's a lot more to Alaska than the Dalton Highway."

"I know. I plan to head north and east, check out the National Wildlife Refuge, maybe stop in a town or two to soak up some local flavor."

Jess laughed. "There are no towns around there. Just a few small villages."

"Perfect." He smiled, and Jess felt the noose tighten around her neck. "I'd like to get a sense of the local heritage."

Damn it all to hell. The man wanted to visit her backyard. And she was way overdue for a visit to Fort Yukon. Jess set her to-do list down, knowing Ren Gallini had somehow found her soft spot—the one thing that would convince her to take the afternoon off and spend it in close confines with him.

"All right. You want to compromise, then here's my compromise. I'll play tour guide today *after* the bus heads back to Fairbanks. Tomorrow, we're up at the crack of dawn, and I *will* work you hard."

He nodded and stood. "Done."

Jess wanted to wipe that smile off his face. She didn't know how, but he'd managed to snooker her. She was sure of it. She just didn't understand why.

With a glance at her watch, Jess rose. "The breakfast rush is just about to start. Why don't you join us in the kitchen in about an hour and we'll get lunches made for the bus' return trip." She got up and made to pass him, but he stalled her with an arm across the doorway. He leaned in, and it took all her strength to remain standing on the spaghetti her legs had turned into.

"Don't you think we should shake on it?" His voice, so close to her ear, felt like velvet brushing her skin.

"I—I trust you."

His face dropped to within inches of hers. "Trusting me could be dangerous."

Jess stared into eyes that were a kaleidoscope of ambers and browns. The world tilted off its axis and slowed to a snail's pace as she got lost in them. In those lips. Lips that were so close, she could touch them without any effort.

She licked her lips, and Ren's audible intake of air snapped normal back in place. Jess put her game face back on, or hoped she did. "Move your hand."

When he hesitated, Jess gnashed her teeth and pushed his hand out of the way.

He stepped aside as she tilted her chin up and willed herself to walk slowly past him and into the kitchen.

Chapter Six

It had been a hectic couple of hours cleaning up from breakfast and making lunches for the passengers, but by nine a.m., the tour bus had moved off. Jess had to give Ren credit. He dug in and helped just like he said he would, even pushing up his sleeves. There had been times when she'd found herself staring at those forearms as he stuffed boxes with food. Dark hair accented muscles that moved in ways she found difficult to ignore.

After seeing the bus on its way, everyone retreated indoors except Jess, who stood on the porch and watched clouds skate across the sky. They didn't have the look of snow—yet. Storm possibilities would be more finely tuned this evening, and Jess made a mental note to call Fairbanks then to discuss that final tour bus.

She shivered as the cold filtered in despite her well-insulated coat, knowing she should be getting ready to leave. Mary had been quite transparent in her pleasure at the idea of Jess touring Ren around the wildlife refuge. She'd even offered to put together lunch for them, as well as indicating she might have a box or two Jess and Ren could deliver to Fort Yukon.

Jess had mixed emotions about spending this time with Renzo Gallini. The man was arrogant and much too certain of himself. She didn't like him.

Even as Jess thought it, she knew it wasn't true. She didn't want to like him. In reality, she reacted to him in a way she'd never experienced before. Not to this degree, at any rate. Her body forgot the cold, forgot the station, forgot everything when he was near.

Unable to shake the doldrums that had settled on her shoulders, Jess wondered again where her father was. He should be here. He'd know how to handle this Gallini situation.

Her gloved hands clutched the porch railing. It seemed like every time she stopped and took time to think, she understood less. She shook her head in frustration at this inability to keep life from throwing curve balls at her. Used to taking action when things weren't right, she was stuck in a rut of inactivity that was driving her nuts. If her father wouldn't come to her, maybe she should go in search of him. First on her list was a little talk with John and Rocky. She glanced at her watch. If she hurried, she had just enough time before meeting Ren.

It wasn't like Dad to up and leave without some method of contact in place. If he'd taken off to meet a woman, well, guys talked, right? She pictured them sitting around, beers in hand, discussing their conquests. Out of the blue, her mind plunked Ren into the picture. He would look out of place amongst the small group. Did Ren Gallini kiss and tell?

"Worried about the weather?"

Jess's heart skipped about three beats as she spun around, and her boot caught on a lose board. She threw her arms out to regain her balance, but it was too late, and she fell directly into Ren's rock-hard chest. Solid arms cushioned her, held her steady and, for a fraction of a second, seemed to pull her in closer. She could have sworn she heard him groan.

An unfamiliar ache surfaced as she spread her fingers over his chest, feeling the twitch of his muscles, even through the coat. Jess balled her fist, willing the strange feelings coursing through her to go away. Several seconds longer than it should have taken, she stepped back. When she looked at Ren, his brown eyes were dark and filled with emotion. He took a long, somewhat ragged breath, then let go of her and turned to the gravel expanse in front of them.

"Looks rather gray out today," Ren said.

Jess shook her head, in part to clear it. "You just don't see the colors," she answered him, her voice no more than a whisper.

A raised eyebrow showed his disbelief. "What colors?"

Her lips curved upward in a half smile that seemed to divulge some secret Ren was not yet privileged to understand.

"There's color all around you."

Ren looked. He saw buildings in need of paint, with gray gravel covering the distance in between. Shrubs that looked more like weeds gave way to bare hillsides.

She reached for his gloved hand and walked to the stunted bushes that surrounded the camp. "This is willow."

"I thought willow was a tree. This can't be, what, four feet tall?"

"It's a ground shrub, and a major source of food for moose around here." She touched one of the branches. "Stop thinking with your head. Look. See the hint of yellow in these tips? When the sunlight hits it, it stands out like polished gold ore. And when there's no sun, the echo of that color remains." She threaded the branch through her fingers before looking up to the hills. "You see a barren, shrub-infested hillside there, right? Well, I see remnants of fireweed, Autumn's most vibrant color, a red that defies definition." She didn't wait for his response, but walked ahead, her arm waving to encompass the land around them.

"I see the colors of sustenance for moose, caribou, and all manner of creatures that survive the harsh winters here in Alaska. And because they survive, we survive. We have food. Did you know that sausage you had this morning was caribou?"

"No."

"On a sunny day, the sky is bluer than blue. At night, the black is a welcome darkness, broken by a million pricks of light. Then," her voice lowered, "if you're lucky, the lights make an appearance. Have you ever seen them?"

"Not really." Technically, he'd been more focused on Jess than the northern lights.

"The colors are amazing. Mostly greens and whites, but if the spirits are in a good mood, the deep night sky can be alive with different colors."

Ren didn't see the landscape. Instead, his attention was riveted on the animated face of the woman in front of him. Jess Jenkins was an innocent. So in love with this place, she would never see its flaws. Ren got a sense she never cared to be anywhere else but here. Hell, he would bet a year's profits her father had to force her to leave this place, even for R&R, once in a while.

If that was the case, then Jess had lived a very sheltered life. He watched an eighteen-wheeler pull in and wondered if her life had always been sheltered. What kind of education had she gotten from these road warriors? He frowned. Had any of them tried to teach her what men had to offer? That thought made him tighten with an instant tension he was unaccustomed to. He jammed gloved fists into his pockets.

Jess watched the truck's arrival and appeared to have forgotten Ren was here. He took advantage of the rare opportunity to view a profile devoid of her usual attitude. She had an upturned nose and a smattering of freckles that made her appear even younger than he supposed she was. There was a wholesomeness to her that appealed to him much more than it should. Certainly much more than Kathryn had ever sparked in him.

Jess's forehead furrowed, and he wanted to wipe the worry away.

"What's got you so worried, beautiful?"

Rolling her eyes, she moved away, or would have, if Ren hadn't stilled her with a hand to her arm.

"It's possible I can help."

"Not with this, you can't."

"Try me. If nothing else, it's easier if you don't carry the burden alone." He waved an arm at their surroundings. "This is too much for someone as young as you to take care of."

Ren suppressed a smile at the flash of fire in her eyes. Damn, but he enjoyed sparring with her. Now, though, was not the time.

"I'm old enough to take care of this place just fine."

"You shouldn't have to," he said. "Your father shouldn't leave you alone like this. Too much can happen in a place this isolated. I consider that a poor decision on his part."

"My father takes very good care of me. Has since I was a baby. Even more so since my mother died. Besides, I'm not alone. I've got Aunt Mary and the guys to help me."

"But the responsibility, and the choices, fall on your shoulders alone, don't they?"

Jess straightened. "Yes. And I gladly accept them. This is my home."

"A home that your father seems to be selling without giving you the benefit of an argument." That was the moment when Ren Gallini started to feel like a true asshole. Brown eyes that had bewitched him since first notice now filled with tears.

Jess swiped the tears away as if they stung. "My father wouldn't do that."

Ren looked across the expanse of gravel, then back at Jess. "I've seen people do some pretty strange things in my business."

"Not my father. You ask anyone. He's a stand-up guy. Hell, he never even plays practical jokes." She looked up at him, wide eyes showing signs of hope. "Do you think that's what this is? Some colossal practical joke?"

"I don't see how. The intent is clearly documented in the paperwork."

"Paperwork can be forged." She gripped both Ren's arms. "You saw him, didn't you? You had to, to do the paperwork. Where—"

He hated to disappoint her. "I didn't see him."

"Then how did you come by those papers?"

"My mother handled the transaction. I had no idea this place existed until she called me three days ago. By then, the deal was already beyond the negotiation stage. The contracts were signed."

Jess clapped her hands together. "Then we can call your mother."

"I've already tried."

"And?"

"And, like your father, I don't seem to be able to reach her."

"What does that mean?"

"It means I've left several messages, and she has not yet returned any of them."

"Is that normal?"

He cocked his head. "She doesn't do it often, but she has been known to disappear for a few days here and there."

Jess shook her head. "Just like my father. Do you think they know each other?"

"How? This isn't meant as an insult, but..." He waved his hands again, across the landscape in front of them. "They come from different worlds. How would they ever meet?"

"I don't know."

"I'll continue to try to locate my mother, but I doubt she has any information that will help find your father."

Jess hugged herself. "I...would like to know where he is, what's going on. And his side of this...issue."

Ren couldn't stand to see Jess give in to the worry. He wanted to remove all the stress from her face, all the worry lines from her eyes, and all the pain from her heart. So he did the only thing he could think of. Stepping up to her back, he wrapped his arms around her. She resisted for a moment, then melted into him. The feeling of trust between them, however fleeting, held him under its spell, and neither of them moved for several long moments. He leaned down and relaxed further at the surprisingly light, flowery scent of her hair.

She snuggled deeper and a new, more urgent sensation began as a spike in his groin, growing and spreading out until it threatened his sanity. Not good. Not good at all. Ren straightened and set her away from him before she could feel his need.

He could see confusion written in the little lines that bridged her eyebrows as she clutched her arms in front of her.

"I'm sorry," he said. "I shouldn't have done that."

Before she could voice the question in her eyes, he walked away from her, aware she watched him.

What the hell was he thinking? No matter how good being near her made him feel, he had no time for this. Besides, Jess wasn't what he wanted, who he dated. She was too young. Too naïve. Too...virginal.

Ren stopped short. Could she be a virgin? He kicked at the gravel. This place was basically a truck stop. And she had an innocent attractiveness that was hard to turn away from. She must have been propositioned. The flare of green that shot through him dimmed any leftover ardor as he thought of her having to deal with all the travelers, all the men, who passed through Last Chance Camp.

Jess had proven she could hold her own, though. If he'd learned anything in his short time here, he'd learned that steel lay beneath the beauty. She'd hold her own. And if she couldn't, Mary, John, and Rocky had all proven she had people around who would make certain she wasn't bothered. Especially Rocky. There was a story there, one he wasn't sure of or how Jess'd been involved.

Ren continued on to his trailer-turned-hotel room, letting that thought reassure him that Jess was at all times safe to make her own choices here. Still, for her father to disappear regularly as she indicated was unconscionable. Ren couldn't fathom what would make a man so well thought of do this to his daughter. It was a mystery, and one he'd very much like to help solve.

Chapter Seven

Jess watched Ren abruptly stride off, shaking her head. *And they said women were complicated?* She rubbed her arms, the lingering comfort she'd gotten from his embrace soothing her and irritating her at the same time.

He'd said she was too young for this burden. Her entire life defied that belief. No one could accomplish what she'd done here on such a shoe-string budget. She didn't need Ren Gallini, or anyone else. She would take care of this camp and find her father without the man's help.

First though, she had a flight to endure. She glanced at her watch and realized she was about out of time. She went in search of John to have a quick conversation, finding him and Rocky both working on generator maintenance.

"Hey, guys," she said. "How's it looking? Are we set for the weather?"

John shrugged. "As set as we can be or ever were. You know how cantankerous the generators can be, but they look good at the moment."

Jess nodded. "And we're good on fuel?"

Rocky nudged her with his elbow. "Gee, boss, seems like the person who does the ordering should *know* how much fuel we've got."

"Ha ha, very funny," she said, giving him a playful shove. "You can be replaced, you know."

"Nah. Who'd have your back if you kicked me out? Besides, I'm too cute to get rid of. I'm good eye candy for the ladies."

Jess rolled her eyes and laughed. "In your mind, kid. Only in your mind." Okay, so he was cute, if you went for that kind of trendy, disheveled look. At least, that's what she'd been told. Rocky was puppy-dog adorable to her and she loved him like a baby brother. Not that she'd tell him that. If she did, he'd be insufferable for days.

John clapped him on the back. "How about you go dip the stick to verify our fuel levels, Mr. Eye Candy?"

"Wait," Jess said, forestalling Rocky. "I'd like to ask you a question." Geesh, now that she had them together, she didn't even know what to ask or how. "I, um, well, do either of you know where Dad went?"

Rocky's headshake was immediate. John took a moment, looking down as he considered, making Jess wonder what he knew.

"I don't have any idea where he's at," he finally said.

"It's just so unusual for him to leave when something important was about to happen. Did he ever mention...selling this place?"

Rocky guffawed. "No way the old man would sell this place. This is your home."

"Well, the guy who's here right now—"

"The one who's been bugging you?" Rocky asked.

"Well, sort of. Anyhow, he says Dad's selling this place to his company."

"Doesn't sound like something Owen would do," John said.

"I know. Which is why I don't understand his absence. Do you...does he have a woman he visits?"

Both men began shuffling their feet.

"Aww, that's not a fair question, Jess. You can't ask

guys to rat on each other. Even if we knew, we couldn't tell you. It's the guy code."

"I'd just like to stop wondering what's going on. I'm starting to worry."

John put a comforting arm around her shoulder. "I'm sure your dad's fine. He's never mentioned having a woman friend to me, but it's not outside the realm of possibilities."

"Yeah, I guess it isn't."

"Would you be okay if he did have someone he...visits?"

"Sure. I mean, I don't expect him to be alone forever. I just figured he'd tell me if he did. We haven't had many secrets between us."

Rocky laughed. "Hard to have any secrets period, here."

"Try not to worry, honey. And give it some time. He'll turn up eventually. He always does and this will all be resolved then."

"I guess. Well, thanks. I'll try to be patient."

A half hour later, she left her trailer still wondering. John and Rocky had offered no useful information. Trying to decide what she should do next to find her father, she rounded the corner of the restaurant and bumped into Ren. "Sorry I'm late," she mumbled. "I got busy."

"No apologies needed," he said as he held up a basket. "Food from Mary. Feels like there's enough for an army."

Jess peeked inside. "There is. I'd say she packed enough for Fort Yukon to have lunch."

Ren nodded. "You ready?"

She wanted to run in the opposite direction. "Sure. I just need to make one quick stop on the way to the airstrip."

They walked across the road to the Visitor's Center, where Jess introduced Ren to her friend, Meg. "She's one of two state troopers stationed here."

Ren shook Meg's hand, and Jess smothered the irritation she felt as her friend's eyes kept darting from Jess to Ren and back again. When Meg winked at Jess in full view of Ren Gallini, Jess was ready to pinch her.

"So, Mr. Gallini," Meg said. "How do you like our little piece of Alaska?"

"Please. Call me Ren." He glanced at Jess and grinned. "Alaska definitely has some redeeming features to it. I could get used to it."

Jess didn't find anything amusing in his answer, but Meg let out a hoot of laughter. "I bet you could," she said as her phone rang. "Last Chance Station."

By the way Meg's eyes lit up, Jess guessed that Rod was on the phone checking in. When she hung up, Jess could tell by Meg's face that Rod had once again kept it all business. She'd promised Meg she would stay out of it, but if that man didn't realize what was standing right in front of him pretty soon, he was going to lose it.

Somber-faced, Meg returned to the counter. "What brought you to Alaska, Ren?"

"I'm here on business."

Most people wouldn't catch the subtle changes in Meg's face, but Jess knew her friend had put her professional hat on. "Really," Meg said. "What kind of business are you in?"

"I help businesses re-organize or maximize their assets to sell."

"You're not in the oil business?"

That was the point where Ren Gallini turned on the charm, Meg's smile returned, and Jess's attitude went further south than it already was. Why did it bother her that he was leaning on the counter having a conversation with Meg when he could easily chat from an upright position?

"No, I'm not in the oil business. This trip is at the request of our CEO. I came here in the hopes of speaking to Owen Jenkins. I was quite surprised to find him absent when I arrived."

Meg turned to Jess. "Your Dad take off for a few days again?"

"It seems so," Jess answered. She chewed her lower lip. "It's strange this time, though. I can't seem to get hold of him."

Meg frowned. "That's not like your father." She turned to Ren. "Did Owen know you were coming?"

"I believe so," Ren said.

"Any reason he would not want to be here to meet you?"

"None that I know of."

"Why do you need to speak to him?"

Jess stifled a grin at the grilling Meg was giving Ren. Maybe this day wouldn't be so bad after all.

Ren held up his hands. "I confess," he said. "I set this all up. I lured Mr. Jenkins away so that I could swoop in and seduce his daughter."

Oh, God, no. Jess felt the flush creep up her neck and settle in her face as she watched Meg's eyes turn owl-like in their surprise.

Jess really wanted to kill Ren Gallini at that moment.

"It's not like he's suggesting, Meg," she said, in an effort to stop what her friend was thinking.

Meg raised her eyebrows. "It should be."

Ren's laugh iced Jess's attitude-cake, and she refused to look at him. "I just stopped by to tell you I'll be gone for the afternoon. Mr. Gallini—" She could feel him smiling behind her.

"Mr. Gallini wants to see a bit of Alaska so we're doing a flyover for a few hours and stopping up at Fort Yukon."

"Ah, so that's what the plane is for. I saw it come in. You know Rod's up in that area?"

"He mentioned this morning he was headed that way."

Meg pointed to the phone. "Rod said he'd be in Fort Yukon by dinner. If you see him, tell him...tell him everything's fine here."

Jess placed a hand over her friend's for a quick moment. "We'll be back by dinner. Are we on for tonight?"

Meg straightened. "You bet. You two have fun, now. And don't do anything I wouldn't do."

Jess turned to leave and saw the wide smile on Ren's face. Rolling her eyes, she trudged past him and out the door to the airstrip.

A blue and white Cessna Super Cub stood ready next to the landing strip. Jess didn't recognize the pilot, but that wasn't unusual. Bush piloting seemed to be the new extreme sport these days. There were always new pilots looking to stretch their wings. He greeted Ren, handed him some paperwork and muttered something about weight limits as he loaded one final box in the plane. Before Jess had a chance to introduce herself, the man walked off toward the Visitor's Center.

She turned to Ren, who was walking around the plane, checking it out from wing to wing. Why was he doing pre-flight?

"Ummm, where's our pilot going?"

"Across the road. Apparently, your restaurant has a good reputation." Ren checked the tail rudder and kicked the tail-dragger's rear wheel, then walked around to the far side of the plane. "He's gone to get some food and relax for a while."

"But aren't we leaving?"

Ren smiled as he checked the wing. "Yes. I'll be flying us today."

"You? You're a pilot?"

"That surprise of yours is mildly insulting, you know. Yes, I'm a pilot."

He lifted the engine hatch. Then he checked the propeller. Jess followed close on his heels. "This is Alaska. It's not some casual daytime flight territory. Bad things can, and do, happen here. It takes a certain amount of training and understanding of the unique elements at play. Flying in the Alaska back-country is not for the faint of heart."

He turned to her then, amusement showing in his eyes and his mouth. "So now you think I'm faint of heart?"

"No. That's not what I'm saying. It's just...there's a lot of wilderness up here. And planes get lost all the time."

"Don't worry, beautiful. I think I've got enough know-how to handle what Alaska has to offer."

"Do you even know where we're going?"

"I take flying pretty seriously, so I've studied the maps and have spoken at length with a seasoned bush pilot about the best route for where I want to go. If it will ease your mind, we also discussed what Alaska can throw at pilots and how best to navigate around those possibilities, as well as what to do if we can't get around an issue. Always expect the unexpected, especially in Alaska."

The idea of spending the next few hours in such close quarters with Ren Gallini, without another person to provide distraction, made Jess feel just a little bit...well, edgy. Somehow, the man had gotten under her skin. And if she didn't watch it, he'd find her heart, ensnare it, and leave it to shrivel up and die when he left.

"Ready?" The passenger door was open and Ren had one arm on a strut and the other held out to assist her. Working hard to tamp down her emotions, she took his hand.

Time slowed to a crawl as he brushed his thumb along her fingers. A new kind of warmth tingled its way up her arm. She could sense the strength in his hand, yet he held hers as if it were precious. This one simple touch made her feel protected. Like she was home in camp and nothing would hurt her.

She glanced up, certain Ren would catch her with her mouth gaping open and be thoroughly amused. She was surprised to find him staring at their hands. His brow was furrowed, as if he were sensing something he didn't particularly want to feel. So maybe it wasn't just her. Maybe this, whatever it was, affected both of them?

When he looked up, the businessman quickly took over as he smoothed his face and smiled. "Up we go," he said.

Once she climbed in, he secured her seat belt, and Jess noted the pains he took to not touch her as he helped. She hated to admit to the sting that realization caused and reminded herself yet again the man was trouble.

After a smooth liftoff, Jess forgot any misgivings she'd harbored. Opportunities like this were rare and no one could be immune to the landscape from this vantage point. Any tension disappeared, and Jess gave herself over to the experience.

Alaska had a lot of mountains. It also had a lot of flat tundra areas, and she doubted anyone could see that expansiveness without being touched by it in some way. The mountains in the near-distance were blue and white, but the tundra was alive with color. Browns and yellows and greens played tag with the winding silver ribbons of rivers. This beauty never ceased to amaze her.

"I thought we would skirt the southern edge of the Brooks Range," Ren said.

"That's a good idea. Those mountains can be pretty nasty."

"We'll head north for a bit, then westerly into the wildlife refuge, finishing up a semi-circle with a stop in Fort Yukon."

Jess was too busy looking out the window to care which way they went. "Sounds good to me."

"The Brooks Range looks pretty amazing from here."

"At Last Chance, we live in the shadow of those mountains, and we've learned to have a very healthy respect for them. We've outfitted more base camps for rescues than I like to think about." She glanced sideways at him. "A lot of people think they can come up here and hike into the mountains and it will be no different from what they do in their own backyard."

He raised his eyebrows in apparent acknowledgement that she'd put him in with the foolhardy.

She pointed across him. "See the snow line?"

Ren nodded.

"It's already lower than normal for this time of year. Another indicator that we'll get weather early."

"But not today. I do err on the side of caution, you know. I took your concerns about imminent weather change seriously and checked further. Both with NOAA and with a local pilot."

"Who?"

"Rod. I spoke with him last night."

Jess nodded. "I trust his opinion." She grinned. "Maybe we'll see him today."

Ren worked hard to silence the curiosity raging through his mind. He could tell Jess and Rod were close. The question was, how close? "Why is he up in this area?"

"Just trying to keep things peaceful. He got wind that there's an oil-driller snooping around the ANWR. Thought whoever it was might try to talk to some of the locals." She shook her head. "That would be more foolhardy than heading off into the mountains with nothing but a GPS and a granola bar."

A deep twinge of guilt hit Ren. Was he the "oil-driller" scoping things out? He'd only agreed with William that they should take a look in order to decide if the company they'd contracted with should be sold off whole or in pieces. If he was the target of these rumors, how did anyone even know?

Ren needed to call William. The man could be ruthless, but he'd never turned that streak toward Ren. If that had changed, they would be having a long conversation.

He watched Jess. She was trying to play it cool, but he could see her excitement bubbling over. She pointed out ridges and rivers. She explained what tundra was.

"See." She pointed at the peaks to their left. "The Brooks Range is filled with these jagged tooth-like mountains. And yet," she arched in Ren's direction, "if you look down, the land leading up to the range is full of color."

Her enthusiasm was infectious. He leaned forward to see where she pointed. Did she realize how intoxicating that perfume of hers was? All flowers and spring, with a touch of spice to keep people on their toes.

"Ren?" She turned to him. She was only inches from him. If he moved he could touch lips that had begun to claim his nights and take over his days. Lips that must taste like heaven.

"A-hem?"

Caught in the middle of what was quickly becoming a daydream, Ren responded in the only way he knew how. "You smell good."

Hell. Even her blush turned him on. The shade of pink complimented her hair color, her lip color, everything.

"Be serious."

"I am being serious."

Shaking her head, she pointed. "Look at the tundra. Up close, it's not just brown. It's like life. It has shades of brown. A hint of red. Some leftover green, gray, and even some blue, leading into the hills."

Jess sat back and closed her eyes. "The color is amazing. Even the snow. It isn't just white. It's shades of blue and black, too."

"Ummm—"

"Yes. Snow has black in it. Have you ever stood on a glacier?"

"Yes."

"Then you know," she said, nodding her head.

"I think I do."

She grasped his sleeve as he checked the horizon. "See. You aren't color blind."

Ren laughed. Who would not be affected by enthusiasm like this? "All right," he said. "Maybe I see a little color."

"I knew you had it in you."

They spent the rest of the flight in an easy camaraderie, enjoying the view. Ren found Jess captivating. Somewhere, in amongst watching Jess, he managed to keep them aloft.

"Oh, look!" She squirmed in the confines of her seatbelt. "Caribou." Ren followed her gaze and watched the herd slowly move along the tundra. "Is this the herd that migrates between here and the Arctic Ocean?"

"Part of it. And we're lucky to see them this close to Fort Yukon. This time of year, they're moving through to their winter grounds in the forests."

"So they are migratory."

"Yes, and Fort Yukon, as well as most outlying villages in Alaska, survive the harsh winters because of the caribou." She turned to Ren. "That's why most folks don't want to expand drilling in the ANWR. Any chance that it might disrupt the herd, the eco-system, and our subsistence, is too great to take."

She watched Ren closely. Most people didn't get it, didn't understand life on this most basic level. "You understand, right?"

He took a moment before answering. It felt like a lifetime to Jess.

"I do understand. I'm...not sure I believe that drilling would affect the herd that strongly, though."

Her heart plummeted. She wasn't sure why she needed him to understand. She just knew that she did. "Accidents can happen. They have happened. Look at Valdez."

"True." He nodded. "So most people here think drilling is a bad choice?"

"The people I know do. I'll be honest. It's a tough decision. The money would come in handy. But money runs out. The caribou replenish themselves."

"Money invested well could help out for a long time," Ren countered.

Jess slumped back in her seat and stared glumly out the side window. He didn't get it. Ren Gallini was like everybody else. Something deep inside her started to hurt and she felt the sting of tears. She closed her eyes to keep them at bay. "But it's not our way."

Ren's hand covered hers. "Look at me."

She didn't want to.

"Please?"

She turned to him, tears held in check but unable to keep the unshed sheen from showing.

"I don't disagree. In my job, I play devil's advocate on a regular basis."

She blinked and waited.

"It's kind of hard to take that hat off and, to be honest,

I'm not sure I want to. I think it's smart to look at both sides of the issue."

"And have you?"

"I'm working on it."

She crossed her arms over her chest and looked away. "Let me know when you make a decision, all right?"

His hand under her chin nudged her face back toward him. "We called a truce, remember? Today is for fun, not for fighting." His hand covered hers again.

It wasn't in Jess's makeup to let a disagreement go unresolved. She fought to win, especially now. This was important.

But Ren was right. She was nervous enough that he would meet her extended family. They'd be making all sorts of assumptions and she'd be working hard to straighten them out. Going in butting heads with Ren would not make things any easier.

So she nodded. Slowly. "You're right."

When she tried to pull her hand out of his, he held on. And she had to admit, the warmth felt good. If she tried hard, she could almost ignore the underlying tingle that was working its way through her body.

"That's Fort Yukon, I believe." Ren tipped his head toward her window.

Home. Jess's smile returned in full force. She hadn't realized how homesick she was until this moment. The town looked good. Very good.

When she turned back to Ren, he stopped breathing for several seconds. Jess in fighting mode was breathtakingly beautiful. With her face full of joy as it was now, she was the shining star he never wanted to let go of.

That scared the holy hell out of him.

He looked out over Fort Yukon as they circled to land. From the air, it seemed a small community. Jess mentioned there were only five to eight hundred people living there. He recognized pretty quickly that it would be hard to be anonymous in a place like this. By the time the propeller stopped, and well before Ren had a chance to disembark, Jess was out of the plane and surrounded by people. He rounded the plane, but she was gone, pulled along by a swarm of women. She turned back briefly, threw up her arms in supplication and he laughed. Waving her on, he hollered that he would follow shortly, but doubted she heard him. It was obvious the people here loved her.

He pulled the parcels out of the plane, astounded at the amount of boxes and bags Mary had packed, apparently items Last Chance had that were scarce or hard to come by in Fort Yukon. Grateful that a few of the men stuck around to help, they made quick work of loading everything into a truck. Slapping Ren on the back, the men invited him to sit on top of the boxes for the short trip to the house Jess had disappeared into.

He found Jess ensconced at the kitchen table, the central focus of a mass of women of all different ages.

"Yes," Jess said with a melodious laugh. "I am still studying. I do it online now."

Studying? Ren's interest was piqued, and he stood silent at the edge of the group, hoping for more information. Jess, however, tuned into his presence and turned briefly in his direction. Just as quickly, she changed the subject, leaning over to take a months-old baby from the young woman who sat next to her.

Ren was content to stand back and listen. This was Jess in her element, and she was more animated here than she was in Last Chance. He enjoyed seeing her in her native environment. And he understood more now about why she was so...real. She was well loved by family and friends alike.

When food appeared, Ren realized just how hungry he was. A combination of local dishes and the basket Mary sent was laid out on the table and passed around. The meat was caribou, he was certain of it. It was a different flavor, but not one he minded. In fact, the way they seasoned it added a unique taste that would probably do well in an urban restaurant. After all, buffalo was making a comeback as the new meat. Why not caribou?

"—supplies in order for this year? Weather is coming."

A woman answered who appeared to be the elder, if age was any indication. "The caribou hunting has been good. Our elders have foretold an early winter, so extra supplies are stocked. We are ready."

"Good." Jess patted the woman's hand.

His appetite satisfied, Ren became acutely aware that he was the only male in the house. That feeling strengthened when the women began gazing back and forth from Jess to him and back again. Curiosity would soon get the better of them and the questions would start. Excusing himself, he went outside and found several men standing around. One of them pulled a beer out of a cooler and handed it to Ren.

"We wondered how long it would take for you to tire of women's talk." He smiled and held out a hand. "I'm Carl. This here's Mark and that's his twin brother, Matt.

That's our wives and kin inside, and since they love to henpeck as a group, it's usually safer to hang out here."

Ren shook Carl's hand and tipped his beer to the others. "It didn't take me long to figure that out. I think they were about to throw me to the wolves."

Carl laughed. "You got out just in time, then."

They watched as another plane, this one with pontoons, circled and settled in for a landing on the river.

"Busy day for visiting," Jim observed.

Mark and Matt headed for the truck and went down to pick up the newest visitor. It wasn't long before they returned, crunching to a stop and throwing up gravel and dirt. A state trooper who could only be Rod Willson hopped out of the truck, and Ren got some perverse pleasure out of knowing he wasn't the only one remanded to riding in the back.

Rod greeted the local men easily, then turned to Ren. "Gallini," he said with a nod. "How was the flight up?"

"Excellent. Thanks for the weather help."

"You come up alone?"

Ren shook his head. "I wanted to see more of Alaska. Jess offered to be tour guide. The afternoon has been quite...enjoyable. She's inside." He pointed to the house.

"With the other women," Jim said.

Rod held both hands up. "I've been the brunt of their plans before. I know better than to go in there."

"What brings you to Fort Yukon?" Carl settled on a wood crate.

Rod glanced at Ren. "We heard a rumor that someone from one of the oil companies might be up here stirring the pot. I've just been in Arctic Village. They haven't seen any strangers around there. Have you?"

Carl shook his head. "No one's come in except Jess and her boyfriend, here."

Rod's eyes narrowed, and he glared at Ren. The grin Ren flashed had nothing to do with boardroom negotiations. I win, it said, and Rod knew it. For an instant, Ren felt some primal urge to pound his chest. He and Rod might have actually squared off, if Carl hadn't interrupted.

"Those people sure don't know the meaning of 'no', do they?"

"Not when they want something, it seems," Rod answered.

"This is about drilling for oil in the ANWR, isn't it? Forgive me for sounding ignorant, but I'm curious what your take on the situation is."

Carl took a long pull from his beer before waving the bottle at the surrounding landscape. "The ANWR provides sustenance to a lot of herds, most importantly the Porcupine River herd of caribou. Each winter, the land provides survival food. In the spring, they migrate to the coastal plains of the refuge, where their birthing and nursing grounds are. The elders call it *The Sacred Place Where Life Begins*. Even if this area weren't considered sacred ground, the people here will not survive if the herd is diminished...or worse, if man's intrusion causes them to move."

"Is the herd that sensitive to humanity?"

"We hope to never test that hypothesis. You have to understand. We are an economically depressed area. It would be nice to have the money the oil-drillers offer. And they have offered a lot as recompense. But honoring our heritage, and the hard work of those who now reside with the Great Spirit, is more important. I hope we never yield to the oil-drillers."

Ren could feel Rod watching him as Jim spoke, recognizing that he may well suspect Ren was the "person of interest" he'd heard about. Hell, Ren himself suspected the rumors were about him. William would get an earful as soon as he could get cell service and some time alone. Ren didn't play lackey for anyone.

Feeling the burn of Rod's stare, Ren decided it was time to end this conversation. He turned to the trooper. "Will you be back in Last Chance tonight?"

Rod shook his head. "No, I think I'll hang around here overnight and see if anyone...else shows up." He glanced at the sky. "Flying at night in Alaska isn't advised, especially for a rookie."

Ren bridled at the veiled insult. He glanced at his watch. "I'm sure Jess and I would be just fine, but you're right. It's time we started home."

He turned to go indoors, but Rod beat him to it. "I'll get her for you. I need to pay my respects, anyhow."

Ren shrugged and sat down next to Jim on the crate to wait. He set his nearly full beer down behind him.

It took several minutes for Jess to show up and the look on her face told him Rod had said a few things she didn't like before letting her go.

The short ride to the airport was quiet except for the un-muffled truck engine. He did a once over of the plane as Jess buckled herself in.

A quick taxi, and he pulled the wheel back. Before long, they were aloft and on their way back to camp. All during takeoff, Jess stared straight ahead and didn't say a word.

"You giving me the silent treatment?"

"No."

It took several more minutes for her to ask what was on her mind. "What do you really do, Ren?"

"Right now, or in general?"

She scowled at him. "You know what I mean. What is your company about?"

"I explained that before we left. We sell businesses."

Her scowl didn't lessen one iota.

"If you're thinking along the lines of Richard Gere in *Pretty Woman,* that's not what we do. We come in at the request of the company leadership, sort of as consultants. Generally speaking, we facilitate the sale of the company. Either it's in trouble or the leadership simply wants out, or to retire. There are a lot of reasons. They hire us to market the sale and negotiate the price. Sometimes, as with your place, we buy it outright." He had some serious questions about why his mother would do that.

"So you don't deal in oil commodities or companies?"

Ah, so that was it. Rod had bent her ear about his reason for being here. Ren smiled. This, he could handle.

"No. I do not deal in any commodities. Only real businesses."

"Any of them oil businesses?"

"You're worried I'm the person who was sent up here to scope out the local attitude, aren't you?"

Sitting stiff in her seat and looking straight ahead, Jess nodded.

Ren reached for her hand, and she didn't resist. "I'm

not going to lie. We are in the process of bartering the sale of an oil business that has not done well in this new economy."

Jess's hand tensed under his.

"Let me assure you, Jess. There is no financial advantage to my company getting involved in the controversy here."

Jess turned to him then. "Really?"

"Really."

Jess's answering smile triggered a quick hit of guilt in Ren. He knew he hadn't been totally honest. And he fully intended to kill William when he got back home for suggesting such an incendiary errand.

Chapter Eight

Jess believed Ren. Maybe she shouldn't, but she did. He'd made no mention of the ANWR and drilling until she brought it up. Relaxing back into her seat, she determined to enjoy the rest of their trip home. Ren still held her hand, and her leg felt warm where they rested. His hands were lean and long-fingered. He stroked her palm almost absent-mindedly. She wanted to pull her hand away, acutely aware of the calluses hard work had given her. Her nails could use a manicure, too.

She forced herself to leave her hand there.

"What are you studying?"

So, he had caught that conversation with the women. Jess didn't like talking about this. She wasn't ready. Not until she accomplished what she needed to. Not until she graduated.

"Touchy subject?"

She let out a sigh. "No. Not touchy. Just something I haven't really talked to anyone about. I've been taking online courses."

"In what?"

"Business administration with a minor in hotel management."

Ren nodded. "Nice. How's it going?"

"I'm in my final quarter." Jess couldn't quite keep the pride out of her voice.

"For your B.A.?"

"Uh-uh. Masters."

"I'm impressed."

She turned as much as her seat belt would allow, careful not to disturb their entwined hands. She found she liked them like this. "Dad's not going to want to work forever, so this helps to ensure I've got the knowledge to run the place. It'll be all mine one of these days."

Jess realized what she'd just said and what unfinished business still lay between them. She felt the warmth of red flood her face.

Ren laughed. "Don't worry. We'll sort it all out."

Reminded of her father's part in her current situation, Jess couldn't help but wonder again where he was. Ren's hand tightened on hers for a brief moment.

"We'll find him."

For the first time in days, Jess felt real relaxation ease muscles that had been tense for a long time.

Too soon, Ren pulled his hand away to land the plane. As they climbed out, the pilot joined them, and it took very little time to turn the plane back over to him. After a quick word with Meg, they walked back over to camp. The air was chilly, and Ren pulled her hand into the pocket of the coat he wore, along with his own.

That action made Jess just about melt. She could have kept walking halfway to Fairbanks and not felt the cold.

Except there was a yard filled with trucks, most of which probably made the run to Deadhorse and halfway back before hitting the mandatory rest period dictated by law. Even without a bus full of tourists, it was bound to be busy for Mary and the guys.

"I'd better go see if I can help with dinner."

They stopped at the restaurant's porch and Jess tried to

pull her hand back. Ren tightened his grip. "Your hand is still cold," he said. He reached for her other hand and pulled them both up to his lips, cocooning them while he blew warm breaths into her palms.

Jess felt frozen, not by the cold, but by the sensation his action caused. A slow burn consumed her body, starting with the hands he held, then moving up her arms. She could feel an ache in her chest as the gentle heat wrapped itself around her heart. She pulled her hands out of his. "Umm, I need to get inside."

"Yes. You must be cold." Ren leaned down and Jess's heartbeat jumped to double time. Did he mean to kiss her? Instead of touching her lips, he kissed first one cheek, then the other.

Her lips felt the lack.

Straightening, he put his own hands in his pocket. "I had a nice time today. Thank you for showing me another piece of your world."

Jess felt like she was dreaming. Everything seemed to be moving in slow motion. She picked leaden legs up one at a time to climb the stairs. At the top, she turned to find Ren still watching, his own face filled with bemusement before he walked off.

What the hell just happened? She'd enjoyed the afternoon, hadn't even thought about camp. Well, not much. And the two of them had gotten along. Worse, she'd really liked spending the time with him. Seeing him smile when she pointed something out. How he handled the curious stares of the women. The warmth of his breath on her hands...

Jess was so screwed. She'd never be able to sort this all

out if she went all ga-ga over the new guy in camp. No. This couldn't happen. She tamped down the smile trying to force its way out. This. Would. Not. Happen.

After dinner, she headed for Meg's and a much needed mani/pedi girl's night. Except Meg didn't have relaxing on the brain. She was in total snoop mode and completely unrepentant about it.

"So you spent the entire afternoon with that gorgeous hunk of a man, and he never made a single move on you?"

"I've told you this already," Jess said, swiping red polish along a well-shaped toenail. "Why would he make a move on me? I'm the one who hates his reason for being here, remember?" That was easy to hate. The man himself was another story altogether.

Meg eyed her closely. Too closely. Jess started to squirm.

"Hating the reason is not the same as hating the man," she said, speculation rampant in wide eyes framed by her friend's short brown hair.

"It's close enough for me." Jess crossed her fingers that Meg would stop there. She didn't want to delve too far into how she felt about Ren Gallini. It was confusing enough without having her friend trying to dissect it. Meg, however, was first and foremost an investigative cop, so her next question didn't surprise Jess one bit.

"So, do you like him?"

Jess rolled her eyes. "The man says he's going to own my home. What do you think?" She finished the toes on one foot and moved to the other one.

"I think," Meg said, adding clear polish to her fingernails and nodding, "you like him."

Jess wanted more than anything to blow that statement out of the water. But she couldn't, because she didn't know what she felt about Ren. Meg was the only friend she could talk to about anything, and she owed her the truth. "Maybe. I don't know, Megs. It's confusing."

Meg stuck the brush back in the bottle of nail polish and placed her hand on Jess's arm. "Oh, boy. I know what that's like."

"Yeah, you do. Have you gotten any indication from Rod that he's interested at all?"

Shaking her head, Meg took the red from Jess and began painting her own toenails. "None. I've done everything but throw myself at him."

"I'm sorry," Jess said, knowing it probably wasn't enough to dull the ache of unrequited love. "Maybe you *should* throw yourself at him."

"I can't. You know the rules about officers fraternizing."

"Yes, but in outposts like this, isn't that rule bent on a regular basis?"

Meg nodded. "I've heard rumors to that effect. But it can also be career-ending." She hugged her knees. "I'm going to have to do something soon, though. I can't stay here like this."

Jess looked up from the cuticle she was edging. "You're not thinking of leaving?"

"No. Well, maybe. I don't know."

Jess grabbed her friend's hands. "We're quite a pair, aren't we?"

Meg nodded, the sheen of unshed tears brightening her eyes. "Yes, we are. And my problems can wait until we solve yours."

"Ugh. I tell you what. Let's hold off on solving anything until we find Dad, okay?"

Jess saw the career officer take over Meg's face again. "Good idea. You haven't heard a thing?"

"Nothing at all."

"It's not unusual for him to take off like this."

"True, but after signing papers to sell our home? And without telling me?"

"Somebody has to know something."

"I've spoken with John and Rocky. And Ren. None of them seem to have a clue."

"What about Mary?"

Jess frowned. "I think I asked her about it."

"Sounds like a good next step, then. Let me know what Mary says and, if need be, I'll put an official missing persons out on him. If you want."

Jess felt better with somewhat of a plan. Now to put it into action. First though—she slipped into her thongs for the quick drive across the compound to her place—she needed to get through with this season. She had one last bus of tourists coming in tomorrow. After they were gone, she could focus on finding her errant father.

Chapter Nine

By morning, Jess had no answer to her questions. In fact, she'd spent the better part of the night trying to figure out what was going on between her and Renzo Gallini, and now she was paying for that lack of sleep. The breakfast rush was over. The truckers had all headed out and camp was, for the moment, empty.

She stood on the porch in less winter wear than she should, snuggling close to the steaming cup of coffee in her hands.

Daytime had begun to look more like early twilight than morning as the north moved closer to the polar night. That effect was enhanced by the lowering cloud layer. She loved how the gray made the last bits of yellow in the willow seem almost on fire. Fall colors lasted a very short time here as they gave way to the long dark of winter.

"Why so solemn, beautiful?"

Jess jumped, spilling her coffee. She hated that he could startle her with such regularity. "Stop sneaking up on me, Gallini."

He smiled. "But it's so much fun. I don't think you know just how cute surprise looks on your face."

Her eyes narrowed, even as she felt grateful for the return to normal in their relationship. She could handle him this way. The other...well, that felt like a danger she didn't need. "Can I help you?"

He held up her coat. "I think you forgot something?"

Trust the man to ruin a perfectly good annoyance by

doing something nice. "Thank you," she grumbled as he helped her into her cold-weather coat. The added warmth felt good. Damn him.

"So I ask again. Why so solemn?"

Jess shrugged. "I don't know. It's kind of an end of season thing. We've been going gangbusters since May. Each year, it seems to end so abruptly that it's hard to make the shift."

Ren nodded. "You've still got one bus coming in today, right?"

"Yes, and that's part of my worry. They're already en route, but I'm not sure the bus should have been allowed to come."

"The weather reports all indicate the storm should hold off until at least tomorrow, right?"

Shaking her head, Jess pointed skyward. "Have you looked up lately?"

They both glanced up. The clouds showed very little white to contrast the gray and not a wisp of blue peeked through. "I don't care what the weather service says. Weather is coming, and I think it's coming sooner instead of later."

She held her hand out flat and watched as a few stray snowflakes settled on her glove. "You see this? Snow. Snow we shouldn't have yet. If I'm right on the timing, and they're right on the early cold front coming in behind it, we could be snowed in."

"Can we handle being snowed in?"

An uneasy pleasure threaded through her at his use of the word "we." She missed her father more than she could say. It felt good to share the burden, even if it was with Ren

Gallini.

"Last Chance is well stocked, and we can accommodate a group for longer quite easily. As long as they don't get too surly."

The real question was whether or not she could get everything done they needed to before snowfall hit. She should never have taken the afternoon off to go gallivanting around the state with Ren. According to her snow nose, they'd just about run out of time.

Her watch indicated she had about six hours of daylight before the bus arrived and there were precautions she needed to get in place. Mary had the kitchen under control, so now was the time to do the outside work.

"I need to talk to John and Rocky. We've got work to do." She set her cup on the railing and hopped off the porch.

"I'll help," Ren said.

That would be all she needed, some city slicker slowing her down. "We can handle it."

"I said yesterday I'd help, and I will." His lop-sided grin appeared. "I won't hold you up."

Was the man a mind reader now, too?

"Really—"

"I won't take no for an answer," he said. Placing a hand on her arm, he continued. "I can help."

Once again, his touch, even through the layers, sent a warm shiver straight to her heart. No, she did not need him hanging around while she was trying to work. "Fine," she said. "You can help John and Rocky."

An hour later, Jess crawled out from underneath the inn, having given the pipes a once over and an extra wrap where needed.

"What in the hell are you doing?" A red-faced Ren yanked her to a standing position.

"Uh, weather's coming, remember? I'm checking the pipes."

"You should not be crawling around in God knows what underneath these buildings. Let the men do it."

Jess rolled her eyes. "It's all right. I've done this before. A bunch of times."

"Your father allows this? Well, he may not be willing to watch out for you, but I am. You will not crawl under these buildings again."

Jess felt the heat rise in her own face, then flush her entire body with a prickly ice. She pulled one work glove off, then the other before looking Ren in the eyes. "You giving me orders, Gallini?"

"If it's the only way to stop you from being so foolish, then yes, I am giving you an order."

"You," she said, poking him in the chest, "do *not* get to boss me around." She poked him again. "This is *my* place. I've *crawled* every inch of it, both above *and* below." She began enunciating each word. "I will do whatever I need to do to get this place ready."

"Not if I can help it. I'll get John and Rocky. They can finish the job."

"You know full well they're winterizing the restaurant and outbuildings. You're supposed to be helping them."

"I was. I came to see if you needed anything. They can finish the inn when they're done with the restaurant and outbuildings."

"I don't ask my people to do anything I'm not willing

to do myself. Plus, the faster we get it done, the sooner we can all go inside. In case you haven't noticed, there's a bit more chill to the air."

He raised an eyebrow. "A bit *more* chill?"

The man was such a greenhorn. "This is tepid in comparison to the dead of winter. Now, if you will excuse me, I have work to do, and you're keeping me from it."

She turned her back on Ren, reached down for the roll of plastic she'd left on the ground, and went around to the weather side to cover the windows with additional weatherization.

Except the first thing she did was tear a gaping hole in one of the sheets of plastic. Taking a deep breath, she took more care with the next one, then held the translucent material in place as she set the first nail.

Bam! Bam! With Ren Gallini's head as the visual, she set the nail in two hits and picked up a second one.

Bam! City Boy was going to drive her nuts.

Bam! Who did he think he was, telling her she couldn't do what she'd been doing for years?

Bam! Bam! Bam! Before she knew it, Jess had finished the window. She came down off the ladder and turned to see plastic laid out, cut and ready to go, beside two more windows. Ren was on his knees in the dirt, measuring out another strip.

Damn him. Just when she had a righteous hatred worked up, he had to turn back into Mr. Helpful. The man made it very hard to dislike him.

He looked up then, and she could see white teeth from her perch on the ladder several windows away. He stood and walked over. "Wondered how long it would take you to notice me."

"Yeah, well, I was busy driving nails," she answered.

"Into my head, I'd imagine."

Unable to help herself, Jess laughed. "A few," she admitted.

He pointed to the laid out sheeting. "Peace offering?"

She nodded. "A pretty good one, too, if your measurements are accurate. Okay, Gallini, time to prove those muscles you've got are more than just for show."

He moved the ladder and began to climb it. Jess's eyes narrowed.

"What?"

"Down, boy. You get ground duty."

"You think I can't pound a nail? I know I told you I worked my way through college working construction."

"I think I know this building better than you. I know what stresses it can and can't take. And where."

"Touché, beautiful. All right, you win. I'll play apprentice."

She smiled, pleased with his acquiescence. They settled into a pattern that seemed both intuitive and comfortable. He cut and handed pieces to her, and she nailed them in place. She had to give the man credit. He knew how to maximize their supplies. Each sheet fit with just enough overlap for her to nail them down. He hadn't been joking about the carpentry thing.

"Did you know," he said as he measured, "that each of these windows is just a little bit different, size-wise?"

She laughed. "We didn't exactly build this in place."

"Then how did it get here?"

"Camp got its name from the folks heading north. Last

chance to turn around before things *really* get cold. There's
not much north of here. Then, in the early seventies, it
became a work camp. Temporary housing for the folks
building the Trans-Alaska pipeline. Once it was no longer
needed for work crews, it turned into a sort of waypoint for
those heading north to Prudhoe Bay and the oilfields. The
truckers you see come and go? They helped build this place,
dropping off supplies and pounding nails on their way
through. In 1995, when the Dalton Highway became
accessible without permits to the general public, Last
Chance became the success you see today."

"Success?"

"Hey," she said with a huff. "We've made a lot of
improvements since then."

He shook his head. "Name one."

"Bathrooms."

"You didn't used to have bathrooms here?"

She climbed off the ladder and let him move it. "No.
The rooms used to share bathrooms. When the cruise ships
added us as a destination stop, the main thing they required,
and that we lacked, were bathrooms in each room."

"Ah," he said.

"You don't understand what a feat that was. Come on.
I'll show you." Jess headed inside the inn. They each
opened their coats to the indoor heat, and she opened the
door to one of the empty rooms. "Do you see how small
this room is?"

He looked around, and she tried to see if from his
eyes. He probably saw the two single beds that hugged each
wall, with a small shelf attached to the wall in between.
What he didn't see were the high quality mattresses they'd

scrimped and saved to put in place. And yes, the drapes didn't quite close, at least not without help. But they were the best blackout fabric made, something folks appreciated during the summer months when Alaska earned the nickname "Land of the Midnight Sun."

He would see the tiny pedestal sink next to the door, but not the hours spent poring over catalogues and the internet looking for the best look for the fit. She'd cut and framed the mirrors for all the rooms herself.

The bathrooms, though, had been her baby all the way. Originally a much smaller closet, she'd re-designed an antiquated plumbing system to handle a tenfold increase in flow. It was an engineering feat she was still proud of five years later. Each room now had its own shower, commode, and sink.

Jess was proud of these self-contained little rooms, but it was an invisible pride. Ren Gallini most likely did not see any of it. He saw shabby where she delighted in ingenuity.

"You're proud of this room," he said, intruding in her thoughts.

"I'm proud of Last Chance."

"Do you mind if I ask why?"

"Because we turned it into a place people not only have to stop at. They *want* to stop here. For a lot of folks, this is an adventure. One they might not be able to do if things were more rustic."

She saw him glance around again.

"Believe me," she said. "This is a lot better than when it was a work camp. Add in the fact that we're known for solid, down home food and it's a good reputation. I'm part of what made it this way, so yes, I have every right to be proud."

She tapped him on the chest. "And you need to acknowledge the fact that this isn't some backwater establishment."

His hand covered hers and held it to his chest. She looked up into amber eyes that seemed larger than life, shaded by strong brows. Eyes that drew her in with a naked need she felt her body straining to match. She lowered her head, only to stare at a chest well-muscled. She could feel his heartbeat underneath her hand.

Th-thump. Th-thump. Th-thump. It seemed fast. Her own pulse felt like it was racing, catching up, matching his.

His free hand came up under her chin and lifted it so she could see eyes filled with desire...scant seconds before his lips touched hers.

The jolt raced through her body and settled low in her stomach. When he pulled his lips away, hers followed. She didn't want to stop. This felt like heaven.

"We shouldn't do this," he whispered.

"I don't care," she answered, standing on her toes to reach him, needing to pull him down to her. Their lips met and the same flaming desire coursed through her. She kept her hand locked in his hair, giving him no chance to pull away.

He deepened the kiss with an urgency she matched. Oh, Lord, but she'd never felt this much pleasure in a kiss before. His lips moved to blaze a trail down her neck.

What was happening? She felt weak all over, yet energized at the same time.

He pulled the collar of her flannel shirt back and kissed the ridge of her t-shirt, then pulled it back to plant gentle kisses on her collarbone. Tendrils of need wound their way through her body as she melted against him, feeling the bulge of his need.

Crash! Ren and Jess jumped apart as the main door to the inn crashed inward and Rocky rushed in. He stopped short when he saw them. Ren turned away and Jess struggled to straighten her clothes.

Rocky blushed, then anger showed in his face, and his color deepened to crimson. He took a step toward Ren, hands fisted. "You got no right—"

Jess held a hand out to stop him. "We don't have time for this. What's up?"

She watched Rocky fight to regain control. Finally, he ground out the message. "The snow's started. Big time. And the tour bus is in trouble."

The heat drained from Jess's body as his words sank in. "What kind of trouble?"

"The snow's come in from the west and the highway's inundated. It's a deluge. The driver radioed that they're about twenty miles south of here and stuck in a drift."

"Okay. Get the truck ready to go."

"John's gassing it up now."

"Good. Let's grab the supply packs."

"What are you going to do?" Ren asked.

She'd forgotten he was there. "Get prepped and ready, of course." She pulled her coat tightly closed and headed for the door.

She could hear him running to catch up, but she didn't have time. She'd have to explain on the fly.

Ren was beside her. "If they're stuck, what makes you think you won't get stuck, also?"

"I'm not going to get stuck because I'm not going. You are. With John and Rocky."

Ren opened his mouth, then closed it.

Jess continued, raising her voice as she ran. "I need to help Mary prepare for their arrival and I know what's needed better than you. When you all arrive back, you'll need warmth and food."

By now, they'd exited the inn and all three stood there watching the heavy snow fall.

"I don't know the first thing about how to handle this situation," Ren said.

"You follow John's orders. To the letter, got that? He'll get you through."

Ren spoke first. "We're going to drive through this blizzard?"

She turned on him. "Either you do, or I do."

His eyes narrowed, and she knew she'd put him in a tight spot. He wouldn't want her out in this weather. Any other time, she be chomping at the bit to go. But it just didn't make sense when there were three strong guys here. And Mary really would need her help.

Funny, she'd never enjoyed watching snow light on someone's eyelashes quite as much she appreciated it now. Ren Gallini looked good in any weather.

He decided quickly. "I need cold weather gear."

"Rocky?" Jess turned his way.

"Yeah, boss?"

"Go ask Mary if John has an extra set of cold weather gear." She cocked her head toward Ren. "He's going to need it."

Rocky set off at a run and was quickly lost in the

blowing snow. Jess followed, knowing Ren was on her heels. He caught up to her before the door of the restaurant and they walked in together.

"Can this bus make it here on its own?"

"Not without help. It'll take some work to get it out, but hopefully it will be drivable."

"How can you be so certain?"

She nodded. "We've done it before. Worse than this, too. Once, we drove fifty miles north. And the bus was full-sized. This is a small one."

"So you've done this yourself?"

"I've had to. We're inside the Arctic Circle. When someone hollers help, we help."

Ren nodded. "You're right. I'd rather go instead of you." Rocky came in, still glaring, but he tossed him a set of cold weather gear, and Ren started yanking it on.

All of a sudden, Jess didn't like the way things were going. She walked up to Ren and grasped his collar, pulling it tightly closed. She began buttoning it up with a vengeance. "Just be sure you don't do anything stupid, City Boy. You listen to John. He's done this before."

"Yes, Ma'am!" Ren smiled and touched her cheek. "Don't worry, beautiful. I may be a bit rusty at it, but I do know how to follow orders."

Chapter Ten

Half an hour later, Ren was second guessing his agreement.

John seemed to be driving like it was a hot summer day on a paved interstate freeway. In reality, they were traveling at less than twenty miles per hour. But the way they were careening from one side of the road to the other, Ren's stomach was screaming for him to take over the wheel. "Do we *have* to weave back and forth like this?"

"We're rolling with the drifts," John said, talking loud to be heard over the whine of the old engine.

"Is this truck going to hold together?" Oof! Ren wedged a hand against the frame as they went airborne.

"Always has," was John's succinct reply.

Making matters worse, Rocky was squirming like his ass was frostbitten. After a few more minutes of this, John blew out a long breath. "What the hell's wrong with you, Rocky?"

"What'ya mean?" he grumbled.

"I mean, sit still!"

"It's not easy. I don't like sitting next to *him*."

"Me?" Ren asked.

"Yeah. You."

John swerved around another drift, throwing Ren into his ride-partner's shoulder. Rocky shoved him back.

"Stop it," John said, never glancing away from the road. "I don't know what this is all about, but you'd better settle it and quick. Before I throw both of you into a snow bank and pick you up on the way back."

"I caught him making out with Jess," Rocky said. "He's got no right."

With one hand on the doorframe and another one on the dashboard, Ren managed to catch the smile on John's face before the man sucked his lower lip in to quell it.

"So what?" John said.

"So, he's got no right."

"Don't you think that's Jess' call?" Ren asked.

"Well, yeah, but she might not know what she's getting herself into."

That was the very question Ren had already asked himself. And one he didn't have an answer to. Then something occurred to him. "Are you in love with Jess, Rocky?"

"God, no." Rocky threw up his hands. "I mean, no, not like that. Ewwww."

"I'm assuming she's had men interested in her before. Did you react this way with them?"

"Didn't have to. Jess put them in their place good and quick."

"Then, if you're not interested in her that way, and you've seen her handle advances herself in the past, why are you so angry with me?"

"Because she's different with you. And...I've seen this before. I'm not going to lose another family member like this."

Okay, so more was going on here than just Jess and Ren. "Who did you lose, Rocky?"

"He didn't lose her," John cut in. "That's just how he sees it."

Ren looked at Rocky, his face full of misery. "Someone you loved?"

Rocky hunched further into himself. "Yeah. Big time."

"I'm sorry. I know that hurts. But it still doesn't explain why you're upset about a moment between Jess and I."

"Tell him," John said. "It'll do you good. You still haven't gotten over it and it's been two years. She's happy, boy. Time to accept it."

The truck started to slide and everyone focused until John got it straightened out.

"She's my sister. And my responsibility ever since our folks died several years ago."

Ren nodded. "That's a lot of responsibility."

Straightening his shoulders, Rocky huffed. "I was up to it. Still am. Only she went and fell for a British guy. Before I knew it, they were married and headed to England."

"That was two years ago?"

Rocky nodded.

"Are they still married?"

Another nod.

"Happily?"

"Seems so."

"Then what's the problem?" Ren asked.

John spoke up. "The problem is he went from working hard to take care of his sister to having no one to take care of. This boy's a born nurturer."

"Geesh, John. I'm not that bad."

"Near about. Anyhow, that's when Jess and he met. He was thinking of going to school and she was checking out schools."

"Man, she was really homesick."

"Doesn't she ever get away from this place?"

"Not often," Rocky said. "Anyhow, we got to talking. I think I cheered her up, and that felt good. So when she found out I was kind of undecided, she offered me a job at Last Chance. I got here about a month later and been here ever since."

That explained a lot about their relationship. Rocky had clearly taken Jess under his protective wing, just as he had his sister. Ren got the impression Rocky had found a home here, and he didn't want to trample on that. At all. He understood what it meant to feel like you belonged. Especially since he'd been a fish out of water ever since he arrived in Alaska.

"Just so you know, Rocky. I'm not sure what's happening with Jess and I." Ren raked a hand through his hair. "Hell, I'm not sure what's going on at all." He turned to Rocky. "But I would never intentionally hurt Jess. I respect her a lot."

Rocky turned to Ren. "You'd better not. Or you'll deal with me."

"I understand." Ren held out his hand and Rocky, after a moment's hesitation, shook it. The returning smile on John's face validated that Ren had handled the situation in the best way possible.

It took another hour of travel to reach the stranded bus, and they were energized by the hoorays that greeted them.

John and Rocky got straight to work. The small bus held twenty tourists, a driver, and a tour guide. All were a little cold, but otherwise fine.

Thanking the Good Lord for cold weather gear, Ren helped Rocky dig the bus out while everyone stood bundled up outside in their own coats and the blankets they'd brought along. John repositioned the truck, hooked the winch up, and within fifteen minutes everyone was back on the bus and they were on the road leading the way back to Last Chance.

When they pulled into the yard, Ren saw Jess standing on the porch waiting for them. He was first off the bus, the smile she gave him filled his heart with a lightness he hadn't felt in a long time. She jumped the steps and was in his arms before he could say "hi."

Just as quickly, she jumped back and away from him, her head down as if embarrassed at the show of emotion. And Ren felt himself grinning like a damn teenager.

Jess was grateful for the influx of passengers exiting the bus. She'd made this type of rescue run herself on multiple occasions and knew the risks were doable. Still, her head hadn't been into making sandwiches and coffee, and Mary had prompted her a few times to get back on task. Her heart had been out on the highway. Seeing Ren step off that bus felt like landing on a soft pillow after a free fall through empty space.

Feeling that way was one thing. Exhibiting the behavior she had was quite another. She felt the flush creep up her neck as everyone filed into the restaurant. She handed out blankets and poured coffee and cocoa while she tried to reason it out. Had she actually *jumped* into his arms?

"Could I have some more cocoa, please?" The voice belonged to one of the two children who'd come in with the bus. Fraternal twins, she'd figured out quickly. And eternally energetic, by the looks of them. She smiled as she poured. That was what her father always said about her. That she was eternally energetic.

She gave the twins' parents props when the boy thanked her for the cocoa. "Are you warm enough?" she asked the boy's mother.

"Oh, yes. Quite comfortable now." The woman's worried face searched the windows, where falling white flakes filled the view. "Are we stranded here?"

"I was just about to address that with the group." Jess set the pots on the table and tapped one with a spoon until the chatter died down.

"I know you've had a traumatic start to this leg of your vacation."

Murmured assents and nodding heads validated her statement. "Now that you've all had some time to warm up, I'm sorry for the way you arrived, but I'd like to welcome you to Last Chance Camp. I'm the own..." Jess faltered. A glance at Ren told her he knew why, too. Damn him. There's no way her dad sold this place. No way in hell.

"Sorry. I'm the manager here at Last Chance." She raised her eyebrows. "So if you have any issues or questions, I'm the person to solve them."

"Great," a gray-haired man at one of the back tables spoke up. "Can you make sure this snow is gone by the time we have to leave tomorrow?"

Jess joined the chuckle that went around the room. "There are limits to what I can do, I'm afraid. And the news isn't too good. The weather service indicates this unusual storm may stay in place for another twenty-four to thirty-six hours."

A collective groan went through the group. "We're only supposed to be here overnight," said a teenage girl, her long hair streaked with a couple strands of blue. "This side trip was for Mom. We're flying to California the day after tomorrow."

"You might not make that flight. It looks like you'll all be our guests for a couple days, at least."

The girl turned down her lips in a world-class pout. At that moment, Rocky came through the kitchen door in a T-shirt, carrying a food-laden tray, and big eyes and a smile replaced the pout as the girl followed his movements. Jess groaned inwardly when the girl started twirling bits of hair around her fingers.

With his tray empty, Rocky almost made it back to the kitchen when Jess saw him notice the dark-haired young beauty. The slow grin that spread across his face made Jess decide to remind him of the number one rule here. No sleeping with the guests. Ever.

She glanced at Ren and saw his no-holds-barred head to foot appraisal of her, and her body heat went up several degrees as she blushed what felt like a deep scarlet.

No exceptions. She'd better remember that herself.

Most everyone else was looking out the window and thankfully didn't see her discomfiture. Big, white flakes still obliterated any view. At the moment, the inn across the way wasn't even visible. Worry settled on each of their faces.

"I'd like to reassure you that we have everything we need to wait out this storm. Food supplies, fuel for heat, water. It may be a bit more rustic than what you're used to, but I think you'll find your adventure quite tolerable." Jess smiled, trying to ease the additional sting she was about to deliver.

"I know most of you came here for a chance to view the Aurora Borealis. Since you need clear skies for that..." She left the last part hanging as she gestured to the window.

A few sighs rounded the room. "At least," one of the twins parents said, "we'll have television." He gestured to the wall screen at the end of the trucker's table.

"Yes," Jess said, nodding. "We have an extensive movie collection that's available for viewing here in the restaurant. Right now, we have satellite reception, but I expect that will change soon."

"Because of the snow?" The father asked.

"Since the satellites circle the equator, we practically have to point the dish directly toward the ground to get a line of sight connection. So it doesn't take much to disrupt that reception. Snow is pretty hard for signals to pass through."

As if on cue, the television spit, then went to static.

"Like I said," Jess laughed.

A glance around the room reflected some glum faces back to her. She didn't know how to relieve their worry. "Look at it this way," she said. "You'll be able to go back and tell your friends and family that you survived the snowstorm of the year."

She was rewarded with a few chuckles. The door opened and the bus driver walked in.

"Is everyone pretty well fed and warmed up?" she asked.

A few heads nodded.

"Then I suggest we go across to the inn and get you all

situated in rooms. It looks like your luggage has been offloaded and the showers are hot." Jess crossed her fingers behind her back that the new plumbing held. She glanced at her watch. "Dinner will be served in about two hours."

Planning to help, Ren trailed the group that walked across the yard, fastidiously searching out the next marker Jess had mentioned, and the next. Over the following hour, his admiration for Jess grew. She handed out room assignments and dealt with issues with a professional calmness that made her appear wiser than her years. And people listened to her, including him.

"Mr. Gallini, if you could help the Johnsons with their luggage, I'm sure they would appreciate it."

Her face didn't show one lick of the satisfaction she must have gotten in asking that. Ren plastered his best happy-to-help smile on and reached for the suitcases the twins' mother stood next to.

Each room had two twin beds in it. He unknowingly echoed Jess' earlier thought. There were no exceptions, no other room designs to be had. So the family of four split the boys up, putting one child with each parent. *Smart.*

He set the suitcase down and checked to make sure the room was stocked with towels, glasses, and soap. It was.

"Is there anything else I can get for you?" he asked the harried woman as both boys started to bounce on beds.

"Valium?" She shook her head. "Timmy and Jonathan, stop that this minute!" She held her hand out to Ren, and he reached to shake it, but she placed a five-dollar bill in his hand instead. A tip? Ren almost laughed out loud as he stared at it. He started to give it back, but wondered if tips were allowed and if he'd be doing John and Rocky a disservice by refusing it. So instead, he tucked it into his jeans, mumbled a thank you, and ducked out the door.

He no sooner got back to the lobby than Jess sent him off with more luggage. He leaned in close before following the next set of guests. "Do you take tips?"

She nodded, not looking up. "Only those freely given. I give them to Mary, John, and Rocky to split."

"Works for me," Ren said, taking a moment to enjoy the scent of her hair. It still struck him as odd. He expected his beautiful tomboy to smell of axle grease and gas fumes. The light floral and citrus scent of her shampoo seemed a distinct opposite to her character. He followed the gray-haired man and his wife down the hall smiling at yet another side of Jess Jenkins to puzzle through. She was an enigma. One he knew he wanted to understand better.

Even though the busload of guests only filled half the rooms, it was enough to keep Jess, John, and himself hopping. Jess sent Rocky back to help Mary with dinner. John stuck around the lobby to field questions and keep an eye on the hot water, while Ren went with Jess to talk to the bus driver.

He set his mug down and jumped up to pull her into a bear hug that had Ren seeing green. "How's my best girl?"

Jess laughed. "Put me down, Paul."

"Not until you promise to marry me."

Ren wanted to pound the grin right off the guy's face. He raised his hands, already in fists, as Jess slapped the bus driver's hands until he set her on the ground.

"Now, you know I can't marry you."

"Ah, honey, you'd make me the happiest man on earth

if you would."

"I'd make you jail bait. What would your wife say if she found out you had another one stashed up here in the north?"

He leaned in conspiratorially. "Hopefully, she'd say ménage."

"Oh, you are incorrigible."

"You want coffee, Jess?" Ren asked, knowing he needed a moment to calm down. "Sure," she said. "Thanks."

Ren glared at Paul. "You need a refill?"

"Nah. I'm good." He grinned and plopped back down in his chair.

A few moments later, Ren set two coffee mugs down.

"Thanks," Jess said, turning back to the bus driver. "It was a white-out, then?"

"One of the worst I've seen." He took a sip of coffee and stared at the brown liquid in his cup. "Hit us out of nowhere, like a wall of thick cotton batting."

He looked at Jess, but Ren saw the concern in his eyes. The man was worried.

"You know me, Jess." He glanced at Ren. "I've lived in Alaska my whole life. I respect this state. And I *know* the unwritten motto—expect the unexpected. But this thing...well, I didn't even see coming. I think we're in for a storm the likes of which we haven't seen here before, at least not this time of year. I'm not sure even Last Chance Camp can outlast this thing. Look at it."

They all glanced outside.

"It's a blizzard. When's the last time you saw snow hit this hard? Or this early?"

"I've seen bad snow, but you're right. Never this early. Not in the entire time I've been here," Jess answered.

"Exactly. This one's got me spooked."

Ren was starting to get a little spooked himself. Just how bad were things going to get, if macho man here was this worried? "How bad could this get?" he asked.

Jess shrugged her shoulders. "I checked the weather service before the satellite fritzed out. It looked like we were in for a couple days of snow."

"That doesn't sound so bad."

"It didn't indicate it would be at this strength or come in quite this fast. Don't get me wrong. We get snow here. But this is unusual."

Now worry was evident in her face, also.

"All right. This is bad, and you seem to be keeping it low-key for our guests. Let me ask this. Can we weather it here?"

Without hesitation, Jess nodded. He had to give her credit. The woman had spunk. Ren looked out the window at the snow. It seemed to be falling heavier, if that was even possible. They were trapped here for who knew what kind of duration. And there was nothing he could do about it.

Jess's hand on his arm brought him back around.

"We're fine. As long as we can keep the generators going, we're fine."

That resonated with him. "That's something concrete. What do we have to do?"

"Nothing, unless they go out. Then we fix it."

"Well, we can't just sit here and wait."

Jess stood, laughing. "Don't worry, Gallini, you won't be sitting and waiting. You'll be learning what it takes to keep all those folks across the way happy under enforced captivity." She tossed a set of keys to Paul.

"My usual room?"

"Yep."

"Same arrangement as before?" Paul winked at Ren.

Ren's eyes narrowed and Paul's grin widened. He grabbed Jess in a hug and twirled her around. Then, pulling his coat on, he grinned. "Until later, babe."

After his exit, Ren turned to Jess and the dark cloud over his head deepened at her wide smile. Worse, when she looked at him, the smile disappeared. And something deep in his gut twisted.

"Come on. We've got food to prepare." Jess headed for the kitchen and, after a moment, Ren followed her. Something told him he was about to learn a lot more than he ever wanted about the hotel business.

Later that night, Ren shut the trailer door behind him, more tired than he'd been in a long time. In the real world, he worked hard. In fact, his own mother said he worked too hard, that he should take some time to relax and enjoy life. Find a wife and give me grandchildren, she said on a regular basis.

Tonight, shadowing Jess had been an eye opener about how hard they really did work here. And the place was only half full. First had been dinner. Who'd have thought that thirty people could eat that much, drink that much, and create that many dishes. Jess had called a moratorium on excessive energy use *just in case,* so he had spent three hours at the back-breaking work of hand-washing dishes.

There was one thing you learned from kitchen chores. Most people were pigs. Bussing tables proved that. Then, after the camp's rigorous recycling program, you were left with little but scraps of food. Five buckets worth. Didn't these folks know there were starving children in Africa? And that a minor state of emergency had been called for the camp.

He shook his head as he pulled off his jacket. That's right. Jess' rule. If it's bad news, the customer doesn't need to know unless personally affected. Apparently, the fact that they may or may not have power for the entirety of this little emergency didn't warrant a station-wide alert.

After dishes, they'd had some minor hot water issues to deal with, a few guest requests, and had slogged back and forth through camp a few times to make sure everything was ship-shape.

He was more exhausted than he could ever remember being.

Ren turned up the heater in the trailer and sat at the kitchen table, wondering how anyone could live their lives, let alone even short periods of time, in such a confined space...and in the midst of a snowstorm.

He didn't bother turning on lights. It was after one a.m. and he had no plans for anything except collapsing into bed...and a dreamless sleep.

Ren shifted the window blind to glance outside. He had a wide view of the open area between the restaurant and the inn. The snow, while still falling in monster flakes, seemed to be less dense. Maybe the storm was letting up.

He sensed, more than saw, movement in the clearing, well to the left of the sight line between the two main buildings. Peering closer, he couldn't decipher who it was. Could it be a guest trying to find the restaurant?

Concerned now, he pulled himself up off the bench seat. Grabbing Owen's coat, he didn't wait to put it on. The cold hit him instantly once outside the trailer, and he shuffled along slower than he liked while taking precious time to don his protection against the frigid air.

As he got closer, the moving blob in the middle of the snowstorm coalesced into a parka-clad figure, outstretched arms reaching toward the sky. It swayed back and forth, moving in a slow circle. Snow scattered from gloved hands. What was this? Some sort of Aleut snow dance? Who was crazy enough to be out here in this cold?

He grabbed a hold of the coat, turning whoever danced to the snow gods around.

Chapter Eleven

Jess yelped when she felt the yank. She whirled in wide-eyed surprise and came face to face with Ren Gallini. Still in the throes of an emotional plea to the skies, she'd been unaware of his approach. Her heart about jumped out of her chest. No one was ever up this time of night.

This was her time. Here, in the quiet dead of night, she talked to the spirits and asked them to guide her choices. She sent a plea skyward for pity on his ignorance, then glared at him. "What the hell are you doing?"

"Stopping some lunatic doing some sort of snow dance, by all appearances."

Her eyes narrowed as the flush in her face morphed from the candy-red glow of cold weather exertion to the full-faced redness of anger.

"Not a snow dance. A weather-abatement plea. And you interrupted me."

She watched him closely for any reaction to her statement. She'd give him credit. He covered his amazement well. A slight widening of the eyes, just for a fraction of a second, along with a slight clenching of a gloved hand, was the only indication he gave of disbelief.

"You don't believe in prayer?" Jess asked.

"I...don't know how to answer that."

"You either believe or you don't."

He shook his head. "Is this a discussion about God?"

She shrugged. "Whatever you discern him to be."

"It's the middle of the night. I'm tired. And standing

out in a blizzard, in weather colder than a body should have
to stand, defending my religious beliefs?"

"No. All I asked was whether or not you believe in
prayer. It's a simple question." She took a step toward him,
hoping it would make him feel as off guard as she was.

"That kind of question is never simple."

"Sure it is." She took another step and placed her
gloved hand over his heart. "It's—" Even through the
down parka he wore, and her gloved hand, something
passed between them that befuddled her thoughts. Jess
pulled her hand away, only to have it trapped once again as
his glove covered hers. She looked up into eyes of swirled
brown smoke that deepened in color as she gazed into
them.

They were surrounded by the silence of night, and
veiled by a blanket of falling snow. No one, no thing
existed, except their two heartbeats, matched in rhythm.
And in need.

She leaned in.

He lowered his head.

Their lips met in snow-melting desire and the heat
between them ran a ragged path through Jess's body,
settling into a deep ache. One she'd never felt before...not
to this degree. An ache that brought her arms up and
around his neck, only to be frustrated by the wealth of
down stuffing that kept her from feeling skin.

Her body felt as if it was being consumed by fire. They
were outside in the middle of a blizzard, and she didn't
care. She pulled back and began to rip at his coat.

Ren's gloved hands stopped her. "We can't do this.

Not here."

"I don't want to wait."

"Trust me," he said, his voice low and filled with his own need. "I don't want to wait, either."

She reached for him, but he held her off. "Come back to my place." He didn't wait for an answer. Grasping her arm, he started off in the general direction of the trailer he was staying in. Owen's trailer. Her father's trailer.

Ren stopped, knowing he wouldn't...couldn't make love to her in her father's bed. He twisted in the direction of her trailer. "Not my place. Yours."

She planted her feet, surprising him with her ability to stop them mid-stride. "I'd rather not go to my place."

He spread his arms. "Look around, beautiful. Where else do you suggest we go?"

She stared at the ground, scuffling her feet in the snow.

He raised her head. "Why not your place?"

"Because." She lifted her face further, the stubborn tilt to her chin making him want to kiss it. "Because," she started again. "No one goes in my place."

"No one?" Ren paused, some sixth sense trying to break through the haze of desire. "Would you rather..." He didn't finish. Couldn't finish, since he had no idea what he'd been about to say.

She looked down, kicking more snow up with her foot. He waited, giving her time. When she moved closer and raised her lips to his, he knew her choice. And that he liked it. A lot.

He followed her now as they ran the remaining distance to her trailer. With no hesitation, she opened the door and climbed the two steps. He was right behind her.

Once inside, he spent several moments divesting himself of his cold weather gear. He looked up...and froze as his brain tried to fit this new piece into the puzzle that was Jess Jenkins.

Her trailer screamed femininity, from the colors and patterns to the framed pictures hanging in the few spaces available. He'd expected grizzly bears, or caribou. Instead, delicate flowers decorated her walls. Ren leaned in closer. They looked like original photographs. Had she taken them?

He glanced at her as she leaned against the kitchenette's counter, chewing her lower lip.

"Did you take these?"

She nodded.

"They're...very good."

She responded to the hesitation in his voice. "Beauty is in the eye of the beholder."

"Trust me," he said, pulling her into his arms. "I like them. Very much. You've an obvious talent."

She frowned.

"My hesitation had nothing to do with the quality of the pictures, Jess. I'm trying to mesh this completely different side of you with the wrench-wielding, coarse-talking girl I've known to date. This," he waved an arm around her living quarters, "feminine side caught me off guard."

She pushed against him. "I can be a lady."

"Beautiful," he said, unwilling to let her go, "you can be anything you want. I have no doubt of that."

She didn't look up, but stood there fiddling with the buttons on his shirt. Ren took a whiff of her very girly shampoo, then kissed the top of her head. When her arms snaked around him, her head came up a bit. He planted small kisses along the edge of her hairline and she raised up to allow him access.

"Trust me," he said as he peppered kisses along her cheek, her chin, and worked his way down her neck. "I am fully aware of just how much of a woman you are, Jess Jenkins."

When their lips met again, pillows and patterns flew from Ren's mind as the truth of what he'd just said hit him. He wanted this woman more than he'd ever desired any woman before. Too much more. A heart and soul want. He should run. Hard and fast. Yet he stood rooted to the floor. His hands moved of their own accord, pushing her coat over shoulders and down arms until it fell to the floor.

Her jeans were trendy hipsters. He teased the edges of her shirt, his fingers sliding underneath to touch skin softer than fine suede. She shivered, and his already rock hard status jumped to granite.

His fingers blazed a gentle trail up her back. When she arched away from him, he followed the line of her ribs around to the front, letting the shirt ride up as he splayed his hand along her midriff.

She sighed, and he lifted the shirt over her head. When it landed with her coat, Jess closed her eyes and leaned back across the counter. An invitation to explore.

And one he couldn't turn down. He smiled at the bright green, lacy wisp of a bra she wore. Then her chest rose as she took a deep breath and the smile disappeared, replaced by an urge that threatened to overwhelm him. A fierce need to touch her.

He spread a hand over her stomach, and she flinched slightly at the renewed contact. Ren leaned over to feather kisses along the edge of jeans that rode below her waist. His hands settled along her sides, then, as he raised up, he followed the outline of her bra with his hands.

She gasped as he fingered the curve of lace, then wandered to the middle and spread outward from there, caressing, learning, never quite satisfied. Unable to resist, he lowered his mouth and kissed a nipple straining beneath her bra. Jess rose up to meet him, and he took advantage of the opportunity, reaching back and unclasping the hook that held her captive.

She groaned as his mouth let go, so he quickly disposed of her bra. When he glanced down, he almost lost it right then and there, and still fully clothed. His hands reached out to cup breasts that fit like perfection and were capped by rosy nipples so taut they begged for his attention.

He ran a hand across one and she jumped, raising her legs to tightly circle his hips. Granite hardness became molten lava. He kissed the spot between her breasts and felt her breath catch. Feathered kisses along the underside elicited jumpy gasps. When he reached her nipple and took it between his teeth, she moaned.

"You like?"

"Mmm-hmmm."

He sucked her into his mouth.

"Ah, damn. What are you doing to me, Gallini?"

His hand moved to play with her other breast as he alternated between bites and kisses.

Her hands wound into his hair, pulling him in, begging

him to take more of her. He sucked and kissed his way to her other breast as he untangled her legs and moved to her side. His hand wandered along the top of her jeans until he found the clasp and unbuttoned it. The zipper slid slowly down until he could feel some gauzy cloth underneath.

He glanced up and saw eyes staring at him from beneath lust-laden lids. She was so beautiful. Ren almost growled as he reached under her legs and picked her up. He carried her to the back of the trailer, barely registering the floral bedspread and eyelet lace pillows.

Her arms around his neck would not release, so they lay on the bed as one unit. As he renewed his interest in her body, she began to unbutton his shirt, faltering as his hand moved to settle between her legs.

She fumbled at the buttons until he backed away and shed his shirt for her. Instead of pulling him closer, her hands began to move across his chest, embedding themselves in his hair, lightly caressing his own nipples to stiff nubs. He stayed still, awash in the ecstasy of her touch, especially when her hands moved to his jeans and surrounded him. He would explode if this went on much longer.

"Am I—" she whispered, "pleasing you?"

Just like that, Ren's libido hit the showers. He pulled back and reached for her hand. When she murmured her dislike, he pressed her hand to his chest. "We need to talk."

"I think," she said in a smoky, passion-filled voice, "we are way beyond talk." She tried to move, but he held her hands captive.

"What, then?"

He could see irritation adding lines to her beautiful

face and wanted to wipe them away. He wanted more than anything to bring back the darkness of lust that had shone in her eyes only moments before. But he had to know.

"Are you a virgin?"

She stared at him. "Seriously? The fact that I'm a virgin is what's worrying you?"

Ren sat up and ran shaky hands through his hair. "Oh, my God, you *are* a virgin."

"So? I thought guys liked making love to a virgin."

"We do. I mean, no! Damn. I can't believe this," Ren muttered. "Who would've thought that someone who worked in a truck stop like this would be a..." His voice trailed off as he realized what he'd just said.

Jess yanked the floral quilt off her bed and wrapped it around herself. She rounded the bed and advanced on him and Ren felt the unusual desire to back up.

"You think—" she jabbed a finger into his chest. "That because I work in what you see as a truck stop, that I sleep with all the guys?"

"You're misinterpreting what I said."

"You took me to bed tonight thinking I was an easy lay."

"No. That wasn't—"

"Tell me something, Mr. Gallini. Is that the only way you get gratification? By bedding a whore?"

"No, you're just—"

"Out! I want you out *now!*"

Ren held up his hands. "You're upset."

Jess growled.

"I can see that." He grabbed his shirt and pulled it on. "So I'll leave. For now. But we will finish this discussion.

You *will* understand that I don't think of you that way. That this is a colossal misconception."

Jess did the only thing left to do. She slapped him. Hard. She stared at her hand briefly, as if surprised she'd done that. Then she pointed to the door. "Get. Out. Now!"

Chapter Twelve

Jess would have loved to slam the door on Ren Gallini's ass, but that was a problem with trailers. The doors opened outward. Still, a nice boot to his jeans seemed like a good idea. Except he turned around just as she raised her leg. So instead, she just pointed again. Once he was outside, she yanked the door shut. The motion was highly unsatisfactory, though, and she kicked the cabinet beside the door, caving it in.

"Arghhhh!" Shaking her fists in the air, she cursed the day that Ren Gallini had driven into her camp. Jess slumped down to the floor, still wrapped in the quilt, and tried to feed the anger. Anything was better than the aching need that thrummed through her body. How could she still want him after what he'd said? She pounded on the floor. This was exactly why she'd never given her heart to anyone. Falling in love meant nothing but pain.

Her head came up as she clutched the blanket tighter around her. Love? Had she really thought that word? How could she possibly be in love with someone who thought she was…loose.

Misery settled over her like a cold, wet, snowy mist. Jess wasn't sure how long she sat there, but when she started shivering, she pulled herself up and got dressed. She looked at the damage to her cabinet and, with a sigh, went to get her tools.

The next morning, Jess woke feeling like she'd been out on the Iditarod trail for three nights straight. Her eyes were filled with grit and her neck felt like she'd been slung over the bar of a sled for about twenty hours past the mandatory rest period. Even after the hour or so it took to fix the cabinet she'd let her foot loose on, sleep had eluded her. Working on her masters studies had also been a futile effort.

Finally, she'd shoved the books away. Glancing out the window, she'd found the light on in her dad's trailer. Gallini was still up. Gritting her teeth, she said a silent prayer that frustration was keeping him from sleeping. Maybe she'd have the pleasure of seeing him do a snow dunk to cool down.

Jess nodded. That, she'd like to see.

The curtain across the way moved and she dropped the blinds as if they flash-froze her hands. Drawing back, she realized that he could also see her lights on. So she'd turned them all out and spent the rest of the night tossing and turning and coming up with new names for him.

So, after no more than a couple hours sleep, she took a quick shower and got dressed, selecting a peach, polka-dotted thong and matching lacy concoction that the store had called a *Wunderbra*. She slathered herself with body lotion to combat the dry cold, then covered up with thermals, jeans, turtleneck, and flannel shirt. Stocky work boots came next, then her coat and work gloves. Leaving her trailer unlocked as always, she headed for the kitchen.

"Hi, Auntie," she called when she walked in.

"Hello, yourself," Mary replied. Mary stared at and around Jess, as if expecting someone else...or someone different.

"You're up early," Mary said.

Jess cocked an eyebrow. "Uh, this is my normal time. I always help you prep food for breakfast." Jess pulled hat, gloves, and coat off, tossing them onto a chair.

"Yes," Mary said, nodding. "It's just that, well, I expected you might want to sleep in this morning."

Jess turned slowly around, a suspicion growing like a water-filled sponge in her gut. "And why would that be?"

"It seemed like you were up late last night." A smile played at the corners of Mary's mouth and Jess's eyes narrowed.

"So?" Jess said. Mary would speak her mind, but in her own time. Rushing had never gotten Jess anywhere. She washed her hands, then went to retrieve eggs from the cooler.

"Word is, you weren't alone. Thought you'd want some additional time this morning."

Jess slammed the eggs on the counter and winced. A cursory glance indicated they all seemed unbroken. She whirled on Mary. "You spying on me?"

"Don't get huffy with me, girl. I can still take you over my knee."

"You can try." Jess muttered the words under her breath, but saw by Mary's reaction she hadn't been quiet enough. "My life is my own," Jess countered.

"Not here it isn't. You been here your whole life. You ought to know by now that what happens to one happens to all."

Jess felt the deep blush rise up into her cheeks as Mary continued.

"So don't you get uppity with me. My John saw that city-boy follow you into your trailer. He'da come knockin' but I told him to leave you alone. That it was about time you started learning something about the ways of the world." One side of her mouth crooked. "Course, didn't matter much. City Boy wasn't there very long."

Jess whirled away from Mary so she wouldn't see the flames that seemed to have engulfed her face. She cracked an egg into the bowl, then had to dig out some shell.

Another egg. And more shell.

Jess grabbed the edges of the counter and held on for dear life, praying for some semblance of calm. Not only had the man humiliated her in private, now the whole camp knew she'd been...left untouched.

A remembered flash of flesh reminded her she wasn't untouched. And that was all it took for the fire to rage anew. Damn it! She tried to tamp down the flames and pounded her fists on the countertop so hard the egg cartons bounced.

When she turned, it was to Mary's concerned face. "You all right, honey?" She threw the towel she was holding over her shoulder and walked over to stand next to Jess.

"Yes. I'm fine. I just..."

"You got any questions about, you know, stuff?"

Crimson took on a whole new layer of hot on Jess's face. She could feel it. "Geesh, Mary. I'm twenty-four years old."

"All right. All right. You know I had to ask."

"Besides, knowing didn't make a difference anyhow."

"How's that?" Mary placed a hand on her shoulder, but Jess shrugged it off.

"Fool thought I was some bed-hopper. Made a

comment about this being a truck stop and all." Her embarrassment grew to colossal proportions when she felt the sting of tears in her eyes.

Mary's hand tightened. "And here I thought city-boy had more sense than that."

"So did I," Jess said.

"You want me to have John set him straight?"

"Taken care of. Trust me, he won't want anything to do with me anymore." Jess struggled to quell the spike of pain that staked her heart at the comment. She turned away from Mary and started cracking eggs, this time with a barely managed calm.

The older woman watched her for a long moment, then returned to her own preparations. Jess let out a slow breath, grateful that the grilling was over. She didn't want to think about Ren Gallini. Or about last night. Ever. "He'll probably stay a long way away from me after that," she muttered.

"Who will?"

Jess whirled to find Ren Gallini standing in the doorway. She tried to work up some righteous anger, but the damn chill kept pooling into liquid heat in her groin. The man looked like Adonis, and it was only four-thirty in the frigging morning. That irritated her even further. "What are you doing here?"

He kept his eyes focused on her. "I thought I could help."

Jess opened her mouth, then closed it again. This place ran like a well-oiled machine...usually. Mary was the chief cook, but Jess helped her in the mornings. John checked the generator and gathered any supplies they'd need for the day. Rocky prepped coffee, water, juices, and dishes.

Her father? Well, over the last couple years, she realized now, he'd stopped doing a lot of the work. Instead, he spent his time socializing with anyone who'd listen. The truckers always hit the road early, but Owen would be up having coffee with them and see them on their way. He'd backed off from much of the responsibility of Last Chance Camp. Jess had taken that over a long time ago.

Had her father been getting tired of this place? Was he ready to retire? Was that why he'd sold?

No. She scowled at the man standing in front of her. Her father would not have sold the place without telling her. Something else was going on here. The problem was, until she could find her father, she would get no answers. Jess shook her head. She had no idea where to start with that.

"A-hem."

"What?" Jess cracked a couple more eggs against the side of the bowl.

"That wasn't my head you just cracked, was it?"

"Why would I want to do that?"

"Oh, maybe because last night I acted like an idiot."

"Yes. You did."

"I'd like to—"

Jess held up her hand to stop him. "It's done. Forget it."

Eyes gleaming with danger stared at her for a long moment. Then he leaned in. He was so close she could smell his aftershave, expensive and alluring. At this hour of the morning?

"We *will* talk about this. And we will also talk about the

other thing. You remember? Those papers I gave you?"

"Not until my father gets home."

"This isn't home, beautiful. This is a waypoint."

He stood a foot taller than her, but she stared him eye for eye. "This may be a, what did you call it? A truck stop, to you. But this is my home. If you don't like it, you can leave anytime."

He backed off with a chuckle. "Would that I could, darling. Have you looked outside lately? It's stopped snowing but everything's just about buried, including my SUV."

"Then stay out of my way and you can hit the road as soon as the plows come through." She went back to cracking eggs. "Can't be soon enough," she said under her breath.

"If I didn't know better, I'd think you wanted me gone. It sure didn't feel that way last night."

The egg in Jess's hand crunched as she crushed it. Yellow ooze slid out beneath her fingers and, for a fleeting moment, she considered throwing it at the arrogant man standing in front of her.

As if sensing her thoughts, Ren backed up, held up his hands and turned for the kitchen door. "I think I'd better go help Rocky with the coffee."

"Oooh!" Jess tossed the egg in the trash and went to wash her hands. "The man is insufferable."

"Yeah, but no one's riled you up that much in, well, ever," Mary said.

"So?" Jess realized the discussion had come right back around on itself.

"So, I'm just sayin'."

Jess pointed at the swinging door. "You cannot think I have any interest in—in him," she said.

"You know what they say," Mary said, chuckling. "There's a fine line between love and hate."

Jess raised her hands up in the air. "I am beset from every angle," she said to the heavens. "What did I ever do to deserve this?" As soon as breakfast was over, Jess resolved to check on when the plows would come through.

The next few hours were spent keeping the buffet stocked with food. She was hot and tired and feeling decidedly cranky. She'd pulled her hair into a ponytail while working and could tell that bits and pieces of it had escaped. She looked down at the food-spattered apron she wore. Hadn't it been clean a couple hours ago?

Rocky came through a few times to get more juice, trailed by the teenage girl from the bus. He'd promised Jess the night before that he would be on his best behavior. Looking at the way the girl giggled every time he said anything, Jess figured she'd better remind him at least twice more today.

Hands from behind covered her eyes. "Guess who."

Jess smiled. "Hmmm. Rocky?"

"Not a chance."

"John?"

"Now I'm insulted."

"The only guess left is Smokey the Bear."

"You really do know how to wound a man."

She laughed as she turned into the arms of dark-haired, dark-eyed Rod. "Aw, you know I love you."

"If that's true, then why won't you marry me? We'll travel the world, living on nothing but our love for each other." He dipped her in true movie fashion, and she smiled up at him.

"What? And leave all this? Besides, we can't live on love alone."

"Sure we can, when it's strong like ours."

She slapped his hands until he let her up. "Sure, and that explains why you've come over here to raid the breakfast buffet, right?"

He leaned toward her conspiratorially. "Ach! But a man has to have sustenance in order to satisfy a woman such as you."

Jess turned, still laughing at Rod's jest, but the laughter died when she saw Ren Gallini standing just inside the door. The man looked like a powder keg ready to blow. Energy and darkness seemed to gather around him. He stared at them, his eyes dark and unreadable, then turned on his heels and left the room without a word.

Jess shook her head, sent Rod out to get some food, then took off her apron. "You need any more help?"

"No," Mary answered. "Rocky and I can finish up here."

"Okay. I'm going to call and check the weather and roads, then go help John clean rooms. Send Rocky over when you're done with him."

"Will do."

Chapter Thirteen

Ren stood in a corner shadowed as dark as his mood. He'd greeted Rod with a curt nod when the man entered. Had he known the man would try to manhandle Jess, he'd have bounced him out of the place instead. He watched the man load a tray high with food, juice, and coffee. Rod sat down at a table with tourists and shoveled food into his mouth, chewing while he answered their questions about the wilds of Alaska. The man must have a decade on Ren, putting him in his mid-forties. He laughed like an explosive charge that rumbled on and on before it died out.

This man and Jess were friends and Ren didn't much like the abnormal jealousy he felt over that. That whole proposal thing may have been a joke, but it rankled. Jess didn't need an uncouth state trooper. She needed someone who would take her away from all this and show her what life had to offer beyond Alaska. He remembered the slippers. Jess Jenkins needed someone who would allow her to be a woman. Show her what being a woman was all about.

He'd fallen back into deliberately baiting her this morning, hoping it would keep a necessary wall between them and cool his ardor. It hadn't helped. Not one bit.

Jess walked out of the kitchen at that moment. She stopped by the table reserved for the long haulers and her laughter floated over to him as she responded to some joke.

"I'll check the road situation and let you know when it will be clear."

"Thanks, hon." One of the men patted her arm and Ren wished it had been him. He wanted to touch her. To be touched by her. Damn. He was in serious trouble here.

The twins, turning the restaurant into their own little indoor racetrack, barreled by Ren's corner, rounded a table, and tried to skate past Jess. She managed to grab both of them around the waist, lifting them off the floor as she quietly explained that, if they stopped running inside, she'd have Rocky help them build an igloo later.

"Really? Cool, man!" As she set them back on their feet, the wide-eyed boys trounced over to their parent's table and sat down. The way they were fidgeting in their seats, though, Ren didn't think they'd be still for long. By the look on Jess's face, she didn't either. She glanced up and saw Ren in the corner and the happy smile on her face faded.

She walked past him without a word and entered her office. No time like the present to hash things out, he thought, following her. He shut her office door behind him.

Phone in her hand, she didn't look up, but finished her conversation with her head stoically pointed at a blank computer screen. After saying goodbye, she glanced at him. "I'd rather you left the door open."

"You're not going to want this discussion overheard," he countered.

Jess didn't say a word, but the sound of the landline hitting the cradle put her solidly on the still-pissed side of the emotion scale.

Ren sat down in one of the chairs in front of her desk. "How are the roads?"

"Looks like it'll be drivable tomorrow, barring more snow." She stood up.

"Are we expecting more snow?"

"Hang on." Jess opened the door and disappeared into the restaurant, returning moments later. "I needed to let the guys know when they could be back on the road. There'll be a line of trucks heading out early in the morning."

She sat down at her desk, still looking at her desk instead of him. "The weather service says we're done with snow for a while. So it looks like our busload of tourists will be heading south tomorrow, too."

Ren stood and again closed the office door she'd left open, then sat on the corner of her desk. "We need to talk."

She folded her hands primly on the desk and looked up at him, a resolve that bordered on extreme stubbornness wiping any lines of emotion from her face.

"Not with you sitting on my desk, we don't."

He couldn't resist leaning in and had to hide the grin when she stopped herself from backing away. "Afraid of me, beautiful?"

Her chin came up. "Never."

Her hair smelled of citrus flowers and spring sunshine. When he leaned in closer, he realized the floral fragrance wasn't her hair. It wafted from her neck. Perfume? His lips crooked up in quick acknowledgement that there was a very feminine side to Jess Jenkins she kept well hidden from almost everyone. As he stared, a pink tongue darted out to wet lips that he'd spent what little sleep he got last night dreaming about.

Ren hovered over those lips, close enough to feel her

breath. It would be so easy to kiss her. And she would respond with an eagerness that drove him crazy. "You should be afraid."

"W-why?" Open eyes stared at him with an innocence that tugged at him in a way nothing, and no one else had.

"Because you're beautiful. Alluring. Intoxicating. There's something about you that I can't quite stay away from."

She licked her lips again and it was his undoing. Just as their lips would have touched, she turned her head away.

It was as effective as her slap last night. Ren thrust himself off the desk and turned away. He sat down in the chair, wrapping his hands around the arms in an attempt to apply controlled brakes to his libido. She didn't want him. And it was better this way for both of them.

Then he looked at her. Saw her eyes focused on him, the heightened color in her cheeks, the way she gripped her fisted hand on the desk.

Maybe she wasn't so immune to him after all. He drew a deep breath. Tomorrow would not come soon enough. He needed to get out of here before he did something they would both regret.

The time to get back on track was now. "I need to apologize for last night."

Her color deepened. "For what? For seducing me or for the fact that you called me a whore?"

He flinched, then nodded. She had the right. "It was wrong of me to make assumptions." He waved an arm. "I've never been in a place like this before."

"In a truck stop, you mean."

"Yes. I came here with preconceived notions I should

never have applied to you." He bent his head in a sign of acquiescence. "For that, I am deeply sorry."

Jess didn't say anything for a long moment, then grunted a quick, "Fine. Apology accepted."

He shook his head. The woman seemed to dislike backing down from any high emotions, including anger. That would be interesting to test in the bedroom.

Which would only get him in trouble, he reminded himself. "We need to talk about the sale of Last Chance to Gallini Enterprises. My mother sent me here to determine what must be done to bring this place up to the standards of our other properties."

Jess stood then. It didn't matter that she was only, what, five-foot-four? Her character added an imposing wall of strength when she needed it to. And she looked larger than life at the moment.

"You will not be changing any little bitty thing in my camp, Mr. Gallini."

"It's not your camp anymore."

"It is until my father tells me differently."

"You have his signature on the papers."

"Signatures can be forged."

Ren's eyes narrowed. "Now you accuse me of being something I'm not?"

All he got was a blink, but it was enough to know she understood his meaning. Then the fire was back in her eyes.

"I don't accuse you of anything. I'm trying to tell you. I know my father. Ask anybody here. Ask Mary, John, even Rocky. They'll tell you what I've been saying is true. There's no way my father would sell this place, especially without telling us, and then disappear. I...need some answers before we can talk about this."

The quaver in her voice threaded its way straight to Ren's heart. He almost went to her, pulled her into his arms. He held back, but only because he knew her pride would not allow it.

"I wish I knew where he was," she said. Her head dropped to her arms, and her voice lost all its fierceness. "It's starting to really worry me."

This Jess, the vulnerable one he'd never seen before, pierced his soul and an overwhelming protective instinct reared up. Ren rounded the desk and pulled her into his arms. Her body argued at first, but within seconds she had melted against him.

"Where is he, Ren?" Her voice was nothing more than a whisper. Ren patted her back, unable to think of any way to reassure her. He found himself making promises he didn't know if he could keep.

"I'm sure he's fine. Probably holed up somewhere on a three day binge."

She shook her head against his chest. "Dad doesn't drink."

"Then there's another reason...a less volatile reason, for him to not be here. We'll find him, beautiful." There was that take charge attitude of his, getting him in trouble again. Helping her meant spending time with her. Ren wasn't sure he could be in Jess's company much longer and maintain any sort of perspective.

"I don't even know where to start looking," Jess said.

That take charge attitude of his was twice as deadly when coupled with a protective instinct. Ren knew he was screwed. He'd never taken something on without seeing it through to the end, though. He turned Jess's face up so she could read the resolve in his own. "We'll figure it out."

"All right."

The conversation had come to a conclusion and it was time for him to let her go. His arms refused to listen. The way she kept staring up at him held him captive. Eyes painted in a myriad of colors darkened as pupils opened up and innocence gave way to desire. He felt her breathing quicken, tuning in to her heart rate. Hell, matching his heart rate, which, at the moment, seemed about to leap out of his chest.

Before he could stop himself, before he could think, he leaned down. The kiss never touched tentative. It went straight to white-hot.

He devoured her lips.

She opened them to let him in and began exploring on her own. Her arms traveled up his back as her mouth sought for deeper understanding.

He met her need move for move. At first, his embrace was supportive, then need drove his arms down. He cupped her bottom and pulled her against his raging desire.

Jess pulled back briefly, eyes and mouth forming perfect circles of surprise. He waited, letting out one long, slow breath. Giving her time to adjust. To decide.

When she grasped each side of his face and pulled him back into the kiss, he almost whooped with joy. He cupped her more tightly, raising her off the ground until she twined her legs around him. Settling her on the desk, he kissed his way to her throat, again catching the floral whiff of her perfume. He found the racing pulse at the base of her neck and kissed there. His hands pulled aside her work vest and t-shirt to gain access to her throat, her clavicle, and lower.

"Hey, boss?" The door pushed open at the same time Jess flew off the desk. Papers scattered and Ren backed up against the wall in the small office. There was nowhere else for him to go.

Rocky turned about three shades of red before his face settled on scarlet. "Uh, I'm sorry, boss. I, uh, well, uh—"

"Spit it out, Rocky. What do you need?"

He looked at the ceiling, the desk, anywhere but directly at Jess. "Um, the guests are, uh, starting to question, um, when they'll be able to go back to Fairbanks."

Jess sighed and it did absolutely nothing to cool Ren's libido. "All right. I'll head across the way in a couple minutes to give an update."

By now, embarrassment had faded and Rocky's attitude did a one-eighty. A smirk morphed into an all out grin as he answered her. "Um, thanks." He leaned in closer. "And don't forget the rules here, okay, boss? We don't need any trouble with the guests."

His grin faded a bit as he looked at Ren, but he didn't scowl. He just nodded, then dodged the ball of rubber bands that Jess threw at him and laughed his way out of the restaurant.

When Ren turned back to Jess, her scowl was firmly in place, but tinged with pink. She glanced at him, then bent down to pick up the desk items that had hit the floor. She set it all on her desk then edged by him.

"I think I'll, um, go update the guests on the weather and the roads." She reached the door and looked as if she expected him to leave with her.

"If you don't mind, I'll stay here for a bit."

"Why?" Her gaze dropped to about zipper level. "Oh! Okay. Um, really, stay as long as you need. See you later."

With that, she flew out of the room. He heard the restaurant door open mere seconds later. Did she even bother to grab her coat?

Jess rushed across the yard in the chilly weather. Unwilling to take even a minute to grab her coat from the kitchen, she was feeling the effects of the frigid weather on her jaunt to the inn. Her cheeks still flamed with the same slow burn as other parts of her body. Well, not all of her was affected by the cold.

What had gotten into her? She knew how to handle guys. How to discourage them in a nice way. She'd never accepted any of their advances. What was different now? What sort of spell had Renzo Gallini put her under that she wanted to rip her own clothes off every time he kissed her.

She ran up the stairs and into the lobby with no answers. Several guests were there. She saw the teenager that had cemented herself to Rocky's side and asked her to knock on doors and tell them she had an update.

"The storm has moved east."

A general cheer went up, so she held up her hand.

"It doesn't mean you get to leave today. As you know, it's an eight-hour drive back to Fairbanks. Maybe longer with the roads like they are." Jess glanced at the bus driver. "Paul?"

"If we get no more weather, we should be able to leave for Fairbanks tomorrow, nine A.M."

More cheering.

"And," Jess interrupted them, "have you looked outside lately?"

"No," the twins' father said. "Why?"

"The skies are clearing. If that keeps up, you have a shot at seeing the Aurora Borealis tonight."

That seemed to please everyone, if the ensuing noise was any indication. She loved making the customer happy.

"Just remember to write your room number down on the notepad here." She pointed to the ledge where it sat. "Only the room numbers written down will be notified."

Jess smiled at the flurry of activity. As folks headed for the sign-up sheet, she grabbed supplies out of the closet and began cleaning rooms. On her fourth bathroom, she was down on her knees, scrubbing the floor, when a throat cleared behind her.

Ren. Her head came up too quickly and connected against the pedestal sink with a sharp thud.

"Ouch!"

Before she could react beyond that, Ren was at her side. "Are you all right?"

"I just whacked my head on a sink. What do you think?"

He started feeling her head and, when he touched the already growing lump, she yelped again. "Stop it," she said pushing his hand away.

"I need to see if you've cut yourself." He kept trying to check out her head.

She tried to get up, but fell back down to the floor.

"See," he said. "You can't even stand up. We need to get you to a doctor."

"First, there is no doctor here. We take care of

ourselves or medivac and that's certainly not necessary. Second, I'm fine. And lastly, I can't get up because you're kneeling on part of my shirt." By now, she was frustrated enough she was grounding out the words. "Would you *please* move?"

He did, but not very far. When he tried to help her get up, her irritation hit the roof. "Get away from me, Ren. You're trouble."

She stood and was gratified to feel the room only dip and sway for a few seconds, then right itself. She looked up at the concern on his face and realized she might have been a bit tough on him.

"Sorry," she mumbled. "I'm cranky when things hurt."

"That's not when you're crankiest," he said.

Jess straightened. "Really?"

"Really. You're crankiest when you perceive something, or someone, you love is being threatened. Like this camp of yours."

He was right. No one messed with her home. Or with her people. She smiled. "Don't you forget that, either."

Ren rubbed his cheek. "Don't worry. I won't." He grinned then. "So, you think I'm trouble, eh?"

Oh, yeah. To my head, my heart, and my world. She couldn't tell him that, though. So she tapped her head. "Yep."

Ren smiled, and Jess could have sworn the world around them dimmed. Only his smile mattered. Seeing the little lines crinkle at the edges of his eyes and a light fill the light brown color with amber highlights.

This Ren Gallini was even more dangerous than the brooding one. That one, she could handle. This one yanked the rug of her defenses out from underneath her.

She turned to pick up her bucket of cleaning supplies. "I need to get back to work."

"I left your jacket in the lobby for you," Ren said. "You forgot to grab it when you ran out."

Figures he'd think of that. "Thanks. I'll get it later."

"Can I help?"

"What? Clean rooms?" She didn't even try to mirror her surprise.

"I do understand what it takes to clean a room, you know."

She shook her head. "You surprise me on a regular basis, Mr. Gallini."

"I'll take that as a compliment, Miss Jenkins."

"All right. Grab a pail out of the supply closet down the hall." She consulted her list. "Rocky and John have the other wing. Why don't you take rooms twenty through twenty-four? I'll pick up the rest. Make the beds, clean the bathroom and sink, and empty the trashes. Because of the snow, a lot of folks are still in their rooms. Knock and make yourself known first, okay? We can come back later if the room is occupied."

He saluted her. "Got it, boss."

"Don't you forget it."

Once he left, Jess went to work making up the twin beds. They would wash bedding tomorrow, once the bus had started on its return journey to Fairbanks.

After a long afternoon of cleaning and food preparation, things were finally winding down. Everyone was fed except the crew. Jess grabbed a tray and put together a salad. Too tired to eat it, she sat down and cupped her mug of coffee, staring into its depths.

"Penny for your thoughts?" Ren Gallini took the seat across from her.

"I was just thinking about Dad."

He reached over and covered her hands around the mug with his own. "I'm sure he'll turn up. You said he's done this sort of thing before."

"Not by being totally out of touch. And not when...well, the kind of bombshell you laid on us is about to hit."

She shook her head. "I just don't understand why. Why would he sell this place? It makes no sense." She looked at Ren. "I considered the possibility that you might have been involved in his disappearance."

"And discounted it, I hope."

"Not completely." When he pulled his hands back, she felt the chill settle around her. "But anyone who's willing to clean toilets to help out, well, how could they be involved in kidnapping an old man?"

"Thanks for the vote of confidence," Ren said. "We know he left his cell phone here."

"Yes. That's unusual."

"Is that the only way you ever know how to contact him?"

"Pretty much."

"He never left an address? Or told you *where* he was going?"

Jess shook her head at each question he asked.

Mary walked out of the kitchen, wiping her hands on a towel, as Ren asked the next question. He happened to be looking up or he might have missed her reaction. "And no one else has any clue where your Dad has been going?"

Jess's aunt turned on her heels and disappeared into the kitchen like a fire had been lit under her. Ren frowned.

"No," Jess said.

"Are you quite certain of that?"

"Yes. If anyone here knew something, they would tell me."

"Then why did your cook just hightail it back into the kitchen when she heard me ask you about your Dad?"

"Aunt Mary?" Jess's chair toppled over as she jumped up. "She couldn't know anything. She would have told me."

Ren spread his arms. "I'm just relating what I saw."

"Come on. I'm going to prove to you she doesn't know anything." She grabbed Ren by the hand and pulled him up and after her into the kitchen.

"Mary?"

"Just a minute," the muffled voice came from the storeroom at the back. When Mary came out, carrying napkins for holders Jess knew were already filled, Jess's eyes grew wide.

"You *do* know where Dad is!"

"Why would you even think that?" Mary did a poor job of looking shocked as she plunked napkins on the counter.

Ren answered before Jess could. "Because you look guilty as hell."

Mary was busy planning Owen's funeral. Because she surely would put him in the ground for making her hold out on Jess like this. Nothing about this felt right. If he hadn't held the ultimate ransom—Jess's happiness—over her head, Mary would never have gone along with this. She pulled the towel from her shoulder and started to wring it in her hands.

"Mary, all this time? You knew where Dad was?"

"I know. I couldn't say anything."

"Why not?" Jess asked.

"He made me promise not to tell you."

"He? You mean my *father*?"

The shrillness in Jess's voice made Mary cringe. I'm really going to kill you, Owen. Really and truly.

"Yes." Mary slumped to a stool. "I'm sorry, honey. If it had been anyone else asking, I'd have told them to go fly a kite. But Owen had a pretty convincing argument."

Ren settled on a stool, apparently deciding Jess could handle this grilling without his help.

Jess opened her mouth, then closed it. Opened it again, then her lips became thin lines. "Did John know? And Rocky?"

"Rocky couldn't keep a secret for anything, so no. John...well, John didn't like it much, but he did what Owen asked us to do."

"And what, exactly, is that?"

"He said it was for your own good," Mary tried to explain.

"What was?"

"Putting this place up for sale."

Jess turned white as a sheet and sank onto a stool.

Tears welled in Mary's eyes. Nothing was worth seeing this girl, the girl she'd raised after her mother's death, in this kind of pain. "I'm so sorry, baby." She tried to wrap her arm around Jess but Jess brushed it off.

"No, Mary. You don't get to be sorry. You get to dish.

What's going on? What's this grand plan of Dad's and what in the hell does it have to do with me?"

Completely torn between the promise made to her sister's husband, the man responsible for all their livelihoods and whom she loved like a brother, and the daughter she'd come to think of Jess as, Mary couldn't decide what to do. Protect Jess. Help her grow into a woman her mother would be proud of. Those things Mary knew. She'd done a pretty good job of it, too, up to this point.

But Owen's argument had worn Mary down. John, too.

She'll never leave this place on her own. She'll never fulfill the life she's supposed to, whatever that's meant to be, if she continues to bury herself here. She'll never fall in love, Mary. Who's she going to find here? We need to help her see beyond Last Chance. And under no circumstances can you tell her you've got that cell phone. I need her to come find me, not call me.

"I can't tell you," Mary whispered.

With her eyes the size of saucers, Jess fidgeted, then got up and started to pace. "You can't? Or you won't?"

"This is something you need to find out for yourself."

Ren apparently reached his boiling point. "I don't know what's going on, or how I got involved in all of this, but I'm damn sure going to find out. Now, Mary, I'm going to ask you a very simple question and I want a very simple answer. How is Jess supposed to find out what she's supposed to when we have no clue where to start."

"Well, um, Owen left her a note."

"He what?"

Mary nodded. "I'm so sorry, baby," she said to Jess. "He told me not to give it to you until I absolutely had to. You have to believe me. If I didn't have your safety, your happiness foremost in my mind, I'd never have gone along with this."

Jess shook her head. "Auntie, my life has been turned upside down these last few days, and I find you're part of the reason." Taking a couple deep breaths, Jess stood in front of Mary. "I know you love me. And you took over the job of mother after Mom died." Jess gulped. "But I'm old enough to decide things for myself. Whatever...manipulation my father is orchestrating at the moment has to stop. I don't know why he'd do this. It's completely out of character for him. But I want to see the letter he wrote. Now."

Mary didn't hesitate. In fact, it was a huge relief to have it all out in the open now. Well, almost all. She reached into a drawer and pulled out the note.

"Thank you," Jess said.

"Can you forgive me for holding back this information?" Mary asked.

"Auntie, you will always be like a mother to me. I know you did what you did with me first and foremost in your mind. How can I be mad at you for that?"

Jess hugged her, and Mary held on tight. "I love you, little girl. You'll always be the daughter I couldn't have."

"I know." Jess pulled back, clutching the letter, and turned to Ren. "Give me a few minutes, okay?"

Out in the empty restaurant, Jess slumped down onto a chair and opened the letter, honestly not sure if she really wanted to read it. What could possibly make her father sell Last Chance Camp, and how did that equate to Jess's happiness?

Hi, honey,

Well, if you're reading this, Mary's told you a few things that have probably surprised you. About her, about John, and mostly about me. Don't be angry with her. I pretty much forced her to play along.

You see, I've looked at life from a lot of different angles. I...I don't really want to run Last Chance anymore. I know it's your home. It's been mine, too. You're mother and I made our lives here. You were born here. But I've been thinking about retiring.

Then leave the place to me, Dad! Jess almost cried the words.

I know you'd like me to leave the place to you, but I can't do that. Well, not in good conscience. At least, not until you've had a chance to see life from a different perspective. So come find me. Mary knows just enough to get you on your way. Don't try to get more out of her, because she doesn't know.

And if, when you find me and you understand, you still want Last Chance, well, then I'll see what I can do about that.

I love you with all my heart,

Dad

Great. No answers and a whole bunch more questions. Jess crumpled the letter in her fist, sitting there for several minutes trying to decide whether or not to go on the scavenger hunt her father seemed to be pointing her toward.

Finally, she headed back into the kitchen, where Mary, still subdued, and Ren, curiosity and anger at war in his eyes, waited. She handed the letter to Ren.

"There's not much there. More mystery, no answers."

"What the hell is going on?" Ren scanned the note.

"It seems I'm going on a wild goose chase, compliments of my father."

"This is insane," he said.

"Yep. It certainly is." Jess turned to Mary. "So. Where is he?"

"He's in Mexico." The words came out in a rush, as if releasing pressure.

"Mexico?" Jess and Ren said it at the same time.

Mary nodded again. "Cabo."

Jess' lips were thin lines by now. "Where in Cabo?"

"I didn't understand what he said."

"Just tell me," Jess said quietly.

"He said he'd be at the Me."

Ren's head snapped up. "I know that place," Ren said. "The ME." He frowned. "My mother vacations there. Regularly." The words trailed off as he tried to pull his thoughts together. He'd tried several times to call his mother, to no avail.

Jess echoed his thoughts. "The mother you can't get a hold of?"

He nodded. "This doesn't make any sense."

"We should be able to call Dad in the morning, right? Now that we know where he is?"

"He said he wouldn't take any calls. And that he's staying under a different name."

Ren turned to Jess. "I guess that means we're going to

Mexico."

Damn it. Jess had way too much to take care of here. She didn't have time to go galavanting around the globe in search of her wayward, and misguided, father. And she sure as hell didn't want to spend that much time with Ren. She was barely holding on to her heart as it was.

"I can't go to Mexico." Jess said, her voice a tiny slice of its normal self. "I've got a camp to run here."

Ren didn't have a clue what spooked her, but his instincts were screaming to handle things with kid gloves. "All of your guests are leaving tomorrow, aren't they?"

"Yes."

"You've got a crew that can manage this place while it's empty, right?"

"Well...yes."

He kept his voice low, soothing, rubbing her back as he spoke. "Then come on, beautiful. Let's go find your father."

Double damn. This was getting worse with each passing moment.

"Why don't you go find him," she said to Ren.

"Because that's not what he wants, apparently. And something tells me we're not going to get anywhere with your father unless you are there in person."

With a deep sigh, Jess nodded. "I think you're right. I guess that means I'm going to Mexico."

"We're going, beautiful. Together."

Wonderful.

Chapter Fourteen

Late that night, Jess bundled up and stepped outside. Camp was in full night mode and dark except for the bare lights needed to cross the compound. She walked past those lights and looked up at a clear sky filled with stars. There was something about this time of year. The cold made everything skyward look clearer, crisper, more focused.

There! She saw it out of the corner of her eye. The thin ribbon of color snaking its way across the sky. The spirits had chosen to come out and play tonight.

The lights didn't move, and yet they did. They grew from a ribbon to a field and undulated across the sky. Yet, with the naked eye, she could not discern movement. It was the most beautiful thing she'd ever had the privilege to witness.

Jess twirled in a circle, arms high in the air, dancing with the shadows as the spirits played their game, taking this one selfish moment to enjoy nature's majesty. She held a finger up to the sky. She could almost hide the ribbon, yet in ten minutes or less, she knew her entire hand would not be able to mask the mischievous brilliance of the spirits' play.

Remembering her responsibility, her shoulders slumped as she realized her time alone with the lights was over. She cocooned the oneness with nature deep in her heart, kicked an imaginary ball up into the sky for the spirits to play with, and went inside to wake the guests.

She walked almost silently down the long, slender hall, knocking on doors one by one. It appeared they all wanted to see the lights. After all, that was what they were here for.

As doors opened, her whisper carried down the hall. "The northern lights are visible." Guests hurriedly dressed. Or went in sleepwear, boots, and with blankets wrapped around their shoulders, just as always happened. One by one, they headed outdoors to share the mystery of Mother Nature. To see the night sky alive with color. To watch the spirits play.

Having tapped on the last door, she glanced one last time at the list, then froze. A handwritten note had been added to the bottom.

"Owen's trailer."

Ren wanted to see the lights? Jess felt the air freeze in her lungs and walking became all but impossible. No. With his papers and authoritative voice, he'd yanked her life out from under her feet. Add in the weird feelings she got whenever she was around him, and she didn't want to go wake him up.

She did not want him to see her lights. Didn't want to share them...with him.

Even as she thought it, though, she began to move. Others would talk about the sights in the morning, and he would know she had chosen not to wake him up. He would make her pay with that smug assuredness of his. No, she'd rather take her chances with the lights.

She hurried across the snow-packed ground and tapped on her father's trailer. She leaned against it briefly, wondering again what her dad could possibly think was right about selling their home.

A sleep-tousled Ren opened the door, and Jess gaped at him. He had no shirt on. Renzo Gallini dressed was a force to be reckoned with. Naked to the waist, he was Adonis glorified. He didn't give her the impression he'd done much hard work, but he must work out. Shadows reflected off finely honed muscles. Muscles she itched to run her hands over. Jess sighed.

Eyes filled with sleep crinkled with pleasure. In spite of the frigid cold, he leaned casually against the counter as he uttered one word that felt like an invitation to look all she wanted. "Yes?"

"Um...The, uh..." She stopped, forced her eyes away from the chest hair she wanted so badly to touch. She looked down at the ground and tried to remember why she was here. Lights. Oh, yes. The northern lights.

"The lights are out. You, um, wrote down that you wanted to be woken up?"

He grinned and nodded. "I did."

"Well, um, they're out."

He straightened, and biceps she'd only seen on the cover of romance novels flexed.

Jess's mouth went as dry as the desert.

"Do you mind?" He indicated the door she held open with a tightly gripped hand.

"Oh, sorry." She backed away.

"I'll get dressed and join you momentarily."

"Um, sure. Great." Face flaming, she whirled and ran as fast as the snow would let her.

Ren got dressed with lightening speed. He knew attraction when he saw it. And seeing the change in Jess when it hit her full in the face had sent his libido into overdrive. He'd bet his share of the family business, if he'd invited her in right then and there, she'd have come without a backward glance.

He'd almost done exactly that, he thought as he pulled on his boots. He was hard as granite with just one sultry look from her. Trouble was, she didn't even realize what effect she had on him. It was so much more than a physical reaction. She'd tapped into his heart and the recognition floored him.

He needed to keep his distance. Getting involved was not smart. Not by any definition. He didn't want to be the guy who broke Jess's heart, damn it.

Ren pulled on his coat. He closed the door behind him and jammed a knit cap on his head, compliments of Owen Jenkins. Remembering that tomorrow they would be stuck in his SUV together for some eight hours, Ren shook his head. It was going to be a very long trip to Mexico.

As he walked over the frozen snow toward the inn, the lights went out. He blinked several times, then his eyes adjusted to the darkness. A glimpse of green caught his eye, and he looked up.

And saw the majesty of the earth reflected back in green striations rising out against a stark night sky. It wasn't just that this color was splashed across the heavens. It was also the depth of the color. It was green, yet any attempt to describe the actual shade of green was impossible.

Ren did not know how long he stood there, but the chill of the night finally got through the coat he wore, and he started to shiver. He ran his tongue over lips that felt as if he'd slept with his mouth open.

He walked closer to the inn and saw guests gathered there, all silently staring up at the show. And all with their jaws hanging slack. Even the twins stood still and watched the display.

The urge to be with Jess, to share this with her, threatened to overwhelm him. He needed to find her. Now. He picked his way slowly through the groups, making a complete circle of the area. No Jess.

Then he caught the hint of movement. There, off to the left. On the side of the building. Someone stood apart from the group, and he would bet the ownership papers on Last Chance it was Jess.

He moved closer. She was hidden from just about everyone, except him. Did she enjoy watching others see the lights for the first time? As he got closer, he realized she wasn't looking at the others. She was looking up, at the lights. Her arms were wrapped across her chest, and she swayed slightly back and forth. She was so intent on the sky view that she didn't appear to hear him approach.

And Ren got an unfettered look at Jess Jenkins in a state he could only describe as enthralled. She didn't even see him, though he was less than ten feet in front of her. Her eyes stared unblinking, as if she refused to miss any single moment. Eyes that were filled with wonder. And something more...some sort of connection.

He walked around her. Still she didn't acknowledge him. He did, however, see a shiver run through her body. She was cold.

He moved to stand behind her and wrapped his arms around her.

She didn't run. Hell, she didn't even jump. Instead, she

shocked him by grasping his arms, pulling them tighter around her, and leaning into him.

God help him, it felt good. Jess's body was a perfect fit, and his body knew it. It took every ounce of willpower Ren had to stand there, hold her, and not take it any further. Especially when what he really wanted to do was carry her off to his bed.

Her hips moved against him, and he jerked in reaction. He could feel the underswell of her breasts through the thickness of her coat. He longed to trace those curves, to kiss them again. To hear her gasp as he drew first one and then the other into his mouth.

Filled with an agonizing need, Ren held his ground as Jess watched her lights until they almost completely faded away. Then she turned in his arms, reached up, and tangled her fingers in his hair as she pulled his head down. There was no tentative in this kiss, only the sureness of a fevered need.

Ren met it with a need of his own, tightening his arms to pull her against him. As he did so, Jess parted her lips, giving him permission to explore.

She sighed, and he felt it in his soul. His brain shut down and instinct took over. He broke off the kiss, letting his lips trail across her cheek. He found her ear and gently sucked the lobe into his mouth.

"Oh!" Jess leaned her head to the side, allowing him more room. Ren took full advantage, trailing kisses down the side of her neck and along the collar of her coat. He tried to pull it back, but there was simply too much bulk.

"My place," she whispered.

"Oh, yeah." Ren scooped her up in his arms and ran as

fast as their combined weight and the snow would allow him. He tried to open the door, but couldn't get the right angle on the thing. Frustrated, he set her on the ground so she could get at the door.

Once inside, coats fell off and into the stairwell at the trailer's door. Jess sat down in the recliner and reached down to unlace her boots, but Ren's hand stopped her. She looked up at him.

"Let me."

He untied and unlaced her boots. With a quiet voice, he explained that what she was offering him, this first time, was the greatest wish any woman could grant. He stopped unlacing twice to look up into her face. "Are you certain you want to do this?"

The emotion on his face seemed timid, like he wasn't used to showing that side if himself. And had she heard a bit of a quaver when he spoke? This vulnerability, in a man who rarely, if ever, showed a soft side, made her more certain than ever that she wanted this.

Jess gave him a smile.

"No, beautiful. Smiles won't do, although yours is amazing. I need to hear the words. From you."

"Yes, Ren. I want this. Almost more than I've ever wanted anything." Everything about this felt right.

He pulled off each boot slowly, asking her if she knew there could be some pain associated with this first time.

Jess nodded. She wasn't a prude. She knew enough. And she didn't care. This overwhelming need to be with Ren was a new feeling for her. She didn't care about anything else except being with him. Here. Now.

She reached for him as he knelt before he, and he obliged her with a long, languorous kiss. It wasn't enough. She needed more. And faster. Her body felt like it was on fire.

But he broke away from her lips and once again trailed kisses down her neck. "I want this to be as pleasurable for you as it is for me," he said in between molten touches along her skin.

"Trust me," she whispered. "It is."

"Trust *me*," Ren answered, glancing up with a smile that had turned decidedly wicked. "There's a lot more to come."

He reached beneath her shirt and inched it up, his fingers leaving fire trails along her skin. When he could raise it no further without help, she raised her arms and allowed him to slide it the rest of the way off her. He gazed at her and she felt the heat of a blush color her face. When he smiled, she looked down and realized he was grinning at the very lacy, very sheer peach-colored bra she wore. She reached behind her to unsnap it, but he stilled her hand.

"Sometimes," he said, kissing her fingers, "it's more fun with clothes on. Let me show you."

Ren returned to the feather kisses, sending bolts of pleasure straight to her core. He kissed his way from neck to shoulder, from shoulder to bra strap, then began to follow the bra strap downward. By the time he reached the top of her bra, which barely covered her, her need was so great she arched into him, her body begging him to capture her, to taste her, to give her release.

"Please," she begged.

He pulled a tight bud into his mouth through the lace

and she gasped. His hand moved across her other breast and she shuddered with need. She reached for him, but he was too far away. Finally, after long, torturous moments of exquisite agony, he reached behind her and unclasped her bra. As he pulled it off her shoulders, his own intake of breath signaled his pleasure at the sight of her.

His eyes moved up to hers, filled with smoky desire. He cupped her face in his hands and lightly kissed her. "I can stop this right now if you want. But if we go any further, I'm not sure I will be able to stop."

"Quit talking, City Boy." Jess reached for the edges of his shirt. He took over and she watched firm muscles flex as he pulled it over his head and tossed it onto the pile of coats and clothes.

"I—" She hesitated.

Ren kissed her. "Ask anything. There are no limits to what we can do. To what *you* can do."

She touched his chest. "I would like to feel you against me."

A slow smile spread across his face. "I'd like that, too." He pulled her up from the chair and into his arms. Chest to chest.

The sensation of being skin to skin with a man, with this man, was unlike anything she'd ever felt before. The coarseness of his chest hair against her nipples sent shards of desire racing through her body. She could feel the ripple of his muscles, and his arms tightened around hers.

When he kissed her, it was like a slow, rolling, freefall. Safe, but not safe. She felt...oh! His lips dipped to kiss her neck and she moved to give him access. Jess ran her hands up and down his back, learning his body, relishing the feel of his golden muscles.

Before Ren got back to the exquisite torture of
enjoying her breasts, he stopped and pulled back. Jess tried
to pull him close again. Instead, he reached for her hand,
brought it up to his lips, and kissed each finger. Then,
turning, they moved until they stood at the foot of her bed.

Suddenly nervous, Jess stood still, unsure of what to
do, but when Ren kissed her, urgency took over, and she
reached for his jeans. His hand stilled her fingers, and she
moaned against his mouth. Instead of giving in, he
unclasped the top button on her jeans.

Jess jumped at the feel of his fingers against her skin as
he lowered her zipper. No one had ever touched her there.
She'd never wanted this before. Now, the need was so
great, she wanted to cry out with it.

Even the act of sliding her jeans down was a sensual
experience. Ren knelt in front of her and made slow work
of it. Jess wanted to rip them off and toss them away. She
wanted skin against skin...to feel the hair of his chest as it
excited her beyond anything she'd ever felt before.

Finally, he nudged her feet up, one at a time, so she
could step out of the denim. Her hands went to cover the
tiny wisp of a thong she'd put on this morning, but Ren
captured them, holding them to her side as he gazed at her.
The heat of a rosy blush crept up her body, but Jess didn't
care. Just having him look at her this way was a turn on.
And she was about as turned on as she could get. She
reached for him, and yet again he pulled her hands away,
this time behind her back. He held them loosely with one
hand while his other began to roam again. Down the side
of her leg, then around back and up the middle. His other

hand joined in and, as he flirted with her, never touching her where she wanted him to, she fought the urge to guide him.

When he kissed her thong, she jumped. He looked up at her with a lazy grin spread across his face. His fingers toyed with the edges of her panties, then dipped underneath and Jess's legs turned to pudding.

Ren must have felt the shaking in her limbs, because he stood and guided her onto the bed. She lay down, arms across her stomach, waiting. When he reached for his own jeans, she held her breath. He slowly pulled them off, keeping eye contact with her.

Her own gaze dipped to the insistent bulge in his low-rise boxer briefs. Then he pulled them down, and her eyes widened at the size of him. Could she... Would he... Could they?

"Yes," he said as if reading her mind. "We can." He laid down beside her and ran a finger along the curves of her face. "We won't do anything tonight that doesn't feel good, or right, to you. Do you believe me?"

"Yes." She said it without hesitation.

"Good."

Then his lips found her breast, and the feelings built again inside her as she tangled her hands in his hair, pulling him closer. When his hand moved along her stomach, she mimicked his movements with her own, curling into his chest hair, then following the line down around well-defined stomach muscles.

He reached beneath her thong, and she gasped as he touched her. Her hands felt along his shaft, and he stilled.

"I'm sorry. Shouldn't I—"

"Trust me. Everything you're doing is perfect. Need stills me, beautiful. I don't know how long I can hold out, so maybe we'll save some of your education for next time." He grasped her hand and moved it until it lay on the blanket over her head. "For now, let me show you what it feels like to make love."

Her mouth went dry, and she only had time to nod her acquiescence as Ren's hands started to move. He watched where his hands roamed, and she watched his face.

He caressed a breast, sending tingles through her as he lightly brushed her nipple. "You're more beautiful than I ever imagined." He glanced up and she saw the smoky haze of need in his darkened eyes. "And I imagined quite a bit."

She smiled, but he had already returned to his exploration of her body. His lips joined hands that were driving her crazy with need. He played with her, running his fingers lightly up and down until she squirmed with a sweet ache she'd never before experienced. She closed her eyes when the feelings grew so strong she thought she would explode. It took everything she had to keep her one hand above her head.

When he shifted away from her, she looked at him with questions in her eyes. He used the separation to pull her thong off and bare this last bit of her to his gaze. A natural instinct had her closing her legs, but he stopped her with his hands. "Let me see all of you," he said, his voice husky with his own desire.

She tried to relax, but it was hard. When he bent down to kiss her thigh, she wriggled underneath his touch. He didn't force her. He simply kissed her. First one thigh, then the other, getting closer and closer to her core, until she was so on fire, she begged for more by opening her legs.

He kissed the triangle of hair. She reached down to pull him up, but he twined their fingers together. To have him touch her like this, using only his lips, was almost more than she could stand. Her legs widened even further, and she arched to meet his tongue. "Oh!" The rolling sensation took over as waves of climax washed over her again and again.

Her fingers clenched in his, and he tightened his grip. Finally, after a time she could not count, he pulled back and the feeling ebbed. Jess's body relaxed into the bed as she tried to make sense of what had just happened.

"Did you like that?"

"Mmm-hmmm," she said as she disengaged her hands and stretched out, reaching to grasp the headboard of her bed.

"I thought you might."

Since he was still settled between her legs, Jess raised herself onto her elbows. "What about you, though? What about your satisfaction."

His eyes gleamed. "I get satisfaction from seeing the look on your beautiful face when you come. And feeling the shudder in your body as the orgasms overtake you."

"But—"

"Don't worry, beautiful. We've only just begun this night." And, with that, he lowered his head again. Unsure she could take any more, she protested. His lips quelled any thought as they pulled her in, and she began the climb back to an even deeper, even more sensual need for him. His hand joined his lips, at first caressing, then centering. She felt his fingers enter her, and the motion sent a new sensation coursing through her. His mouth continued to heighten her need as he moved further inside.

"You like?"

"Oh, yes. I definitely like."

He nodded.

A shadow must have crossed her face because he stilled. "There will be a little pain, beautiful. We'll try to minimize it, but it's part of the process."

"I know."

"I'll make certain it's worth it for you," he said.

She reached for him and pulled him up to join her, staring into his face, making sure he saw her resolve...and her need. "You already have."

He kissed her then, slowly at first. His hand moved back to her core and entered her again. Jess's hands found him, and she moved along the ridges of his penis, in time with his own movements.

This time, it was Ren who groaned. His thumb rubbed across her, sending her whirling into sensual overdrive. "I don't know how much longer I can hold out," he said, grinding the words out.

"Then don't," she answered, driving her hips into his need.

He grabbed a condom and sheathed himself, then moved over her, stopping just at her entrance, leaning down to suck on first one breast, then the other.

Jess, however, was beyond waiting. She grasped his hips and pulled him into her. He didn't resist. Her body did, but only for a moment in time. Later, she would not even remember the bit of burning she felt.

He moved slowly as the momentum built, both in their

actions and their desire. She wrapped her legs around him, and his movements grew more and more frantic until he cried out with his release. Jess joined him scant moments later in another long wave of pleasure.

Chapter Fifteen

Ren held himself over Jess and watched her face as she climaxed, awestruck by the strength of their love-making. He'd been single a long time, and his love life was witness to that. Still, tonight felt...different. His release, their release together, had rocked his world like nothing before.

Her eyes were still closed as he moved to lay beside her, and she snuggled in deeper, while Ren tried to make sense of what had just happened. Desire had flooded him beyond his imagining. Could he attribute that to her being a virgin? It was a first for him, and it was easier to believe than the other possibility. That he was starting to care for her more than he should.

Jess laid an arm across his chest, and Ren tightened his hold on her.

"Is this what love feels like?" Jess's voice was no more than a whisper, and the last words trailed off as sleep overtook her.

It took every ounce of strength Ren had to keep from tensing up. Hell, right at the moment, he wanted nothing more than to cut and run. Love? He was having trouble breathing and had to focus for several long moments to let his lungs settle down. Still, the cold, clammy sweat that covered him verified the panic that her words had set in motion.

He didn't love. Ever. The complications were too great. Hell, the one time he'd thought himself to be in love, it had turned out to be someone with more interest in his non-human assets, and that had cost him almost everything. Ren learned from his mistakes. All women wanted something. He shoved the picture of Jess in the throes of a climax to the furthest reaches of his mind. Jess wanted something, too. She wanted Last Chance. And she'd probably do anything to get it.

His body flinched, screaming at his mind. He knew that wasn't true. Still, he did not love Jess. The vision of her staring up at the Northern Lights came to mind. He. Did. Not. Love. Her.

But he'd made love to her. He'd let her believe his heart matched hers, and she had given him the greatest gift she had to give. And he'd taken it with barely a thought about the ramifications.

He would have to tread carefully to be sure he didn't damage this budding heart.

Ren extracted his arm from underneath her and eased out of the bed. No, he'd have to be very careful how he handled this. He liked her. Maybe even a lot. And he sure as hell didn't want anything bad to happen to her. But there could be no relationship.

She looked even younger, more innocent in her sleep, curled up like a baby. Jess stretched then, settling her arms overhead and, as she did, the quilt uncovered one breast.

Ren sucked in his breath as he stared. One perfect breast with one very sensitive tip that his hand could mold around like a second skin. Damn. He was hard again just standing here staring.

Disgusted with himself, he backed out of Jess's bedroom, got dressed, and left for his own trailer...and a semi-cold shower.

There was no early morning light in Last Chance this time of year, only the ever-encroaching shadows of the long, dark winter. Waking up was more of an instinct or an alarm clock than a body's sense that the sun had risen.

Jess rarely woke ready to take on the world. For her, it was a slower process. When her alarm clock went off, her body reacted first, slamming the snooze button. By the time it came on again, her brain had struggled up from the depths of REM sleep. Jess stretched long and hard and finally opened her eyes to the dark gray of early morning.

Then she shot out of bed as memories of the past night flooded back in. Ren! She grabbed the quilt and wrapped it around her, staring at her sheets.

Her hands flew to her cheeks, the memories heating her skin. They quickly moved to cover her mouth as she let out a guffaw of disbelief, mingled with joy. What had she done?

A triumphant smile settled in as her mind relived the past few hours. Ren's body was even better looking unclothed than clothed. And the things he'd done to her...Jess's whole body flushed. If that was what making love was like, she was sorry she'd waited so long.

She had lots of time to make up. Jess glanced out into the trailer, realizing Ren was not there, and her stomach hit the floor. Why hadn't he stayed? Had he taken what he wanted and then left? No. She was a better judge of character than that. Still, he'd shown up in camp with papers saying he owned the place. And, until yesterday, had shown little concern for the whereabouts of her father.

Flashes of lips mingling, hands caressing, and

emotional heights she'd never felt before ran through her mind. He had been inordinately gentle with her last night. A man couldn't be like that in bed and ruthless out of it.

Could he? Could he have duped her in this, too? Jess didn't have much experience in the fine art of making love. Hell, she didn't have any. But she didn't think loving and then leaving was proper etiquette.

Jess glanced at the clock and started grabbing clothes. She would be late to help Mary, and she knew exactly what Mary would be thinking. Sorting out her relationship with Renzo Gallini would have to wait.

Except she ran smack dab into her dilemma, breaking eggs into the mixing bowl. Jess willed her face to maintain normal color and tried to mimic her normal stroll as she entered the kitchen. "Hi, Mary." She glanced at Ren, whose attention seemed focused on the eggs. "Hi, City Boy."

She had the satisfaction of seeing him momentarily tighten his grip on the counter. Of course, said satisfaction went out the window when he turned and, in a slow drawl, said, "Morning, beautiful."

Jess blushed a deep, crimson red.

Okay. So the man had more composure than she did. Point to Ren. She glanced at Mary, who watched the two of them with way too much interest. Tossing her coat on the rack, Jess opted to turn and run. "I'll check the coffee."

Making coffee, something Jess had done day in and day out for years, turned out to be an impossible feat this morning. First, she was out of filters and had to go back through the kitchen, walking right past Ren and seeing Mary's smirk. Once she got filters, she realized she was out of coffee. So back she went. When she finally got everything situated, she hit the button and started stacking food trays until she heard the hiss of water coming from behind the machines. Jess threw the trays she was carrying on the floor and the loud clatter brought Mary out from the kitchen.

"Everything all right?" she asked.

"Fine," Jess ground out as she crawled behind the machine to turn the water off. "One of the pipes feeding the coffee machine broke again. Just a freaking water pipe."

By the time she got it turned off, her jeans had lines of wet in various spots. Mary stood there grinning. "What the heck are you grinning about? You think this is funny?"

"No," Mary said with a chuckle. "I think the coffee pot is as out of sorts as you are." She turned back into the kitchen, her laughter staying behind to taunt Jess.

"Ooooh!" Jess picked up the trays, dropped them on the kitchen counter without a word to either Mary or Ren, and stomped off to get some more copper tubing for the coffee.

By five thirty a.m., the truckers had been fed and were warming up their rigs in anticipation of hitting the road. The busload of guests were starting to trickle in when Ren freed himself from kitchen duty and went in search of Jess, who seemed to have done everything possible to make herself scarce for the past hour or more.

He knocked on her trailer and was treated to a growl. "What?"

He opened the door and stepped inside to an almost naked Jess Jenkins. She gasped and whirled away from him, and he caught a very delectable glimpse of black thong before she yanked her jeans up to cover them.

And all of Ren Gallini's resolutions flew out the window. What was it about Jess Jenkins that put his penis in the lead over his brain? The slow burn of an erection threatened his sanity as he moved closer. "Hey."

When Jess turned around, her arms covered her breast and fire flashed in her eyes. "What the hell? Do you always enter apartments without permission? Get out of here."

He stood in front of her now, but couldn't quite pull his eyes away from the swell of breasts above her arms. When he caught a glimpse of a bit of rosy nipple, it almost undid him.

Ren ran his hands lightly up and down her arms, hoping to convince her to drop them.

Instead, she tried to shrug him off. He looked up at the thin line of her lips and frowned. "What's wrong?"

"Nothing. Nothing at all." She'd barely moved her lips as she spoke.

Was she having second thoughts about last night? He'd thought it had been as...perfect for her as it had for him. "You didn't like our little interlude last night?"

His question was answered by the rosy glow that peppered her chest. "Last night," she said, "does not give you the right to enter my trailer and...and accost me anytime you want to."

He continued his light caresses along her arms. "Is that what you think I'm doing? Accosting you?"

Her chin came up. "If you're doing something I don't want you to do, then yes."

He grinned, and she looked away. "Even as innocent as you are, your body says something different."

He watched her chest rise and fall. Even her breathing was turning him on. Once. Twice. A third deep breath.

"Why did you leave last night?" Her voice was hushed, as if she was afraid asking the question would shatter a carefully built wall. "Why didn't you stay?"

It had the effect of a dousing with ice-cold water, even though he knew it was a question he needed to answer, for both of them. Ren backed up a couple steps and leaned against the kitchen counter, running one hand through his hair. How the hell did he explain this? He'd hoped to do this on the drive back to Fairbanks. She'd be unable to run from what he needed to say and they could talk it out until they came to some sort of terms.

He shook his head. It was just like Jess to force his hand. She still stood there, arms across her naked chest, eyes wide in question. She was the best kind of seduction and the worst kind of innocence.

"What we had last night...what you gave me, that's something I will treasure for the rest of my life."

Her eyes narrowed slightly. "But?"

He nodded. "Yes, there is a but. I don't do relationships."

"What does that mean?" He had to give her credit. She wasn't yelling. Although the 9-1-1 operator calmness to her voice unnerved him just as much.

"It means I'm not good at relationships. So I don't do them." Some deeply buried piece of him tried to claw its way to the surface and deny the statement. He tamped it down. Hard.

It was Jess's turn to nod. "So you're the love 'em and leave 'em kind of guy then."

Ouch. She knew how to cut a swath to the truth. "I wouldn't say that. I'm more the dates with benefits kind of guy."

"But you always wake up alone in the morning."

The desire to stay last night had been abnormally strong. He still hadn't figured that out. It certainly would have been easier to stay than to have this conversation. "Always. I'm sorry. I don't know how else to say it."

"All right. So it was a one night stand."

"It doesn't have to be."

She moved then, spreading her arms and giving him the view he'd been waiting for. His mouth went dry. Damn, but she had the most perfect breasts Ren had ever seen. Her nipples were tight and straining as her chest heaved. "Go ahead. Take a good look. Because, City Boy? I don't do friends with benefits. So this will be the last time you'll ever see these." She grabbed a wisp of black lace that coalesced into a bra.

Ren almost groaned when she covered her breasts and hooked the bra in the back. It turned him on even more to see that little bit of black and to know she would be wearing it underneath her shirt. He felt the ache in his groin. It was going to be a long eight hours driving back to Fairbanks.

An hour later they were ready to get on the road. Jess's only luggage was a backpack. Mary handed them a bag of sandwiches and other food, then hugged Jess. Ren saw the sheen in the corner of Jess's eyes as she said goodbye. When she turned toward his SUV, any tears dried up. She snatched the keys out of his hand before he could react. "I'm driving the first leg."

Her voice said "don't argue with me" and Ren was a smart man. He took one last look around a place he'd never have figured he'd end up liking, waved to the motley crew left in charge of Last Chance Camp, and climbed into the passenger side.

.

Chapter Sixteen

Jess jammed the accelerator to the floor in frustration. All she managed to do was send the SUV into a circular spin and make her friends jump back to keep from getting a coating of compacted road snow.

"You sure you know how to drive?" Ren asked.

She didn't answer. She couldn't. Speaking to the man was way beyond her abilities at the moment. Having to sit in the same vehicle with him for the next eight hours would be damn near impossible. Equally as pissed at her father for making her go on this wild goose chase, Jess felt pretty much done with men. Period.

She gripped the steering wheel like it was a lifeline, straightened the SUV out and drove out of camp with only one glance in the rearview mirror. Once on the road, she kept her focus forward, knowing that finding the right speed for the conditions meant shaving time off their commute.

Spending less time cooped up in a car with City Boy was second in her mind only to her concern for her father. She might not be sophisticated, or very experienced, but she wasn't as naïve as Ren Gallini thought. She knew when someone didn't want anything beyond casual. And it cut deep that he thought she would settle for that.

Jess Jenkins was no sex-starved adolescent. And it wasn't like she wanted to get married or anything. Her brain froze for a moment as a vision of him standing naked by her bed last night blazed a path through her anger. She shoved the picture to the deepest, darkest recesses of her mind.

Marriage would take away her independence. Right now, she could do anything she wanted when she wanted. No, she wasn't the marrying kind.

She took her eyes off the road long enough to glance at her one-night lover. His nose seemed more aquiline in profile. More...aristocratic. His face, when he smiled, appealed to her in ways she tried not to think about. And in the throes of passion, he exuded a fierceness that compelled her to match it. This all-business face that he wore now, and she suspected, most of the time—well, this wasn't the face of someone she wanted to love.

The problem was, her heart had its own mind. Going by the shafts of pain radiating out to every nerve ending in her body, love was a word she would not like for a long, long time.

Ren chose that moment to change his focus from the road to her. He twisted as much as the seat belt would allow, bringing his knee in close enough proximity that her body started to itch with a need to touch him.

"Are you going to give me the silent treatment all the way to Fairbanks?"

She tossed him a glare and he nodded.

"All right. Just to remind you, we're looking at eight hours of road time."

"No more than seven."

"Ah, so she *does* speak. Seven, then. Still a long time to have silence as your only companion. Maybe..." he tapped her arm lightly and the car lurched as she cringed away from him.

"Oh, for crying out loud. I'm not a monster, you know. I just don't believe in relationships."

Her neck went rigid as she forced herself to stare straight ahead.

"Fine," he said. "How about a different subject? Maybe we should decide what we're going to do when we get to Cabo."

Damn. Leave it to him to find a way to get her talking. "What do you mean?"

"I mean that we know the name of the hotel he gave to Mary. Do you intend to barge in there and demand his room number with no name to go by, since Mary said he's staying under a different name? Or skulk in the corner until you see him enter the lobby?"

"I have no idea."

"The ME is one of the premier vacation spots in Mexico. They cater to those who want privacy and anonymity. Honestly? It's the perfect place to hide."

"Why would my father want to hide?"God." Jess slammed the steering wheel. "I don't understand any of this. I feel like a puppet being tugged this way and that, and in the complete opposite direction that I'm trying to go. I want control of my life back."

"So do I, beautiful. So do I."

"That's pretty darn clear," Jess mumbled.

"What's clear?" Ren asked, his voice filled with the same tension as hers.

"I mean it's obvious you...don't want to be here. Never have."

"Honestly? I should never have come."

The pain sliced through Jess so hard and so fast, her

feet laid into the brakes. The SUV skidded on the icy road and came to a stop perilously close to the edge of a small ravine.

"What in the hell are you doing?" Ren yelled.

Jess clutched the steering wheel, fighting the tears, forcing them back. "You're right. You never should have come."

"You almost got us killed because of that?" Ren shook his head, then opened the door and stepped out of the car. He lost his footing on the ice and almost tumbled into the ravine himself.

Jess was out and around the car in an instant. When she saw him holding onto the door handle and navigating his way to safer ground, she heaved a sigh of relief she didn't want to analyze too closely and turned away from him.

Once he managed to join her in front of the car, he stood there shaking his head. When he spoke, she could hear the undercurrent of control he was using. His voice was low, but dynamic in its resonance. "You've been honest with me ever since we met, beautiful. Sometimes brutally honest. So don't expect me to sugar coat this thing between us. I shouldn't have come. But I did and it's complicated the hell out of things for me."

A finger tipped her chin up to look at him. "You complicate things."

She yanked her chin back. "Then go home."

"I probably should. Problem is, I need to see this through now, figure out what's going on."

Jess couldn't decide if he was talking about whatever plot her father had embroiled them in or if he meant their relationship. Either way, she figured she'd end up on the losing end.

"Yeah, well, we'd better get back on the road if we want to make Fairbanks by nightfall." she said, heading for the driver's side of the car.

Ren held her back. "Uh, uh. My turn to drive."

As he brushed past her, the incidental contact, and her reaction to it, almost depressed her further. This was going to be a long, long day. Jess didn't like inactivity. Especially today. With Ren behind the wheel, there was nothing to keep Jess's mind from trying to sort things out. And that was exactly what she did not want to do. She did not want to think about Renzo Gallini. Or how good he looked in slacks. Or how good he'd looked out of them last night. She tried to distract herself, pulling out her notebook with the short list of things she would pick up before she went back. Might as well get some use out of the trip.

By mutual agreement, they ate on the road. Mary had made them the same box they provided to guests heading out of the camp. The wave of nostalgia at the smell of turkey on white bread almost killed the rumbling hunger in Jess's stomach. She had driven the Dalton Highway to Fairbanks before, but always preferred the homeward bound trip.

They hit the outskirts of Fairbanks by dinnertime. When they pulled up to Pike's Lodge, Jess's mouth hung open. She turned to Ren. "Maybe we should stay somewhere a little less swanky."

"This place will do fine," he said.

"I—I can't afford this place."

"You don't have to. I made the reservation. I'm

covering the cost."

She compressed her lips in an effort to gain some
control. Relaxed them, started to speak, but the wrong
words kept trying to fight their way out. She closed her
mouth tightly, then tried again.

"I really think we should find someplace else."

Ren rubbed a hand across his eyes. He was tired. More
tired than he could ever remember. Hour upon hour of
constant refocusing...on the road, their plan, anything to
keep from reliving last night. When he drove, he kept a
white-knuckled grip on the steering wheel. In the passenger
seat, he'd kept clenched hands in his pockets so he
wouldn't give in and reach for the woman sitting beside
him. His ability to resist Jess Jenkins was getting lost in a
mind-numbing desire to be near her. Hell, he wanted to be
much more than just near her.

"Look, I'm tired. And I can afford this...for both of us.
I need answers as much as you do. The sooner we can find
your father, the sooner we can get this sale resolved, and
the sooner I can get back to my life."

Jess got out and slammed the door of the SUV. When
he got out, she pounded the hood of the SUV and glared at
him over it. "Fine with me, City Boy. If you want to pay the
check for some swanky digs, it's no skin off my back." She
walked around the car and poked him in the chest. "And
the sooner we each get back to our respective *lives*, the
better. In that, I agree with you one hundred percent."

She stalked off toward the hotel.

"That's once," Ren muttered.

"And that will be the only time," Jess tossed over her

shoulder.

Ren shook his head and laughed. Damn, but it would almost be worth staying just to spar with her. If he weren't so blasted tired.

He checked them both in, walked her to her room and opened her door, letting her precede him in. When she gasped, he stifled a smile. So, she wasn't immune to what money could buy. She simply wasn't used to it.

The room was small by his standards, but sometimes cozy worked. Warm colors and a lit fireplace set the ambiance for comfort. She sniffed the air. "It even smells good in here," she said. "Maybe Sandalwood? With a hint of peppermint?" She whirled and threw herself backward on the bed, laughing. "Who cares. It's more luxury than I think I've ever had."

Ren felt the weight of the day shift off his shoulders. With a wide grin, he sat on the edge of the bed. "So," he said. "You like."

She grabbed one of the satin covered decorative pillows and swatted him with it.

He tossed the pillow aside and leaned down on one elbow next to her. Her joy captivated him. Her face, beautiful by any standards, although she'd kill him for thinking that, now glowed in a way that held him rapt. Her smile was real and soft lips he'd like to feel against his skin framed white teeth. Her eyes were alight with her pleasure.

He reached up and moved a tendril of hair that fell across her face. Her smile disappeared as a pink tongue smoothed her bottom lip. Her pupils had dilated, but the spark in her eye had grown into a blaze.

His hand followed the line of her cheek and along her

lower lip. He wanted to kiss her. In fact, the need to do that
threatened to overwhelm him. He leaned in, feeling like he
was moving in slow motion. Their breath mingled. He
could taste the raspberry tea she'd had as they drove
through Fairbanks to the lodge. She parted her lips in
welcome, yet he took a moment to look her in the eye.
What he saw there scared him beyond imagining. He didn't
see lust, or desire. What he saw was trust.

A trust he did not deserve. He'd been that close to
seducing her again, with full knowledge that she didn't want
anything to do with him. He couldn't give her what she
wanted. So what the hell had gotten into him?

He thrust up from her until he was off the bed. "I'm
sorry," he said. "I shouldn't have started that. I'll, um, I'll
leave you to relax for a while and pick you up in, say, an
hour? For dinner."

When she nodded, her face a mask of confusion, Ren
did something then he'd never done in his life. He ran.
Well, he walked out of her room, but it felt like he was
running a marathon in gelatin-filled air.

Once in his own room, he leaned back against the
door, drawing deep breaths to cool himself down. And he
tried to figure out what it was about Jess Jenkins that made
him constantly hard, as well as why he kept letting that
hardness make decisions. Even now he was throbbing with
unquenched need.

She was nowhere near the type of woman he normally
liked. He dated sleek and pliable. She was curvy, albeit in all
the right places, and headstrong. She had a sharp wit and
biting tongue. Hell, sparring with her was more invigorating
than the best arguments in the boardroom back home. But

it was more than that. Back in New York, Kathryn nudged for a change in their relationship, but never pushed. Only suggested. And Kathryn was the type of woman he'd always dated, yet he'd been reticent to take their relationship any further.

With Jess, she didn't want a thing to do with him and she had pretty much become all Ren could think about.

Crap. This trip was going to be the death of him, Ren thought as he headed for a cold shower.

Jess sat up and watched as Ren hurried out the door. An hour ago, she'd been nursing a knife-wound full of anger and pain and yet, moments ago, she'd once again become putty in his hands. Nothing mattered except the delicious feelings that poured through her body when he touched her.

She stretched out on the bed, trying to recapture the desire that Ren's touch elicited before it faded completely away. God help her, she wanted to make love to him again. Even if it *was* only a one-night stand, she wanted that time with him. Her heart would break, but maybe it was better to grab what she could so she would have memories to get her through the pain of separation.

With her mind made up, she spent the rest of her time showering and getting disgusted over the clothing choices she had brought. How could a woman seduce a man wearing work clothes?

Standing in front of the mirror in jeans and bra, she twirled around. Her jeans hugged her well, so that wasn't too bad. And she'd seen him ogling her black bra when she'd put it on this morning. She ran her fingers along the lacy top of the bra. It was low cut and had a bit of a push-up to it. Sexy enough, if she could get him to the point where he would see it. Jess studiously ignored the part of her brain reminding her she'd told him he'd never see her again that way.

Shirts were an entirely different story. She had a turtleneck and a black v-neck, long-sleeved shirt. The shirt would have to do. The neck was a little large, so she could pull it over one shoulder so a bit of black bra strap showed.

She frowned in the mirror. She had a natural tanned look to her skin, and it was smooth from the moisturizer she used year-round. Another bonus. Still, she looked more like a teenager than a sophisticated woman out to seduce her man.

Jess didn't know much about makeup and therefore didn't wear much, if any. She reached for the pitiful little bag she'd grabbed on a whim as she was leaving and applied a thin line of brown along her lashes, then added mascara. She didn't have any blush, but it seemed a natural glow had settled on her face. That would have to do.

She also didn't have any lipstick, but some lightly tinted gloss gave an extra boost to showcase lips she needed him to want. The bathroom had an assortment of perfumes and she tested several, finally settling on one.

She left her hair down, something she never did. This was the one area she could compete with anyone in, as Meg, the hairdresser-turned-Alaska-State-Trooper, said each time she styled Jess's long hair. The layers drove her nuts on a regular basis, but right now, they framed her face in soft coal-colored waves that, when she turned this way and that, she thought looked sexy.

Jess stood back and took one last, long, critical look.
Tonight would be a first for her. She'd never seduced a
man before. By the way Ren had lit out of her room earlier,
she figured it wasn't going to be easy.

She set her vest and boots, both necessary for warmth,
on the bed and went to sit near the fire to wait for Ren. She
first sat in the winged-back chair, but that felt formal and
uncomfortable. So she moved to the couch. It was small,
the size of a loveseat, but when she curled her feet
underneath her, she decided this was the pose Ren would
find her in.

So she waited. As the minutes ticked by, she began to
fidget and the dread of worry settled over her with a
melancholy she wasn't prepared for. She tried to dredge up
thoughts that would keep her in the right mood for
seduction, but it just wasn't working. The problem was, she
wanted so much more than just a one-night stand. She
wanted love. And for Ren to return what she felt for him.

For the first time in her life, being part of a couple
didn't seem so bad.

Chapter Seventeen

When Ren tapped twice on her door and got no answer, he opened it quietly with the extra keycard, wondering if Jess was in the shower. The image of her, naked under the hot spray, stalled him. Shaking it clear and telling himself for the umpteenth time that she was off limits, he stepped further into her room.

He didn't hear the shower running. Then he saw her, curled up on the couch, sound asleep. He stepped nearer and saw red-painted toes peeking out from under a derriere that snug jeans did little to disguise. He held his breath and counted to ten, then to twenty, willing his penis to stop reacting.

Her face, in repose, tugged at his heart. She seemed so young, yet he knew she was in her mid-twenties. He saw the makeup and smiled. Had she done that for him?

This was only the second time he'd seen her hair down. The first had been last night. He liked it this way. Reaching out, he let a lock of it slide through his fingers. Soft. Just how he remembered it.

"Mmmmn." Jess moaned in her sleep and Ren lost the argument with his groin. He settled down on the sofa next to her and waited as her eyes fluttered open.

When she saw him, her tentative smile filled him with a sense of well-being he'd never felt before. He knew this was trouble. He was getting in too deep, getting too emotionally attached. Still, he couldn't seem to help it.

"Good morning, beautiful," he said, his own voice

sounding unnaturally low and husky. Her shirt had slipped and the black bra strap now visible made his mouth go dry at the memory of what she looked like in it...and nothing else. Even now, the bra's lace and her t-shirt couldn't disguise nipples that had tightened with...anticipation?

Ren looked at Jess's face. Wide eyes watched him and that same timid smile invited him. He reached to caress her cheek and let his finger glide over lips that had an understated hint of lipstick on them. He liked it. Jess didn't need much, if anything, in the way of makeup.

There was no noise, except for the gas-crackle of the fireplace. A faint twinkling of night lights from outside filtered in through the dark windows. With only a small bedside lamp on, the mood seemed ripe for seduction.

He moved closer, still focused on lips he needed to taste. Pausing just before he made contact, he whispered. "This isn't a good idea, you know."

Her reply was equally as breathless. "Probably not."

"It only complicates things." The scent of sweet jasmine filled his nostrils. Not a normal scent for her, but it suited her well.

"I know." She closed the distance between them and touched her lips tentatively to his.

He reached up to cup her face with his hand, deepening the kiss. She opened for him, and he lost himself in the fresh, clean taste of her. Ren knew he could remain here forever and be content. He wanted to stay for a lifetime.

He froze. That could not be what he wanted. He pulled back and almost gave in again when he saw the look of hurt confusion in her face.

"I'm sorry," he said, knowing that he seemed to be habitually apologizing to her. "We shouldn't be doing this."

"Why not?"

Even her voice, quiet and low, drew him in like a siren's song.

"Because." He stood and pulled her up with him. "I can't give you what you want."

She followed him to the door and grasped his arm as he opened it. "I'm not asking for anything."

No. But you're telegraphing a strong desire for commitment. He stroked her cheek with the back of his hand. "You deserve much more than I can offer you, beautiful."

"I think I might be falling in love with you."

"I think," he said, feeling the heavy sigh he held in weighing him down. How could he have done this to her? He was a cad of the worst definition. "No. I know this isn't a good idea. I don't want to hurt you. That's why I have to leave. Now."

He stepped into the hall and closed the door, but stood there staring at it. Placing a hand on it, he leaned in, wishing more than life that he could give her what she wanted.

Jess sank to the floor beside the door and let the misery wash over her. She *did* love him. The realization hadn't fully hit her until she actually said the words. God help her, she was in love with Renzo Gallini, a man so outside her world, he might as well be in outer space.

Standing, she started to pace. She lost every sense of herself when she was near him, yet he could disengage with the snap of his fingers. Obviously, he didn't feel the same thing. She'd known that. Known that he was more interested in sex than in any sort of relationship.

She stopped and stared into the fireplace. She'd been willing to waive the whole relationship thing just for another night in his arms.

Jess slapped the wall above the almost silent propane heat. Damn it all to hell. What was the matter with her? She didn't go all wishy-washy over any guy, no matter how good looking he was.

Her stomach rumbled and she took that as her cue, grabbing her wallet and heading for the door. She needed out of here.

Ren stared out the window at the rushing Chena river below him. His room felt too...confining. He needed to go for a run, but it was too dark, too late, and too cold for the clothes he'd brought with him. He glanced at the bathroom, but decided against another shower. Instead, he opted for a drink. Grabbing his leather coat, he headed downstairs to the bar.

As he rounded the corner to the lounge, he heard the soft laughter he'd imprinted on his brain. Apparently, he wasn't the only one who needed a drink. He moved forward until he could see Jess. She sat at the bar holding a glass with amber liquid in it. Whiskey? It figured she wouldn't be a wine drinker. Not his Jess. She didn't conform to a single one of the preconceived notions he had about females. She thought, and acted, according to Jess's rules, no one else's.

And now here she sat, shortly after being shot down by him, laughing at something someone on the other side of her said. He couldn't see clearly who it was, so he sidled into the bar and grabbed a chair in the shadowed back area.

The man she spoke with was twice her age, maybe more. Hell, he could see the graying hair at the guy's temples from here. Ren sat ramrod stiff in his chair. A barmaid sashayed her way over to get his order, but he waved her away, his concentration wholly settled on the couple at the bar.

He couldn't hear what they were saying, but when the man leaned in to get some point across, Ren's hands became tight fists on the table.

Jess nodded, and her companion got up. Ren sighed in relief. He was leaving. Instead, the man walked over to the jukebox. Soon, the quiet strains of some love song filtered through the air. He watched in horror as the man returned to the bar and held out his hand to Jess.

Ren's gut imploded into a tiny, tight little ball, then exploded into a million tiny drops of acid as his vision hazed over. The man pulled Jess into his arms and Ren stood, fists already feeling the satisfaction of pummeling the man to within an inch of his life.

No one touched his girl. No one.

By the time they'd made their second circuit around the small dance floor, Ren could no longer stand to watch. Jess smiled at something the man said, then laid her head on his shoulder.

Ren crossed the space between them quickly, pushing chairs out of his way as he went. He put a none-too-gentle hand on the man's shoulder and backed him away from Jess.

"You're a little old for the lady, aren't you?"

"Excuse me?"

"Beat it. She's not interested in dating her father."

The man surprised Ren by giving him a good look over, from head to foot and back to head again. Then, with a wide grin on his face and a damned twinkle in his eyes, he leaned over and whispered something in Jess's ear, then left without saying a word to Ren. Jess's laughter followed him out the door.

"What the hell did he just say to you?"

His hands curled back into tight fists as she watched the man leave. When Jess turned back to Ren, any lingering laughter had disappeared. Her stare held a fierceness, like she was looking past the eyes, past the skin, straight into his soul. Then her lips relaxed and spread into a slow seductive smile that panicked him more than the guy's flirting with her had.

Jess began to sway to the music, her hips moving back and forth, side to side, in perfect rhythm. Ren was in big trouble. He knew he should run, but he couldn't seem to look away.

When she closed the distance between them, she tapped his stomach with a finger, then began to walk the fingers of both hands up his chest and over his shoulder until she could almost twine them together behind his neck.

"I believe," she said with low-voiced precision, "that you owe me a dance."

That was when Ren started to sweat. He couldn't dance with her. Shouldn't dance with her. Yet his hands snaked around her waist. He cleared his throat. "What makes you think I owe you that?"

"You interrupted the dance I was having with that nice

gentleman, so you owe me a dance to replace it."

She pulled his head down until her fingers could lock together behind his neck. When she nuzzled his throat with her lips, he groaned and pulled her tighter into him. He matched her rhythm, then took the lead. God help him, she was irresistible. His hands settled in the small of her back, but his fingers itched to move lower, to cup that tight ass of hers and eliminate what little open space remained between them.

Chapter Eighteen

They danced, moving to a music that melted from one slow song to another. Someone must have fed the jukebox. It felt good, being in his arms. It felt right. His hands moved a fraction lower as they held her and Jess shivered. She imagined those hands caressing her breasts and more, and began her own exploration, moving up and down his back, feeling the rippling muscles, following them down his arms. She smiled as she felt the goose bumps, even through his shirt, that her light touch evoked.

He was as affected as she. It was time to do something about that.

Jess backed up, and he moved with her. She pulled his lips down to hers and kissed him with an abandon she didn't know she could feel. When they finally broke off, she wasn't sure she had the strength to do what she needed.

Jess pulled Ren's head down to whisper in his ear. "You know where to find me if you want me." Then she nudged him back, turned, and with only one small misstep, grabbed her purse and walked out of the lounge. Once in the elevator, though, she leaned against the wall, willing her body to shore itself up. Her attraction to Ren Gallini seemed to sap all her strength.

In her room, Jess turned all the lights off except one, behind the loveseat. The fireplace was the only other light in the room. She kicked off her shoes and settled in to wait. After several minutes, anxious worry set in, so she jumped up and started to pace. He'd gotten her message. She was sure of that. Was he turning her down? Again? Her hands flew to flaming cheeks as she prayed he didn't have that much self-discipline.

She was by the door when the soft taps came.

Whoosh! All the air left her lungs and she worked furiously to calm her breathing.

He tapped again.

And Jess managed to open the door with what appeared to be a calm demeanor. Still, the delay rankled. "What took you so long?"

He shut the door behind him and pulled her into his arms, turning until she was up against the door. "In case you didn't feel it, which I find difficult to believe, you left me standing alone on the dance floor with a raging hard-on. It took a few minutes to...collect myself, so I could walk and not look like an idiot."

They were pressed together, and Jess could feel the renewed bulge in his pants. "You don't look like an idiot now," she said.

He nuzzled her neck, sending waves of arousal thrumming through her body.

"Woman, you have no idea what kind of monster you're unleashing here tonight," he said in between kisses.

"I think, after the other night, I do." She leaned her head against the door, giving him more room. But he pulled back instead, so she opened her eyes.

"You sure?"

"More sure than I've ever been about anything."

"I can't promise you anything."

"Just promise me tonight," she breathed.

Jess saw the moment Ren gave in to her desire. His

eyes flared and he barely managed a nod before lowering his mouth to hers. She opened herself to him and he took full advantage, swirling his tongue over her teeth, peppering her lower lips with little bites, then delving deeper, letting their tongues dance.

Addictive kisses, light, then hard, deep, then soft tickles, held her in his arms better than any chains. Legs that could barely hold her upright shook with the effort. He cupped her bottom, nudging her up until she wrapped her legs around him. She could feel his hardness and she ground against him, wishing there were no clothes between them.

When he groaned, her arousal spiked even higher.

Ren moved from the door and set her gently in the center of the king-size bed, stripping and joining her without wasting a moment. He traced the collar of her t-shirt as it hung over the edge of one shoulder. The material fell further away with a little tug. She felt his finger dip under the strap of her bra, then follow it until it must have disappeared underneath her shirt.

Keep going.

He didn't. Instead, he reversed direction, making her body follow him, begging for more. His chuckle reverberated through her as he traced a line between her breasts and down to the bottom edge of her shirt. Feather touches along the skin under her ribcage tickled. Jess didn't care. She wanted more and dug her nails into her palms to keep from grabbing his hand and planting it on her breast. The agony of his slow pace was exquisite, but she didn't know how much more she could take.

Her shirt edged up with his hand and he grazed her

breast as he uncovered her. Shards of current spread out through her body until all her nerve endings were screaming.

He fingered the edges of her bra. "I love this bra. I don't know why you hide this feminine side of you from the world, but I love that I'm the only one who gets to see it."

Jess looked at him, tried to let all the love she felt shine through her eyes. "Only you," she said, wishing she could say so much more.

He stared at her a long moment, then gave a small nod, as if acknowledging the gift. He undid the front clasp of her bra, pulled it away, and lowered his mouth to her.

Jess gasped as he pulled her in. She wove her hand through his hair, tugging him in tighter as she tried to mold her body to his.

"Patience, my dear," he said, his other hand swirling around her belly button, then lower, teasing, but never putting her out of her misery.

"Ahhhh!" She'd had quite enough of this and pulled back. She pushed at him until he flipped over on his back, then she straddled him before he could recover and change her mind.

"Are you trying to drive me crazy?" she asked, giving his collarbone a nip.

"Yes."

She glanced up and for a long moment, couldn't move, couldn't breathe, couldn't do anything but be awed by the raw need in his darkened eyes. Need for her. Need no one else had ever shown her.

"I want you to know what I feel every time I look at

you," he said, his voice low and quiet.

She smoothed a lock of hair off his forehead. "I do," she answered. She began to explore him then, and he let her. She learned that the muscles defined by his shirts were real. That he was ticklish if she touched him just so at the edge of those six-pack abs. That trailing her fingers down his chest elicited the same moans she herself had made only moments earlier.

And that, when she moved ever so slightly as she sat atop him, it drove him as crazy as he was capable of driving her.

She kissed his nipples as he'd done to her, swirling them with her tongue.

Ren moved to touch her, but she stilled his hand and continued her exploration. She moved lower, letting his hairline guide her, until she had to relinquish her seat in order to go further.

She slid to his side and smiled when he twitched in response as she grasped him. Stroking down the shaft, then back up, feeling her way, learning how he liked to be touched.

When she licked his tip, Ren gasped.

"Do you like that?" She took the tip inside her mouth.

His answer was unintelligible.

She continued to ride him with her mouth, until he finally spoke.

"Enough."

She smiled up at him.

"You little minx. Come here."

She kissed her way up his side, and his muscles jerked with each bit of contact.

"I see," he ground out, "that you learn quickly."

She straddled him again, running her fingers through the course hair on his chest, and nodded. "Especially when I'm enjoying myself."

He reached to cup her breasts in his hands, and she sat tall, arching forward. When he moved his hand between them, Jess felt like she was going to explode. He reached for a condom, opened the package, and handed it to her. Having never sheathed a man before, it took her several moments, made worse by his jerks each time she came in contact with him.

Finally, she rose and settled onto him. Rose again. Settled again. Loved the feel of him, felt the need in her grow until she quickened the pace. He reached between them again and found her with his fingers, sending her over the edge on one long rolling orgasm. She fought to keep up the pace, then reached behind to cup him just as he came. Even then, she moved, and he moved with her. Two bodies, one motion, paying homage to the sensations vibrating through their bodies as the high melted away.

Collapsing on top of his sweat-covered body, Jess gulped air, trying to still her raging heart. They lay like that until she shivered in the chill air.

"How about we warm up with a shower?" Ren said.

"That sounds great."

"I could scrub your back."

She laughed. "And other places?"

"Oh, yes. Definitely other places."

He gave her a head start, and the warm spray relaxed her. Jess shut her eyes and tried to imprint this night on her memory.

She didn't hear the shower curtain move. Didn't hear him join her. And yelped when she felt his touch on her shoulders.

She tried to turn around, but he forestalled her. "Let me wash your hair," he whispered.

It was by far the most sensual experience she'd ever encountered. Yes, her experience was limited. Very limited. But no man had ever washed her hair before. Especially not while standing naked behind her in the shower.

She tried to hold her head still, but kept moving with his hands. After she'd been thoroughly and gently scrubbed, he whispered in her ear. "Close your eyes, beautiful."

He shifted her until the spray of water was directly overhead. The lather felt like a caress as it washed over her body.

When the soap was rinsed out, he backed her out of the spray and into his body, his arms snaking around to cup her breasts. Jess felt, well... She felt loved.

"Do you know how beautiful you are?"

As he rolled a nipple between his thumb and forefinger, Jess reached back and twined her arms behind his head. "I know how beautiful you make me feel."

"I've never met anyone like you before."

His kisses along her neck and shoulder made it hard to concentrate. "And you never will again, either."

Even his chuckle caused her to shiver as she molded herself against him. His groan was all the encouragement she needed and she turned in his arms. He backed her against the wall of the shower and proceeded to show her yet one more way that two people could make love.

Ren lay awake well after Jess's breathing evened out in sleep. Even in slumber, the feel of her against him could make his body react. Her body molded to his in a way that felt natural. It felt right.

And Ren, a man who always woke up alone, felt the fingers of panic beginning to close around his throat. He swallowed, trying to ease the lump. He did not believe in love. Time and again, the world had proven him right. Love did not endure. It was not a forever thing. And it almost always caused pain.

The room, bathed in faint light that filtered in from the courtyard two floors below, cast an almost angelic glow around the woman in his arms.

He cared for Jess. But he was *not* in love with her.

Jess sighed in her sleep and snuggled deeper in his arms. The vise of pleasure tightened around his chest. He couldn't love her. It was simply his body responding to the sound, he told himself. Still, holding her here felt good. Too good.

Ren eased his arm out from under Jess and stood.

Jess resettled, moving into his leftover warmth. Her face, in sleep, retained all of the beauty, but none of the spitfire personality he loved so much.

Ren froze at yet another thought revolving around a word he never wanted to know, then reached for his clothes, got dressed and slipped out of the room, leaving only silence and regret in his wake.

Chapter Nineteen

Some internal clock nudged Jess out of the realm of dreams she'd been comfortably ensconced in. Her conscious mind registered darkness, but her body knew from long winter months of almost complete darkness in Last Chance, that ambient light...or the absence of it...could be deceiving.

Still not quite ready to open her eyes, she stretched her arms overhead, enjoying the feel of her skin against sheets that were just shy of silk.

Images from last night cascaded across her mind.

Her taking the lead and mounting Ren.

Him joining her in the shower.

She shot to a sitting position, knowing she'd acted like a wanton woman. A smile spread across her face. Ren had certainly seemed to like it.

She turned to him, only to find the bed empty.

Empty? He'd left again? She grabbed his pillow and hugged it to her. His scent lingered. Granted, a rose on her pillow might be something that only happened in the movies, but was a note too much to ask? His empty space felt too much like money left on the bedside table.

A soft tap-tap at the door startled her. *He didn't leave.* Jess grabbed a sheet and ran for the door.

As she threw it open, two things hit her simultaneously. First, that his eyes lit with a smoldering fire as he took in her attire, or the lack of it. And second, that he was dressed. And not just dressed. He was Ren Gallini impeccably dressed.

Dampness at the ends of his hair told her he'd showered again. She tamped down the image of them in her shower. This time, he'd been alone. Had he been trying to wash the scent of her off?

Jess dredged up their earlier conversation and tried to sear it into her mind...and her heart. No strings attached. That's what they had decided. And what she had agreed to. Now, in the aftermath, she recognized just how hard that was going to be.

She watched as Ren's Adam's Apple bobbed and a spark of hope eased the pain in her heart. Maybe this wouldn't be easy for either of them.

"We, um, overslept. We have a flight in," he glanced at his watch, "a little less than three hours."

"Right." Jess nodded. It was back to business as usual, apparently. "Give me ten minutes."

She shut the door, leaving him standing in the hall.

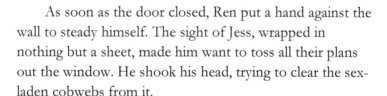

As soon as the door closed, Ren put a hand against the wall to steady himself. The sight of Jess, wrapped in nothing but a sheet, made him want to toss all their plans out the window. He shook his head, trying to clear the sex-laden cobwebs from it.

The sooner he got away from Jess Jenkins and got back to his own life, his own world, the better off they'd both be. In order to do that, though, they needed to find her father. And that meant getting on a plane.

Ren stepped across the hall and leaned against the wall to wait, telling himself over and over again that they were oil and vinegar. They would never mix. He would only hurt her, even though that was the last thing he wanted to do. That's what happened when people invested in others emotionally.

That's what had happened with the only woman he'd ever said the word "love" to. Sheila. Born into society, he'd been smitten from the first time he saw her. Hell, everyone had said they were the perfect couple. She'd professed her love for him. He'd bought it, hook, line, and sinker. Right up until she'd taken him for everything she could.

The only thing that had saved the company was that his mother, in some weird sort of premonition, had legally protected his stake in it. Otherwise, Sheila might have gotten that, too. That was one of the reasons he'd never wanted to be anything more than friends with Kathryn. He didn't need the complications women presented, either financially or emotionally.

Granted, he didn't think Jess was after his money. At least, not yet. But she would be swayed by it. And corrupted by it.

No, it was better to end things now. They would only hurt each other.

The door opened and Jess stood there fully clothed in jeans and a gray t-shirt sporting the logo of some trucking company. Dainty toes with nails painted red were now covered by work boots. Her hair was back in her usual ponytail and her face devoid of any makeup, except for the angry fire lighting her eyes.

She held her parka and backpack in one hand as she shut the door behind her and Ren used the moment to run a hand through his hair.

Oh, yes. This was going to be another very long day.

At the airport, first class tickets—compliments of Ren—got them settled in their seats with little fuss. She'd given him the window, knowing staring outside wouldn't improve her mood. The seats were roomy enough that they didn't even need to touch if they didn't want to. And Jess did not want to. Ren had been stiffly formal ever since knocking on her door earlier and that, in her mind, was beyond rude. Almost more rude than deserting her bed...again.

Almost.

Come on, folks. Get a move on. She drummed her fingernails on the armrest as people boarding the plane filed past her. She couldn't get to Cabo fast enough. The sooner they found her father, the sooner Ren Gallini would go back to his own life and leave her to return home and pick up the pieces of hers.

The man acted like making love to her had been some colossal mistake. The ravenous hunger for him that had raged through her last night still lingered. In her mind, in her body, and in her heart. Apparently, he did not feel the same. She glanced at him. His face was hidden from her as he stared out the window. Did he regret it? The thought made Jess's heart hurt, a slow oozing pain that sapped all her energy. She slunk deeper into the chair as the knowledge hit her once again that he did not feel for her what she felt for him. In fact, it appeared that even the thought of having made love to her was now distasteful.

Yes. It was going to be a long, long flight to Cabo.

It was late when they arrived in Seattle. Ren had pounded a couple of straight bourbons on the flight, then closed his eyes and fallen asleep, leaving Jess wide-eyed and in turmoil. She'd tried to watch a movie, but the romantic comedy just didn't do it for her.

A kind of nighttime hush had settled over the airport. Some restaurants were still open, but the meal they'd eaten on the plane sat like a brick in Jess's stomach. She needed activity. She needed a way to unwind.

She needed a punching bag.

So, with a two-hour layover, when Ren headed for the nearest bar, she plunked her backpack down beside him and lit out for a fast and furious walk. After two passes between security and the furthest reaches of the concourse, Jess realized that airport walking left a lot to be desired. She needed air. Fresh air. With only an hour until they boarded their next plane, going outside was not an option.

Chapter Twenty

When Ren found her, she was leaning against the airport window, staring outside at who knew what. Her head touched the glass, and he could see the sadness in slightly downturned lips and the edges of the furrow between her brows.

He wanted to wipe the sadness off her face, knowing he had put it there. The instinct to make everything right for her threatened to overwhelm him, and he clenched his hands around the straps of their luggage. He did not love her. Could not love her. Love wasn't real. That had been proven to him quite succinctly.

Why was it, then, that every time he saw her, he felt this overwhelming need to be near her? To touch her. To pull her into his arms and make her world a happy place to be.

Hell, even when she wasn't anywhere in his vicinity, he couldn't seem to stop thinking about her.

"Now boarding flight 3736 to Houston."

As Jess pulled away from the window, their eyes met, and Ren watched her swipe at the dampness on her cheek. He felt as if the world had just stopped turning and the backlash punched him in the stomach. Could he actually love her?

God help him.

Dark expressive eyes couldn't hide the pain. Pain he'd inflicted. So instead, she lifted her chin and walked over to him. Taking her backpack out of his hand, she turned without a word and handed her ticket to the flight attendant.

This time, she took the window seat, and Ren didn't argue. He didn't care where he sat. He needed time to think. To sort through this mess and find a...solution.

As it turned out, a four-hour flight wasn't long enough. Jess had curled up as much as possible and slept most of the way. Ren, wide awake for the entire flight, found that, for the first time in his recollection, he did not know what to do.

He loved Jess Jenkins. More to the point, he trusted her. Beyond a shadow of a doubt, he knew she was not like Sheila. Having said that to himself over and over again on the flight to Houston, he still was no closer to knowing what he would do about it.

They disembarked and stretched their legs, continuing the silence between them. At six in the morning, the airport was beginning to bustle.

"We've got another three and a half hours before our flight. Would you like to get some breakfast?"

"Sure."

"It looks like we have several options to eat at. "Do you have a preference?"

"Anywhere is fine," she said, then her lips turned back into thin lines.

Ren picked a restaurant and they ordered breakfast. Jess positioned herself not quite across the table from him and seemed to watch the people passing by. She never once even glanced in his direction.

By the time they finished eating, Ren was quite done with the whole cold shoulder thing. They walked to the first class lounge to wait for their flight. Jess wandered around the lounge until he sat down, then promptly plopped into the chair furthest away from him. She threw her feet onto the seat across from her and slunk down as if intending to take a nap.

Ren had other plans, though. They would have this out. The lounge was empty except for an attendant stocking coffee and juice. As soon as she left, he went to Jess.

Her eyes were closed, but she knew he was there. He'd seen her body tense up.

"We need to talk," he said.

"I'm not in the mood."

He squatted down between the two chairs and set a hand on her thigh.

"Get in the mood."

Her eyes flashed open and she yanked her feet off the chair. "Last I checked, I was in charge of myself. Not you. You don't get to tell me what to do, Gallini."

She jumped up and backed away from him, but her stance and clenched fists proved she was spoiling for a fight.

"I'm not here to fight," he said.

"Well, you're sure as hell not here for any other reason."

Jess backed up another step, but Ren closed the distance between them and grasped her arms.

"Let. Me. Go."

"No." Ren fell back on the thing that had opened the most doors for him. He smiled.

When she struggled to pull away from him, he did let her go. She backed up to what she seemed to think was a safe distance and whirled on him. "How dare you. You have no say in what I do or where I sit. What gives you the right? You don't even want to be here..b-be with me."

He opened his mouth to respond, but she cut him off with a slash of her hand. "You don't want to fight with me. You don't want anything to do with me. That's pretty apparent."

"I wouldn't exactly say that."

"Well, I would. You're making it pretty obvious. You won't look at me or talk to me or...or..."

Jess's lower lip began to tremble and she plopped down into a chair, turning her face away from him. "Oh, just go away, Ren. Please. I can't do this anymore. I'll find my father. Just go...away."

He knelt by her chair. "I can't."

"You're not done screwing with me yet?" she mumbled through the hands over her face.

"No." He nudged her hands aside. "I can't leave because I'm in love with you."

Her eyes widened. "Yeah, right. You don't do love, remember?"

"You're right. I don't." The idea of having to tell her the story didn't sit well with Ren. In fact, it felt like a piece of lead on his tongue. "You need to understand. There's a reason I didn't believe in love."

"You've been hurt, right?" The anger in her voice mellowed just a bit with the question.

"As a matter of fact, yes. And if you'll be quiet for a minute, I'll explain."

"You—"

Ren arched an eyebrow, and Jess clamped her mouth

shut.

"I thought I was in love once. I thought she was in love, too."

"That's happened before."

"You're right. I'm no different from anyone else. When I realized what she really wanted, I told myself that same thing time and time again. It didn't help."

Ren sat in the chair across from Jess and ran both hands through his hair. God, he hated having to rehash this. "She sank her teeth into me really well. Her name made her one of the elite, and I wanted her from the first moment I saw her. I figured it was love. Spent three months pursuing her before she finally consented to a date. I was young, and so thrilled," Ren said, recognizing the derision in his voice, "that I pulled out all the stops. I wined and dined her, bought her expensive gifts, the works. But she wouldn't sleep with me. I was half out of my mind for wanting her. So finally, in what I know now was a desperation move, I proposed."

"You've been married before?" Jess's voice was low and carried no anger in it, but he couldn't look at her. He nodded.

"Why didn't you tell me this before?"

He shrugged. "It's...embarrassing. She initially refused to marry me. Said I probably thought she was only after my money." He laughed, the sound of it harsh in his ears. "She's actually the one who brought up a pre-nuptial agreement." Shaking his head, he let out a deep breath. "That, of course, was the proof I needed that she loved me back so I refused."

"And she married you."

"Yes, and it took an entire month before her fangs began to show. While I was still in the honeymoon stage, she moved out of our apartment and into one of her own she'd purchased as soon as the ink was dry on our wedding license."

"How much did she take you for?"

"Everything."

"But you...well, you don't seem to be short of funds these days," Jess said.

"I'm not, thanks to my mother. She saw through Sheila, but I wouldn't listen. So she got me to sign over my half of the company to her. To protect it, she said. She told me if we were still married in a year, she'd nullify the contract. She didn't give me much of an option, since she held the controlling interest in the company."

Was it getting stuffy in here? Ren got up and started to pace, then stopped to stare out the window at the planes taking off.

"My...wife retained the best divorce lawyer in the country before the ink was dry on our marriage decree. They took all my personal wealth."

"I'm sorry," Jess said from behind him.

"Don't be. It's only money."

"But it dented your pride."

He slapped the window. "You're damn right it did. I should have seen through her disguise."

"That's not always possible."

"It's a necessity if you've lived a life of privilege. You're taught to look for the signs."

"How old were you?"

"Twenty-two."

"And her?"

"Twenty-four."

Jess nodded. "Same age as me."

"Yes."

"Do you think I would do that to you?"

"No."

"But you still don't trust me."

He looked at her then. This was important. He needed her to understand. "I *do* trust you."

"Then what's the problem?"

"It's myself I don't trust."

Throughout the conversation, their roles had gone through a slow metamorphosis. First, he had wanted to reassure Jess. Now, she placed a hand on his arm, trying to reassure him.

"You were young. You can buy into just about anything at that age."

He looked up. Would she tell him the inside track on her story now? "Did you?"

"Did I what?"

"Believe something that brought you pain. Did you get hurt on a trip? Is that why you don't like to leave Last Chance?"

She started to turn away, but stilled at his hand on her shoulder. Instead, she sat on the floor, her back against his legs, and hugged her knees. She nodded.

"What happened?"

"Nothing happened, all right? It's just that...every time I leave, I miss it so much. I was raised there. It's my home."

"What's that saying about home being where the heart is?"

"Well, my heart's in Alaska." Jess had stiffened at his question. Her hackles were up. Now, though, she slumped back in on herself and Ren had to lean forward to hear her.

"Besides, it's where Mom is."

Every instinct in Ren screamed that this was the crux of the issue. It wasn't some guy who'd soured her on the rest of the world. It was a much more primal need...family.

"Your mother died, right?"

Jess nodded.

"How old were you?"

"Twelve."

Ren's father passed away three years ago and it had hit him hard. He tried to put himself in the same situation as a child. It was impossible to imagine. "It hit you hard, didn't it?"

"Sure. It hit everybody hard. Especially Dad. Thank goodness, Mary and John were there. We were all mourning the loss of a wife, sister, mother. But Mary and John had come to help when Mom got sick. They kept the place going...after, until Dad could manage again, then stuck around. They're still a huge part of Last Chance, as you saw. And Mary's become a surrogate mother to me. She filled some pretty big shoes, too. Mom was awesome."

"I wish I could have met her."

"Me, too," Jess said. She looked off into the distance for a while and Ren sat quietly with her.

"Did she look like you?"

"Well, she was an Alaskan."

"I see the beauty of her heritage in you."

Jess warmed at the compliment, nodding her head. "She told me, before she died, the meaning of the lights in the sky. Do you know that Alaskan Indians believe that the Aurora Borealis is the spirits gone before us and that they've come out to play ball?"

He nodded. He'd learned that from her.

"She told me she'd always be there for me, always be watching over me," Jess whispered. "If I ever wanted to talk, all I had to do was look up and her spirit, in the form of the Northern Lights, would answer."

Everything clicked into place in Ren's mind with this piece of information. That's why Jess had such a strong attachment to Last Chance, and why seeing the aurora seemed such a spiritual thing for her. She felt it was her last tie to her mother.

Ren scooted beside Jess and pulled her into his embrace. Jess hung on tightly. "Thank you. I can finally see Last Chance through your eyes. It really is a beautiful place."

She nodded into his shirt, and Ren swore he heard a snuffle.

"You know, though, your mother isn't the only one who can keep you safe. I won't let anything happen to you, either."

Jess lifted her head and smiled at him, a sweet smile that he knew he'd never tire of seeing. "The men in my life are always trying to protect me."

"You're a little sprite of nothing. You need protecting."

"I can take care of myself," she said with a huff that her eyes belied.

"I've seen that firsthand, too. I know you can. But it soothes my male ego to think I need to protect you, so you'll have to allow it sometimes."

She nodded. "I think I can live with that."

They stayed there for long moments, not speaking, just letting the calm aftermath of telling their stories stretch and enfold them.

As Jess lowered her hands, Ren clasped each of her shoulders and stared into eyes that he knew now he wanted to watch for a lifetime. "I love you, Jess Jenkins."

He didn't need to hear the words from her. He could see it in her face. In the way she smiled. In how she looked his face over as if cherishing it. Cherishing the moment. Cherishing him.

"I love you, too, Renzo Gallini."

He pulled her in tight and buried his head in her neck when she clung to him as if she would never let him go. He kissed his way to her mouth, letting all the emotion overflow from his heart and into hers.

"Ahem..."

They both jumped at the noise, and Jess went red to the roots of her hair. A portly gentleman, who looked a little like Santa Claus going to a high-powered meeting, stood there with a gentle smile on his face. "You folks might want to take that somewhere else. I saw several limousines pull up as I was checking my luggage." He looked around. "I'm guessing this lounge is about to fill up."

Feeling very much like a shy sixteen-year-old himself, Ren gathered their bags and grabbed Jess's hand. Thanking the gentleman for the warning, they left the lounge.

And stopped short as the cacophony of the airport yanked them out of their private place and back to the world at large. They had a plane to catch. He grinned and pulled her closer to him. "Let's go find your father."

Chapter Twenty-One

Jess could not believe her luck. This morning, she'd been certain she'd never be happy again. Now here she was, sitting in first class with an Italian god who would barely let go of her long enough to put on his seat belt.

He'd finally managed to doze on this, the final leg of their journey to Cabo San Lucas. But he couldn't be too deeply asleep. He still had a solid grip on her hand. Not that she minded.

She watched him sleep and wondered how it would be to watch him wake up. Maybe now he'd stick around after making love. She grew warm just thinking about it.

Their final flight was just under three hours and passed by quickly. When they disembarked and made it outside, Jess was amazed at how warm it was. Correction. It was hot. The thermometer outside the airport said ninety degrees. Jess had never in her life been in this warm a climate.

"Holy cow, it's hot here." Jess pulled off her down vest and pushed her sleeves up, looking around. "I did not bring the right clothes for this climate."

Ren grinned. "What do you think? Do you like it?"

"I could get used to it. Wow. I bet it's nice to not have to put on three layers just to go eat breakfast."

Laughing, Ren hailed a taxi. "And I think I like the idea of seeing you in less clothing."

The climbed in and Ren gave the address to the man in impeccable Spanish.

"You speak Spanish?"

"Spanish, Italian, even French."

"I'm impressed." She tried not to wonder what she had to offer a man with his many talents.

"You ground me."

"What?"

"You keep me grounded. When I get too high and mighty, you make sure I know my place. More than that, you make me see things in a way I've never noticed before."

"Like what?"

"Like the northern lights."

She smiled.

Ren put his arm around her, pulling her close. "That's another thing you make me remember, too. The importance of family."

"You're close with your mother, though."

"Yes, but not in the same way. My father only passed away a few years ago. My mother and I never really found a common ground until then. She was always involved in her charity work. When Father passed, she took an interest in the business. Turns out she's got a pretty astute head for it. We've worked well as a team. And she saved the company when Sheila tried to get it in the divorce. I owe her for that." Ren tightened his hold on Jess. "I owe her for a lot more, now."

"Why's that?"

"If it weren't for her demanding I go to Last Chance Camp, I never would have met you."

Jess smiled. "Then I owe her a huge debt, too."

"I wish I knew where she was. It's not like her to take

off like this with no word."

"It's just like my father. He's never told us where he was going, but until know, we've always had a way to keep in touch."

The taxi arrived at the hotel. Ren paid the man and picked up their bags. "Ready to go find him?"

Jess turned from staring at a cactus. "I'm beyond ready."

They entered the open-air lobby, something else that awed Jess, and walked up to the desk. Now that they were finally here, nerves had set in and Jess worried her bottom lip. What would they find? She looked around. The hotel seemed pretty swanky, way over anything they could afford unless her Dad had money squirreled away somewhere. Nothing added up here.

"—Mrs. Jenkins are out by the pool, I believe."

Jess pulled herself back into the conversation just in time to hear the last part. "W-who?" she asked.

"Your padre, si? Mr. Jenkins? Y tu madre?"

Jess shook her head. "But my father's not married."

The concierge stared at her in confusion. Ren put a hand at the small of her back and guided her toward the lanai. "Let's go find your father and hopefully he can answer all of your...our...questions."

They walked out into the bright sunshine and it took several long moments before they could see well enough in the mid-afternoon glare coming off the water. They walked slowly around the pool until Jess spied her father.

"Dad!" She ran to him, relief and amazement spurring her forward. He didn't appear to be the least bit stressed, if the tan and fruity drink in his hand were any indication.

When he saw her, he nearly dropped his glass. If Jess didn't know better, she's swear a ruddy glow had started to creep up her father's face underneath that tan. He recovered quickly, though, pulling her into a hug that she had missed so much.

"Ahh, Jess, you made it. Good. I've missed you so much."

"I'm so glad you're okay, Dad. You had us worried."

"I know, and I'm sorry about that. I...didn't see any other way, though. Hey, let me get you a drink," Owen said.

"I don't want a drink, Dad. I want to know what the hell is going on."

Ren caught up to her and started to extend his hand to Jess's father. When he stopped short, she turned to see the look of astonishment on his face. She followed his gaze to an older woman who lay in the lounge chair next to Owen. Who was she?

"Mother?" Ren said.

Chapter Twenty-Two

"Hello, Ren. It's good to see you," Amelie said.

Now that the time had come, that Jess and Renzo found them, self-doubt filled Owen more than at any other time since he set this ball in motion. This past week had been a combination of elation and love, offset by worry about whether or not he'd done the right thing. This time had been hard on Amelie, too. She didn't like keeping secrets from her son. At the moment, she worked hard to look calm. He could see the underlying tension, though. Would her son forgive her subterfuge? Would Jess forgive him?

Owen watched Amelie's son open and close his mouth a few times, speechless at his mother's appearance here. He'd seen pictures, but hadn't yet met the man. He mirrored his mother's Italian heritage with naturally tanned skin tone and dark hair. Amelie had talked at length about his intelligence and ability to feret out the right solution to issues. The stunned look on his face didn't exactly back that up.

Yet, in the face of his mother's duplicity, Renzo remained close to Jess, almost protectively so. Owen smiled. Maybe this would turn out all right after all. He twisted the band on his finger.

"Jess, darlin', I'd like to introduce you to Amelie," he said. He held out his hand and Jess caught a flash of gold on his ring finger before Ren's mother settled her hand in his and stood. "Amelie Jenkins. My wife."

Jess's jaw joined Ren's on the ground. "You—you're married?" They uttered the words simultaneously.

"Yep." It was a simple word, but he couldn't stop the proud-as-a-peacock note in his voice. It had taken him years to find this woman he loved.

"But—" she started.

Ren cut her off. "How do you two even know each other?"

"Well now, that's got a bit of a story to it," Owen said. "What do you think, love?" He turned to his wife. "Should we get them settled first?"

"No." Ren and Jess spoke at the same time again, but Amelie overruled them with a nod of her head.

"I agree," Owen said, infused with energy now that they were all together. Finally, Jess could get to know the woman he loved. But first...

"Come on," Owen said. "Let's get you two signed in." He settled Amelie's arm in his and headed inside. Standing off to the side while Ren and Jess checked in, a peace settled over Owen. He couldn't help but believe, watching them, that he'd done the right thing. "It's all working out just fine, isn't it, my love?"

Amelie worried her lower lip. "I don't know, Owen. They both look pretty shocked...and angry. Especially Ren."

"He'll be fine." Owen pulled Amelie into his arms. "And once we get everything settled, they'll have a chance to enjoy a love like we have been blessed with."

She settled her head on his shoulder as they watched their children. "I hope so. And I hope they will forgive us."

"They have to. After all, how can they resist, seeing our happiness.

"We don't need two rooms," Ren said.

"Yes, we do. I can't even begin to address...us...with my father until we sort out what's going on here." She was gritting her teeth, but didn't seem to be able to help it. "What will they think?"

"I don't care what they think. There is no sense in getting two rooms—" Ren held up two fingers, "when we will only be sleeping in one."

Jess stared at him, seeing the stubborn bent to his head. "Now he gets cost-conscious," she muttered under her breath.

He placed a hand on her hip and leaned down until his words whispered currents of desire through her. "It's got nothing to do with cost, beautiful."

With a glance at her father and Amelie, Jess saw the intense way they both watched the discussion. Mumbling about stubborn Italians, Jess joined her father and his wife.

Amelie put a hand on Jess's arm, pulling her attention away from room arrangements.

"You're as beautiful as your father said you were," Ren's mother said, touching her cheek. "I'm so happy—" She glanced at Ren, then back at Jess. "For all of us."

"Well, I'm not."

"Jess!"

Her father's stern tone was reminiscent of the times when she'd challenged him. Still, she wasn't the one on the hot seat here. "Sorry, Dad, but you both owe us some answers."

"Yes, we do," Owen said. "But you've had a long trip. Amelie and I suggest we all take some time to freshen up.

How about we take some time, meet up for dinner later? I promise Amelie and I will answer all your questions."

No. Jess didn't want to wait. She wanted answers now, and suspected Ren felt the same. When he nodded and placed a hand at her back, nudging her toward the elevators, it shocked her.

She watched her father and Amelie disappear back outside, then hurried to catch up with Ren as he walked toward the elevators. "Don't you want to hash this out? Find out what's going on here?"

"Oh, most definitely. Mother and I will be having a long talk at some point."

"Well, then, why let them off the hook like this?" Confusion and frustration colored Jess's voice. She'd had just about enough of secrets.

"Because..." Ren scrubbed a hand over his face. "Because they're right. I'm tired, and you are, too. We could use some time to take this all in, and some distance. You're angry right now."

"Damn straight, I'm angry."

"Then let's take the time to calm down, so we can sort this all out like adults."

It went against every instinct to give her father this reprieve. Ren's suggestion made sense, though. Anger wouldn't help anything, although Jess didn't know how she was going to quell that emotion in just a few short hours. "Fine. I didn't get a shower this morning. I could use one."

The wide grin on Ren's face really needed to be wiped off.

"Alone," she finished.

She felt a tug at the straps of her backpack and yanked

it out of the hands of the bellman now standing behind her.

"Let the man carry your luggage, beautiful."

Begrudgingly, she let go of the pack. The elevator doors opened, and Ren guided her inside. He had a lot to learn if he thought he could push her around like this.

She was still stewing about Ren's heavy-handed tactics as the bellman let them into their room. At least they hadn't had to explain the whole one room versus two to their folks. Geesh. No way Jess was ready for that. Not until she had some answers.

For the second time in less than an hour, Jess's jaw hit the floor. She'd expected a standard hotel room, maybe even plush considering that Ren picked their room. She entered a palace. Light and airy and spread out, they walked into a sitting area bigger than her trailer. Modern couches gave way on one side to floor-to-ceiling windows looking out onto a deck that seemed larger than the room itself. The other direction boasted a king-size bed. While Ren tipped the bellman, Jess poked her head into the largest bathroom she'd ever seen.

"Does the room please you?"

Jess whirled around with a laugh. "Room? That doesn't even begin to give this...this mansion credit. I can't believe how big this place is."

She ran through the open slider to the deck and stopped short. Curtain-shaded lounging beds and an outdoor hot tub did nothing to take away from the view, which spread from Land's End through the cove to the other side.

Ren caught up with her as she stared out over the expanse of water. He wrapped his arms around her.

"Happy?"

She shouldn't be. She should still be full of anger. Yet, as she leaned against Ren, Jess realized that there was no place else she wanted to be except wrapped in his arms. All problems faded as she turned and pulled his head down to hers.

"I'm still mad," she whispered just as their lips touched.

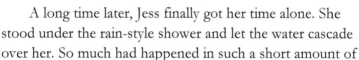

A long time later, Jess finally got her time alone. She stood under the rain-style shower and let the water cascade over her. So much had happened in such a short amount of time, it was almost hard to comprehend. And any time she spent near Renzo Gallini only muddled her mind further.

The man was a force to be reckoned with. He set her heart to racing, her body to sizzling, and fried her brain, all simply by walking in the door.

She stared at the in-shower mirror and some weird fascination with it made her wonder if it was there for shaving and who kept it clean?

Her face did not reflect any earth-shattering changes. She didn't look aged or younger. She didn't look any different than when she'd first stepped into the shower.

But she felt different. She felt...whole. And confused beyond belief. What was her father thinking, selling Last Chance? And what the hell was she doing? She and Ren lived worlds apart. How could they ever be together? She pictured him in Last Chance. No way would he spend more time there than he absolutely had to. So it would have to be New York. How would she ever cope with a city the size of New York? And how could she leave Alaska behind?

She couldn't.

Her father. Ren. Last Chance. Ugh! Trying to sort this all out was impossible. Her heart could find no easy solutions, and Jess crouched into a ball on the floor of the shower, clutching a stomach tight with rolling waves of nausea. She was so screwed.

Maybe it was time to cut her losses with this love thing. Maybe, if she got far enough away from Ren, she would stop thinking about him. She felt the stab of pain that ruled out that option, knowing she would never forget Renzo Gallini.

Jess stood and turned off the shower, more confused and conflicted than ever.

When she and Ren entered the restaurant at the appointed time, she saw her father right away. They'd secured a booth in the back, and he was seated next to Ren's mother. He and Amelie appeared totally engrossed in each other.

As they drew closer, Jess squinted. The two in the booth were quite cozy, as a matter of fact. She cleared her throat well before they arrived at the table, suddenly irritated with the hand Ren had placed at the small of her back.

Her father jumped out of his seat to hug Jess. She had to admit, she'd never seen him smile this widely back home. And she did want him to be happy. Still, the man had some explaining to do.

She returned his hug, then scooted into the booth, with Ren right behind her.

"So, Dad—"

"We must have drinks first. Now that we're together,

you must help us toast our nuptials."

Jess started to override him, but Ren's hand on her knee stopped her. Glaring at him out of the corner of her eye, she sat tight-lipped while her father ordered something fruity for them all, and Ren's grimace when he heard the order almost made her laugh.

She kept her silence until the drinks arrived.

Her father raised his glass. "To my wife, who has given me more happiness than I deserve."

Everyone but Ren sipped the coconut concoction. He raised it to his lips, but Jess could see that he did not taste the drink.

Ren saved her from grilling her father by opening his own inquiry. "So, Mother. Would you like to explain what's going on here?"

"Ah, Renzo," she said, reaching a hand across to pat his. "Always direct and to the point."

"What are you two doing here?"

"We're in love," her father said. "So we got married."

"No." Jess said, waving at the two of them. "What are *you two* doing here? How do you even know each other?"

Her father let a whoosh of air out. "That's a long story, sweetheart."

"We have time," Ren answered for her.

Owen grasped Amelie's hand in his. "Well, first off, this is not something that was done without thought. Your mother and I have known each other a long time."

"How could that be? I would remember if I had met you before," Ren said.

"You have never met Owen," Amelie answered. "He is from...before your time."

Jess watched as Ren stared her father down. She had to give her dad credit. He didn't cower under the blazing eyes of Renzo Gallini. Instead, he sat up straighter.

"Your mother and I knew each other when we were both much younger." Owen looked at Jess. "You know I was raised in upstate New York."

She nodded.

"I met Amelie there." He turned his gaze in Ren's direction. "She wasn't a Gallini yet. In fact, she hadn't even met your father at that time. I worked at the lake where her family spent their summers vacationing. I'd seen her on the beach several times and could hardly take my eyes off her." He smiled at his wife. "She was—is—the most beautiful woman I have ever met."

Seconds passed as they gazed into each other's eyes.

"And?" Jess brought them back around to the story at hand.

"And we fell in love."

Amelie nodded as Owen continued.

"We spent every bit of time, when I wasn't working, together."

"Until my father found out," Amelie said. "It seems he had a strong desire to see me marry into a social status that befitted our family." She glanced at Ren. "You remember him, don't you?"

"Yes. And I know he was all about status."

"Well, he whisked us all off to home. I tried to contact Owen, but didn't know how. I called his job. He was no longer there. I had no home address or any other way to contact him." She clutched at Owen's hand, and he patted hers.

"I wrote her long letters professing my love, but they were never answered. For two years, I wrote."

This remembered pain etched deep lines in her father's face and Jess hurt for him, wanted to smooth them. It took everything she had to keep from leaning over, covering his hand with hers.

"It turns out, my father intercepted each and every letter and destroyed them. Eventually, he convinced me to marry your father, Renzo."

Renzo frowned. "This was a...loveless marriage, then?"

"Umm, do you two want to talk about this privately?" Jess asked. She could see Ren's confusion.

"No, it's all right, dear," Amelie said, then turned to her son. "Please, don't ever think that our life together was anything but pleasant. You must understand. We did not love each other. But we respected and liked one another. In time, that affection became the basis for a strong and fulfilling life together."

"Yet here you are." Ren turned to Jess's father. "Just how long have you two been seeing each other?"

Amelie leaned over the table, countering Ren's aggression. "You will not use that tone of voice with my husband."

Ren sat back and Jess was surprised to see a tinge of red at the collar of his shirt.

Owen reached for Jess's hands. "You know how lonely I was after your mother died."

Jess nodded, feeling tears sting her eyes. "For years, the light was gone from your eyes. You loved her very much."

Her father inclined his head. "I did. I do. And I

mourned her loss for a long, long time. I have been lucky to
have loved two women in my life. One day, while cleaning
out an old storage locker, I found this." He pulled his wallet
out and dug inside, coming up with what looked like half of
a worn theater ticket. "That summer, Amelie and I went to
a lot of movies. It was about the only place we could be
away from the watchful eyes of her father. When I saw this,
all the old feelings filled my heart with a new purpose. I had
to find my first love."

Jess smiled. "And you did."

"Yes. It took some time, since her name had changed."
He nodded to Ren. "Your father had passed away by the
time I started searching, but I located a relative who passed
my contact information on to your mother."

Owen wrapped an arm around Amelie's shoulder.
"The rest, as you say, is history."

Jess felt like some piece of the picture was still missing.
When she realized what it was, she slapped both hands on
the table, startling them all. "That's where you went on all
those little vacations of yours these past couple years."

"Yes. Amelie and I have been getting to know each
other again. Only it never seemed like enough time. So this
trip, we decided to make a permanent commitment. We got
hitched."

Jess folded her hands on the table. She needed to
figure out if she was happy about this or not. It felt like
she'd been left out of a very important part of her father's
life.

"I know I should have told you, honey," her father
said. "Some things, though, are private." He tapped his
heart. "Like matters of the heart. Maybe it was wrong, but I

didn't want to introduce you until I had time to know that this was everything I remembered." His eyes shone with joy. "It is."

Never considering herself to be a jealous person, Jess recognized that she was indeed feeling a bit put out at not having been part of this important moment in her father's life. That was not a good enough reason to diminish the light in her father's eyes. He was happier than she'd seen him in a long, long time. Who was she to dampen his joy?

She smiled, trying to convey the fact that she'd come to make peace with his marriage. "I'm happy for you, Dad."

"Thank you, honey. I know it's not easy for you, but I believe you'll come to love Amelie as much as I do."

Almost as one unit, they turned to look at Renzo. Jess saw the tinge at the edge of his collar deepen.

"I would rather discuss this privately," he said to his mother.

"Whatever you have to say to me, you can say in front of my husband."

The only indication he gave of his displeasure was a slight tightening of his lips. He turned to Jess first. "You remember my history?"

She nodded.

"I need you to remember why I ask what I ask."

"All right."

He turned to his mother. "I heard what you said. And I see that you appear happy."

"I am. Very happy."

He gave one curt nod. "I did not get a chance to protect you before this...event," he said. "So I apologize for having to ask this after the fact, but you left me no option.

No insult intended, Owen, but—" Ren turned to his mother. "Have you protected yourself financially?"

Amelie laughed and turned to Owen. "I told you that would be his priority, my love."

Owen chuckled and pulled out some papers. "I hope you don't mind, but your mother told me that you had a relationship go sour and paid the price with much more than your heart."

Jess reached for Ren's hand under the table and he squeezed back before reaching out to take the papers as her dad continued.

"Understand, we do not need these papers between us. We're in love. What's mine is hers, and vice versa. But to protect you, Renzo, and make you comfortable, we have done a pre-nuptial agreement."

Ren opened the sheaf of papers and glanced at them, nodding his head. "May I?" he asked, indicating the papers.

"Those are for you to keep. As my husband says, we do not need them," his mother said.

"So your business is safe from our love. As is Last Chance Camp."

"Yes," Jess said. "Let's talk about Last Chance. What the hell—"

"First, we must order another round of drinks and toast to our new togetherness," her father said.

Jess bit her tongue and endured the wait while they ordered drinks. This time, Ren ordered himself a double scotch, straight up. His first drink sat untouched. By the time the drinks arrived and dinner got ordered, Jess felt about ready to explode.

"Why, Dad? Why would you sell Last Chance to the

Gallinis? And without talking to me, to any of us. I didn't have the slightest inkling that you were even considering it. If I had, I would have talked you out of it. It's our home, Dad. It's my home."

It was Owen Jenkins's turn to flush a deep red. With his strawberry-blond hair turned more white than golden, it added a comical flare to his face that Jess would have found funny any other time.

"Well, we didn't actually *sell* the place."

"You what?" Ren asked.

Jess clutched Ren's clenched hands. He'd done a good job of keeping any surprise out of his demeanor until now.

"What do you mean?"

"Allow us to explain."

"Explain what? I have papers," He waved the pre-nup papers, "like these that say you purchased Last Chance Station from the Jenkinses."

"A small deception on our part," his mother said.

Ren's voice returned to normal, except for his words being slightly mashed through gritted teeth. "What deception, mother?"

"We just wanted you to be as happy as we are," Amelie said.

Owen looked at Jess. "We thought, if you two met, that you'd see how perfect you are for each other."

Over the past several days, Jess had entertained—and tossed—any number of explanations for why her father would sell their home out from underneath her. Never, in her wildest brainstorming sessions, had she even considered that it was for some sort of...love match.

"You sold it to hook—" She waggled a finger between

herself and Ren. "—us up?"

"And look at how well it's turned out." Her father puffed up and beamed with pride at their accomplishment. "Now you know the meaning of love. Now you can be happy like us."

Jess felt the blush start, willing it to go away. Begging it to.

"See?" Her father continued. "Your blush tells me you're in love."

Too many emotions were rattling around in her brain, in her heart, in her soul. She couldn't breathe. Couldn't think. Were the walls closing in on her?

Jess needed to move, but with Ren sitting beside her in the booth, there was no way for her to stand. And he was so focused on her dad and his mother that he didn't react when she nudged him. She pushed at him until he turned to her. "Let me up."

"We need to sort this all out," he said to her.

"No. I. Need. Air." She glared at him.

For a moment, it looked like he wouldn't budge, but finally he shifted and stood.

Jess just about leaped out of the booth. With a superhuman hold on her anger and whatever else was rumbling around inside her, she lashed out at the only person she could.

"I never thought you would resort to manipulation to get your way, Dad. I was doing fine. I am doing fine. You—" She punched a finger toward him. "You don't get to pick who I...love. Or the direction my life goes in." She glanced at Amelie, then back to her father. "This...concocted story isn't you. It might be boardroom tactics, but you've *never* forced your will on me, or anyone. Ever."

Jess wanted to say more. Needed to say more. But she knew it would only hurt them all, herself included. She opened her mouth, then closed it tight and, whirling, fled out of the room, through the hotel doors and out into the night.

Chapter Twenty-Three

Outside, chaos ruled. People were everywhere. And lights. And music. Some sort of celebration was going on, and she couldn't see any place to get away to, to be alone.

God. Jess swiped at her wet cheeks. Could she find no peace? No quiet place to think? She thought of their room, the one she shared with the man her father had manipulated her into falling for. Ren would probably stay and have it out with his mother, so it was the best option for some alone time.

Jess walked back inside and slipped past the dining room entrance to the elevators. Of course, the elevator was filled with partying, happy people. Oh, and one couple making out like mad in the corner.

Great.

Not satisfied until she'd closed the room door behind her and flopped down on a lounge out on the lanai, Jess finally let the tears fall in earnest. How could he? How could her father do this to her? She curled up, clutching her stomach as she let the hurt of his betrayal roll through her.

He'd tricked her. Forced her to meet a man *he* thought would be perfect for her? He'd never, ever done that before. What right did he have? He was the person she was the closest to, and he'd deceived her. She didn't know her own father anymore. He'd been meeting with Amelie—her new step-mother—for months now and hadn't told her. Then, they'd pushed her into the arms of...Damn it. She didn't need anyone's arms. She could take care of herself.

Jess punched the lounge cushion. She'd been doing just fine at Last Chance. She was happy there, in her home. She didn't need anything, or anyone. What right did they have?

Was this Amelie's fault? Had she convinced her father to do this in order to get him to leave Last Chance? She sniffed. Well, if he wanted to leave, he was welcome to. He could leave Last Chance to her and she, Mary, John, and Rocky would handle things just fine.

Except...it wouldn't be the same without Owen Jenkins smiling and chatting up the new arrivals. She'd miss his hearty "good morning" when he joined them for breakfast prep, even if he did more talking than working. His "time to call it a day" at the end of chores. His wonderful hugs...

Then there was Ren. Jess got up and walked to the edge of the balcony, looking down at the courtyard. Sizzling food scents wafted up. Tiki torches and a three-piece band set playing a slow melody set the mood for several couples who danced. Jess hugged herself, remembering Ren's solid arms as he'd guided her around the dance floor. Had that only been last night?

Ren complicated things for her. Like it or not—and based on the information she'd just gotten, she really didn't much like it at the moment—she'd fallen for him. Big time. She couldn't picture him setting up shop in Last Chance, so what kind of chance did they have for, well, anything? He was New York sophisticated, and her heart was deeply embedded in Alaska.

Not all of her heart, though. Not anymore.

"Damn it, Dad. Why did you have to go and complicate the hell out of everything?"

"Because I want my girl to be happy."

The voice, so familiar, brought the sting of tears back to her eyes as she turned to see her father flashing a keycard. "Ren thought maybe we should talk."

Ren and his mother squared off on opposite sides of the table. For the first time in his life, Ren found himself speechless. There had been so many revelations in these past few hours, he didn't even know where to start. On one hand, his mother seemed happy. She twirled the wedding ring on her finger with a slow reverence and there was a softness in her gaze that he hadn't seen in a long time. Hell, he couldn't recall ever seeing her looking this peaceful. That held a lot of sway in Ren's mind. His anger dissipated, replaced with a numbness that had plagued him before his trip to Alaska. Now, all he had left were questions, and Ren was afraid the answers would not satisfy him.

"Are you going to just sit and stare at me, Ren? Or are we going to talk this out?"

The mother he knew peeked out, direct and to the point. Ren tried to smile, but it fizzled. "Okay. Easy stuff first. It's obvious you're in love."

"I am," she said, smiling.

"And, while I wish you'd come to me, told me what was going on, that's not enough reason to be angry with you, or with Owen. This..." He waved the papers. "Goes a long way toward making me feel better about it all."

Amelie smiled. "We knew it would help you."

"So, setting that aside, we're left with this little deception of yours. Not so little, actually." Ren grimaced. Had his mother really done all this to set him up with Jess?

"Yes, that. I didn't originally think it was a good idea."

"How did you two even cook up something as crazy as this? You're the conservative one in the family, Mom."

Laughing, Amelie took a sip of her drink before answering. "Owen and I have spent these past couple years getting re-acquainted with each other. I was unsure, cautious. We talked about anything and everything during these times. But mostly about our children. His dreams for Jess, my dreams for you..."

"You've never tried to lead me in the direction of your dreams in the past."

"I know. The more we talked, the more we realized how much you and Jess had in common. Yes, it's for different things, but you both have a fire in your belly to succeed. You care about the people around you and consider family very important."

"That's not enough to base a relationship on."

"But it's a start. Except you buried yourself in work and wouldn't take time to even date. I even tried to nudge you in Kathryn's direction." She frowned. "I dropped that pretty quickly. There's something about the woman that doesn't seem right. At least not for you. Anyhow, I figured I'd be dead before I had grandkids."

Deciding to leave the Kathryn thing alone, especially since he agreed, Ren tried to ask what right she had to do this. "Again—"

Amelie held up her hand. "Let me finish."

Ren nodded and remained mute, though it wasn't easy. It grated on him that his mother chose to drop him into a chasm of her choosing.

"Owen said Jess was the same way. Totally focused on

Last Chance."

"She's close to getting her Masters in Business Administration so she can take over running Last Chance. Although, I think she's been running the place for a while anyhow."

"I hear the pride in your voice. That makes me happy. She's good people."

"She's very good people. So, why the deception?"

"Owen knew Jess would never agree to meet you and, in fact, would refuse to leave camp in order to do that. So he came up with this idea. I was hesitant at first, but the more he talked, the more I wanted to see what would happen if you two met. And I see I was right. You are good for each other, aren't you?"

"Maybe. That's for me and Jess to figure out. And we'll do so without any more interference from you and Owen, all right, Mother?"

Amelie laughed. "Yes, yes, all right. We've done our part anyhow. Now it's up to you to decide."

Ren nodded. Yes. He and Jess definitely needed to figure some things out.

"So, do you think I still have a husband, or has Jess sent him running for the hills?"

"Something tells me Owen can hold his own with his daughter. I'm sure he'll be fine."

They'd come to an impass. Ren understood the why now, but needed time to let it all sink in, and to decide what to do. This was too much change too fast. He couldn't process it all. He sat back and sipped his drink. "So, what are your plans now, Mother?"

Jess stared at her father, wondering where her anger had disappeared to. Her father looked unapologetic, but the worry lines on his face were deeper than normal. Even now, she wanted to ease his concern. Jess sighed long and hard, expelling any remnants of resentment. "Yeah, I guess we should talk."

She moved toward the table, intending to sit down, but her body defied her and cut a straight line across the patio, straight into her father's open arms. He hugged her like a starved bear, and her arms tightened around him.

"I missed you so much," she mumbled into his shirt.

He patted her head as he held her. "I missed you too, kiddo. Just as much, maybe more." He nudged them toward the table and they sat, turning their chairs toward each other. Her father grabbed both of her hands and held tight.

Jess took a deep breath and plunged in. "I can't believe you did this. You lied to me."

His face creaked momentarily into that of an old man. "That was the toughest part of this whole thing. I couldn't tell you."

"Why not?"

He chuckled. "Well, mostly because of your stubborn streak."

She tried to sit up, back away. No way was he going to make this about her.

"Now, don't get your hackles up. I'm not blaming this on you. I'm just saying that if I told you about Amelie, and that I wanted to marry her, you'd have balked."

"I like to think I'd have listened."

"And then asked question after question, maybe even

trying to talk me out of it."

He knew her well.

"And then there's Ren. If I'd told you I wanted you two to meet, you know what you would have done, right?"

She nodded. "I'd have downright refused."

"Amelie and I knew you two could be good together. We thought you might be something special to each other. Turns out, we were right."

"You don't know anything about my relationship with Ren."

Her dad laughed. "Honey, if you can't see how he looks at you, and know how you look at him, you're blind." He tightened his hold on her hands. "You look at him the same way I look at my Amelie."

Jess wasn't ready to discuss Ren with her father yet. "Was this whole thing her idea?" she asked.

Owen shook his head. "Actually, it was mine. She wasn't very excited about deceiving either of you."

"Would you—would you really have sold Last Chance?"

He sat back, and Jess steeled herself for the words she didn't want to hear.

"It might be time," he whispered, watching her closely.

"No, Dad. No. That's my home. If you don't want to be there anymore, let me have it. You know I can do it. Please...don't take it away from me." Jess hated the way her voice sounded, but she couldn't seem to stop herself from begging.

"Honey, don't worry. I won't sell the place if you don't want to. I owe you that after what I've put you through. I'm sorry."

She let out the breath she'd been holding. "Yes, you do. And thank you for saying that."

"But...I think it might be time to let go of those reins a bit."

"So you won't stay there?"

"Amelie and I are talking about buying a place in New York. In the country, but close enough so she can still go into work. She's going to semi-retire. She's telling Ren now, while you and I are here talking."

Things were changing faster than Jess could keep up with. "It'll sure be different without you there."

"I know. But...I'd hoped maybe you would consider spending more time away from there, too."

She shook her head. "Can't. With you gone, I'll be needed more than ever."

"Not if we hire someone to manage the place."

"Turn Last Chance over to a stranger? I won't do it. I...don't think I could do it." She continued shaking her head.

"Last Chance is just a place to live. It's not living. You need to get out. See more of the world. And find your place in it."

"I know my place. It's there. Besides, it's home. It's where..."

"You feel closest to your mother. I know. But, Jess, your mother wouldn't want you staying there just because of her. Besides, she'll be with you wherever you go."

"It's not—"

"Yes it is the same," Owen said. "And before you try to deny it, think about it."

She closed her mouth, knowing he was right.

Her father nodded. "Just think about it, okay, honey? And let things unfold with Ren as they will. Give yourself this chance at happiness."

He stood, pulling her with him, and they walked arm in arm to the door.

Jess hugged her father. "Are you really happy? With Amelie?"

She could feel his cheek move as he grinned and pulled back. There was a new light in his eyes. "Yes. I've been blessed with the love of two good women in my life. So now, I'm going to be selfish and spend my time enjoying everything about being married. I hope you can understand that."

"I do. I'm not completely happy about it, but I understand. I feel like I'm losing you."

Owen laughed. "Nope. I'm just relocating. With all the ways of communicating in today's world, I'll never be too far away."

"I love you, Dad."

"I love you, too, honey. Now, I'd better go see if my bride still has any skin left after Ren got done flaying her. And you...you give this thing with Ren a chance, okay?"

Jess shrugged, still unwilling to discuss it. She let her father out, then leaned against the door, no longer angry, but still overwhelmed by all the revelations of the day.

A quiet knock sounded behind her, and she opened the door to Ren.

"Hi," he said, looking uncharacteristically worried. "Can I come in?"

Chapter Twenty-Four

Jess moved away from the door. "It's your room. You paid for it."

"It's our room. I just thought maybe you'd still be angry at a world that included me." Ren closed the door behind him, keeping Jess in his peripheral vision.

"Isn't it crazy, what our folks did?" Jess asked, toying with the piping on the back of the couch.

"Completely crazy. I don't much like being manipulated, but I think I understand enough to let go of my anger."

Jess smiled. "Me, too. The talk with Dad was good. Did you talk to your Mom?"

"Yes. She's planning to retire. Well, mostly retire."

"Dad mentioned that."

Jess wandered out to the lanai, so Ren followed.

"I still feel like I'm reeling from everything. It's too much."

"I feel the same, beautiful." They needed time to decompress from it all. To soak it in and get used to the fact that their parents were married. Then, maybe they could focus on the two of them. Except, Ren didn't want to wait anymore. He wanted Jess in his life now, to see where this could go."

He pulled her back against his chest, cocooning her in his arms as she stared up at the sky.

"I can't see the stars here."

Ren looked up and saw the occasional pinprick of

light.

"Not like at home," she clarified, "where the sky is alive with light. In New York, I'd never see..."

"The Northern Lights."

She turned into his arms, nodding into his shirt.

"It's true," he said. He wouldn't sugarcoat it. "I have a condo in the city, and I've never managed to see the Northern Lights there. But I've heard, out in the country, that it's possible sometimes."

Her sigh dug into his heart like little barbs. How could they make this work between them? Ren couldn't work from Last Chance. He needed to be close to the action. And Jess...how could he ask her to leave a place that she felt so tied to emotionally? This was an impossible situation.

Jess snuggled deeper, her hands moving along his back, and the reassurance from those small strokes bolstered him.

"How about we take this—us—one step at a time," he said. "Come to New York. Come see where I live."

He expected her to tense. Was ready for it. But it didn't happen. Instead, her hands wandered up and down his back, lighter now, seeking, and his body began to answer.

"You've seen my home," she whispered. "So I guess we need to go to New York."

Ren knew she'd just handed him her trust on a silver platter, and he promised himself he wouldn't disappoint her. He tipped her chin up so she would see his resolve and his emotion. "Thank you. We'll figure out a way to make this work. And I won't let anything happen to you, beautiful. I promise."

The last words he heard before his lips touched hers were, "You'd better."

Two days later, Jess and Ren walked off the jetway at LaGuardia and right into a chaotic mess. At least, that's what it felt like to Jess. Ren strode along as though nothing was out of the norm. Like he did this every day. He probably did. But Jess was tired of planes, tired of airports, and just plain tired.

"Do you fly a lot?"

He nodded, grinning. "Yep. Always feels good to be on this end, though. Homeward bound."

She knew that feeling well. Yesterday, when she'd called Mary to update her, she'd found out everything was quiet and fine at Last Chance. Mary's happiness over Jess's plans to see New York had been yet another reminder that everyone seemed bent on her finding a life beyond the arctic circle. She couldn't see it. Well, she could see being with Ren. But the logistics were hazy, and Jess had no idea how they could make this work. The idea of not being with him hurt as much as the thought of not living in Alaska. That was her home, her heritage, everything she'd built.

"The car's waiting outside," Ren said.

With no checked bags, they steered their way through the throngs quicker than Jess had thought possible. People walked fast here. It was crazy. She glanced at Ren. The grin he'd had plastered on his face since getting off the plane widened as they walked outside. It was hard not to catch his smile. His joy was infectious.

Jess's mouth dropped when a long, sleek black limousine pulled up in front of them. "This is for us?"

"Yes," Ren said as the driver opened the door.

"Do you normally—"

"No. But I thought something special was needed this time."

Warmth filled Jess as she returned his smile and settled back into the plush seats. She'd never needed money before, but after first class flights and limos, she could see the advantages. "You're going to spoil me, City Boy."

"That's the plan."

En route to the condo, Jess stared out the window, amazed at all the concrete and towers. It got worse the closer they got to Manhattan. And better. There was a certain flow to the buildings and streets that made sense. But the parks they passed were jokes, concrete triangles peppered amongst the tall buildings.

And the traffic! They crawled along, changing lanes haphazardly, driving through lights no longer yellow. Crazy. The smells, concrete and gas fumes, were almost overwhelming, even with the limo windows closed.

When they reached Central Park, she let out a big sigh of relief. The trees might be different here, but they were trees, and she liked them better than the glass towers and limestone buildings of the city. Maybe they could go for a walk later.

Soon, they were exiting the limo in front of a tall, post-modern structure.

"Home," Ren said.

"Hmmm." It was all she could think of to say, as overwhelmed as she felt at the moment by the sheer enormity of The City.

Ren took her backpack and his case from the driver,

tipped him, and whisked her off to the elevators, then into his condo. Once inside, his phone rang just as he set their bags down, so he answered it.

"William?"

He shrugged to Jess and she waved at him to finish his conversation, wondering who William was and how he'd known Ren was back in town.

"Yes," he said into the phone. "We just got to my apartment."

Jess wandered away from the conversation, showing herself around the apartment. A peek in the bedroom showed a typical man-space. Browns and blacks and a king-size bed. What would it be like to make love with all that room?

The bathroom was tasteful and had the largest shower stall she'd ever seen. Back down the hall, she found a kitchen that rivaled the size of the kitchen at Last Chance but had much higher-end appliances. Who cooked for Ren? She doubted very much that he cooked for himself. It startled her that she didn't know that. They'd been together pretty much non-stop for days...and nights, yet she didn't really know Ren Gallini, did she?

In the spacious open-concept living and dining areas, the furniture and décor—well-made from what she could tell—seemed to match effortlessly.

Ren settled his arms around her, his tone quiet and full of pride. "I picked every item in this place out myself," he said.

"You did a great job. It looks wonderful." She meant it. Jess wouldn't normally think she'd like modern paintings and leather furniture, but it all pleased her eye. She ran her hand along the formal table. The craftsmanship was top-notch.

"I built that."

Jess knew her mouth hung open as she looked at Ren.

He laughed. "Thanks for the vote of confidence."

"I, uh..."

"That's all right. You didn't really get to see me at my best in Last Chance. But I did tell you I worked as a carpenter."

"Yes, but I thought buildings and girders and sheetrock."

He shrugged, running his own hand along the wood. "This is more of a hobby. I like working with my hands."

And oh, what those hands could do. Jess shook herself to stop the thoughts. Now was not the time. Turning to the sliding glass door, Ren opened it and they stepped outside to a view of Central Park with the city surrounding it.

"Wow," Jess said.

"This is the reason I bought an apartment almost on the top floor."

"I can see why." She gazed out over the tree tops. "It's amazing. And a weird combination of nature and man."

"I can imagine it looks strange."

They stood there watching the hustle and bustle below them for a while, until Ren spoke. "That phone call from William...it was one of our lawyers and a friend of mine."

Distractedly counting the number of dogs a dog-walker was trying to rein in, Jess didn't at first hear the concern in Ren's voice. When she did, she looked up at him.

"What?"

"Apparently, there's a welcome back party tonight. For us."

"For you, you mean."

Ren nodded. "I hadn't intended to ask you to meet everyone the first day here." He chuckled. "Figured I'd save something for tomorrow. What do you think? Up for a small gathering?"

"Ummm, how small?"

"I'm guessing maybe forty to fifty people. A few friends, corporation people, their spouses. For cocktails, that sort of thing."

Trying for a relaxed demeanor completely at odds with the turmoil in her stomach, Jess nodded. "I guess tonight's as good as any."

Ren pulled her into his arms. "Don't worry, beautiful. They're only sharks during the day. They're pussycats once the work is done. You'll wow them."

Jess thought about her meager collection of clothing. "Ummm, what do people wear to something like this?"

Chapter Twenty-Five

Jess stared at herself in the mirror, happy to be in girly clothes for once. She'd curled her hair in soft waves, but wore no more makeup than that night in Fairbanks. It was the dress that made her feel special—feminine. She twirled, letting the skirt of the little black dress swoosh. It molded to the curves of her upper body, then flowed out from there in two layers that caressed her bare legs as she walked, but had enough material to swing when she turned. It felt decadent, and so unlike her usual attire. Add to that the killer heels she'd spent the afternoon learning to walk in, and she grinned with pleasure.

Ren had taken her to some exclusive shop and handed over his credit card. She'd refused, and was glad she did. She'd looked at a few prices while he took yet another phone call and almost fainted. Two-thousand dollars for a dress? She could retrofit all the plumbing in Last Chance with that kind of money.

So she'd shooed him out. Told him to go get work out of his system and be ready for the evening. Then she'd conquered the city on her own, hopped a cab to Macy's with her own credit card and found the perfect dress and shoes for a hell of a lot less money.

Jess smoothed the material, nervous about what he would think. Maybe he was used to rough-and-ready Jess Jenkins. Would he like her as much when she tried to blend with his crowd, or see her for a fad, something he needed to get out of his system. Would he still feel something for this Jess?

Shaking her head, she tried to dispel the gloom that had settled around her. The tap at the bathroom door was light, but it startled her.

"Almost ready?" Ren asked through the door.

Jess gulped down her panic and reached for her sheer wrap. "Yes," she answered, opening the door.

Ren's hand froze mid-reach as his eyes traveled the length of Jess's body, warming her as he went. When he brought his gaze back to her face, there was a very satisfying, very hungry fire in his eyes.

Jess pinched skirt fabric in her fingers. "Acceptable party attire?"

Eyes dark with desire, Ren groaned. "God, I wish we didn't have to go. As much as I love this—" he closed the distance between them and ran a finger under the demure neckline. "this dress on you, I'd rather peel it slowly off, tasting every inch of skin as I go. You look absolutely spectacular."

"Right answer," Jess whispered, letting a long sigh follow her words. She pulled her wrap around her shoulders. "As for that whole peeling thing? Later."

"Definitely." His voice promised her it would be a night she would remember.

After a short taxi ride, they stood outside the headquarters of Ren's company in Manhattan. One of the best things they'd done when renovating had been to include their own social facilities on the ground floor. Not only did it allow them to host their own events, it brought in revenue from rentals when not in use by the company.

Right now, revenue was the furthest thing from his mind. He barely managed to keep himself from turning the taxi around and heading straight back to his place with Jess. Holy shit. Jess in camp clothes turned him on. But this Jess, sophisticated and sexy in a little black dress, stunned him. He hadn't been able to draw a steady breath since she'd opened the bathroom door. His hands were clammy, for crying out loud. If he didn't get a handle on things, he'd be a blubbering idiot all night.

He helped Jess from the cab. If her white hands and wide eyes were any indication, she was close to bolting. Considering how she felt about society in general, and how much she'd been through in the past few days, he couldn't blame her. He pulled her into his arms.

"They'll love you. Trust me," Ren said.

Jess took a deep breath and rolled her shoulders. "Just...don't leave me."

Ren flashed her a wide smile. "Not planning to, beautiful. There's no one else here I care about as much as you." Crap. Kathryn. He didn't care about her, not like he did for Jess. Never had. But there had been no time to call her, to apprise her of his newly coupled status. If she was here...

His hand on the door, Ren paused. "I should tell you, in case she's here, that there's someone who thinks—"

He never got the chance to finish, as the door whooshed open, and his friend William whisked them inside, pulling Ren into a quick man-hug.

"About time you got here, man. Party's been going strong for an hour already. Everyone's half toasted."

Ren grinned. "Including you, I gather."

"Just doing my duty, keeping everyone happy while they waited for the person of honor. Sorry. Persons of honor." He eyed Jess, who stood just inside the door.

Something about the speculative way he looked her over made Ren queasy and caveman at the same time. Ren pulled Jess into his side and settled his arm around her waist. "Jess, this is William, the reprobate I was telling you about earlier."

"Ahh, I'm a sweetheart," William said, pulling her out of Ren's arms and into a hug that seemed more seductive than friendly.

"Back off, William."

Jess extricated herself, and William held up his hands and laughed. "Wouldn't dream of it, my man. Wouldn't even dream of it."

A flash of glitz and blonde hair was all Ren caught out of the corner of his eye before Kathryn flew into his arms. *Crap.*

Even worse, she kissed him. Not the peck he'd been used to from her. No, she had to go for the full-on lip lock. He tried to set her back, but the woman's arms were tangled behind his neck. He could see just enough of Jess's thin lips and raised eyebrows to know he was in deep shit. *Double crap.*

With what amounted to superhuman strength, Ren set Kathryn at arm's length and tried to convey a plea to Jess. *Don't read too much into this.* When her raised brows turned to slitted eyes, Ren knew that the dress-peeling he wanted to do later would depend on some very heavy explanations.

Ren stepped to Jess's side and settled an arm around her. "Kathryn, I'd like you to meet Jess Jenkins."

My girlfriend? My lover? They were still trying to figure out their relationship themselves, so how the hell should he describe her to his friends and co-workers. He didn't have a quick answer, and the flush creeping up Jess's neck told him he was too late now, anyhow. He'd screwed up with a simple pause. Royally. *Crap.* This party was not a good idea.

Kathryn, too, looked ready to spit fire at him. But she recovered quicker than Jess, and held out her hand to shake with Jess.

"That's a very strong handshake you have...Jess."

"Comes from lots of hard work."

"Oh, yes," Kathryn said. "You're from that place in Alaska that pulled our Ren away from home for so many days." She curled into Ren's other side and settled her hands on his shoulder. "We're so glad you're back home, honey. It's been too long."

The way she drew out the "too" left nothing to anyone's imagination. Ren needed to rein her in quick. "Kathryn—"

"Ren and I, we go way back, don't we?" She stroked his cheek with a red-tipped nail. "His mother and I are good friends, too." She glanced at Jess, then at William, who laughed.

"Down, girl," William said, extricating Kathryn from Ren's side. "Come along, you two. Lots of people waiting to welcome you home."

They rejoined the party, but Ren held back. "Sorry. I need to explain about Kathryn, I know. But you need to know, there never was anything. She saw more in our friendship than I could ever have given her."

"Yes," Jess said, her face grim. "I can see that."

Ren groaned. "We need to talk, but not here. An hour should be enough for introductions, then we'll slip away."

"Whatever you say, *honey*."

Oh, yes, he was royally screwed.

It took every bit of willpower to let Ren's hand at her waist nudge her forward into what, so far, had been more shark pit than warm reception. Jess just prayed she could keep her head above water. William had taken Kathryn to the far side of the room, but the woman's eyes followed her and Ren as they began to mingle. Anger—and pain—filled them and part of Jess felt for the woman. If she'd expected something from Ren, Jess's appearance had to be one hell of a shock to her. She could understand Kathryn's turmoil.

Didn't mean she had to like the woman, though. She seemed too polished, too sophisticated. Much more so than Jess could ever be. Jess was a fish out of water and didn't belong here.

Ren's puzzled gaze brought her back to the present, and she pasted on a smile as he introduced her to more people. Brad somebody and his wife, Amber. Tom and Sylvia. Mark and Laura. So many names to remember.

"You doing okay, beautiful?" Ren's warm breath in her ear calmed Jess, settled her stomach.

"There's a lot of people here."

"That's okay. There won't be any test on names."

"I'm just overwhelmed, I think."

He pulled her back into his chest and circled his arms around her, and Jess saw Kathryn's eyes narrow.

"I think your friend Kathryn isn't too happy with us."

"I don't care about Kathryn."

"She's not just pissed. She's hurting."

Ren sighed into her hair, and it warmed Jess all the way to her toes.

"You're right. I should have told her about you. I knew she felt...more for me than I did for her. This isn't fair, but it's going to have to wait until tomorrow. You're my concern tonight."

A reassurance Jess needed at the moment. "I feel so out of place."

"Trust me, beautiful. You're fitting in just fine. How about a glass of wine? Will that help you relax?"

"Yes," Jess said, taking a deep breath. "I think it would."

"Great." He moved in front of her and kissed her, his eyes dark. "Don't run off with anyone. I'll be right back, wine in hand to ply you with." He grinned, and Jess couldn't help but smile back.

"You'd better hurry. You promised you wouldn't leave me alone."

"I'll make it quick."

He walked with purpose to the bar. Jess watched him order, then someone she'd met—Tom?—pulled him into a conversation. Their wine glasses sat in front of him without being picked up as Jess watched...and waited.

"So you're the Alaska girl I've been hearing rumors about."

Only rigid control kept Jess from jumping. She'd been so focused on Ren, she hadn't seen Kathryn approach.

"Ummm, I guess I am."

Kathryn nodded. "You know, Ren's mother and I have plans for that man. He's going to take this company to the

next level. And he needs someone strong by his side
helping him. Do you—" Kathryn eyed Jess up and down,
"know anything about corporate business?"

Jess thought about how close she was to getting her
masters in business administration. It seemed like such a
small thing at the moment.

"Well, no matter," Kathryn continued without waiting
for Jess to answer. "He'll tire of you soon and realize I'm
what he needs. His mother knows it. I know it. Ren will
learn it soon enough."

Jess had had just about enough of this woman and her
opinions. She obviously didn't know Ren's mother was in
Mexico, now married to Jess's father. Politeness went out
the window as Jess opened her mouth to reply. Once again,
Kathryn didn't give her a chance.

"I don't even know why he brought you here. It
certainly wasn't necessary. It looks like Congress is going to
agree to drilling in the wilderness, so there won't be any
need to spend time convincing natives how important this
is."

Jess blanched as the news speared through her. "What
do you mean, drilling? Ren came to Alaska to check out
Last Chance Camp at his mother's behest."

"Hardly. William asked Ren to check out the local
attitude, try to plant the seed of change. He's leveraged the
company's resources on a plan to turn around an oil
company with the ANWR contracts."

Kathryn stopped for a breath and stared at Jess.
"You're looking a little peaked. Are you all right? Did I say
something wrong?"

Jess couldn't breathe. Ren had gone to Alaska because

of oil? Ren was *in* the oil business? He'd lied to her, told her
he didn't have an interest in that. Had the whole purchase
of Last Chance been a ruse to...to get in with the locals?
He'd used her! Jess couldn't think, couldn't talk,
couldn't...anything. She needed out of there, out of New
York.

So Jess ran. Out of the building and into a taxi. Back at
Ren's, she called the airport and booked a flight while she
stuffed her meager clothes into her backpack, the dress
crumpled into the deepest part. Every time she left Last
Chance, she got hurt. Well, enough. Less than forty-five
minutes after she'd run from the party, Jess was on her way
to the airport.

She was going home.

It took several interminable minutes for Ren to
extricate himself from Tom's clutches. The man was all
about business. And right now, business was the last thing
on Ren's mind. Jess laughing, Jess sated, Jess in that little
black dress. That was all he wanted to think about. And
he'd about had it with this party. It was time to convince
her out of that dress and into his bed.

By the time he returned to where he'd left her, she was
nowhere to be found. Ren frowned as he scanned the
room. He checked the hallway leading to the bathrooms.
Empty.

A finger tickled its way along his neck in the dark
hallway, and Ren grinned, liking the game she was playing.
If the fingernail felt a little sharper than Jess's work-ready
hands, he chalked it up to her fitting in a manicure today.

He turned and pulled her into his arms. "You little

minx," he whispered before lowering his head. But he
knew, at the first touch, that this wasn't his Jess. Ren
yanked his head back.

"Kathryn!"

"I knew you still wanted me," she said with a definite
purr in her voice.

Ren set her away from him and glanced around,
grateful Jess hadn't seen the exchange. He'd be hard
pressed to explain it. Kathryn tried again to sidle into his
embrace. Ren would have to take precious time away from
locating Jess to deal with this. He could see that now. "I'm
sorry, Kathryn—"

"There's nothing to be sorry about. You may
have...strayed, but you're home now, and that's all that
counts."

"I'm home, yes. But not with you. Jess is the woman in
my life, who I want to be with."

Kathryn stiffened. "What do you mean? How can you
say that you want to be with her? We're perfect together.
Perfect for each other. Together we can conquer
Manhattan."

Ren ran a hand through his hair. "I've known for some
time that you believed there was more to this friendship of
ours. I tried very hard not to lead you on, but I've
never...felt about you the way you want me to."

"You can learn. Affection can come slowly. And we've
got a good basis for a great merger here." Her voice had
taken on a distinct whine, a pleading note, something Ren
knew Jess would never do.

Ren bit back a harsh laugh. "Do you hear yourself? I
am not some business acquisition, and neither are you.

There's no love between us, Kathryn, so why would you even want this?"

"Love? You've never once talked about love being important to you. In this day and age, when businesses are built or destroyed with a single whispered word, love isn't important. Respect is what matters."

"And I do respect you. I don't want to hurt you, but this—" he waggled a finger between them, "isn't going to happen. I plan to marry Jess, if she'll have me."

Her silence lasted only long enough for the timber of her voice to change from pleading to hard. Cold enough to turn the blood in his veins to ice when she uttered her next words.

"Then it's a good thing I got rid of her."

Ren grabbed her by the arms. "What do you mean? What did you do, Kathryn?"

She sniffed, raising her nose higher. "I simply told her the truth. A truth, apparently, you neglected to mention."

"What? What did you tell her?" He fought the urge to shake her.

"I told her what William told me. That you were in Alaska to scout out oil drilling."

Dread filled Ren. Frigid, stone-hard dread. He'd never gone to Alaska for that reason and hadn't yet had a chance to call William on it, to find out what the man was doing. He'd been played. Oh, God, had he been played. And Jess had been the one hurt by that action.

Correction. Ren rubbed his chest. She wasn't the only one aching. He had to find her. But first...

"Leave, Kathryn. Clear out your office and get the hell out of my sight and my life. There's no longer a place for you in it." He didn't look at her, didn't care about her reaction. He had to get to Jess. But he knew already that she was gone.

He called over two security guards, rejoined the party, and stalked toward William. "You manipulated me, wanted me to check on oil rights in Alaska?" He barely managed to keep his voice from rocking the room. "Why?"

William shrugged. "We didn't sell A and M oil. We bought it outright. We're going to make millions once they start drilling more in Alaska."

"I thought I knew you," Ren said through tight lips. "Thought you were my friend."

"Hey, buddy, I am. You stand to double your assets on this."

"The only thing I'm doubling is the security around here once I toss your ass out."

He was momentarily pleased at the stunned look on his ex-lawyer's face.

"Security will escort you to your desk to get your things, then out of the building. You're fired."

Ren's mind was already thinking ahead, trying to determine where Jess would have gone. He needed to find her, to explain. He turned away from William, then paused, wanting just a tad more satisfaction from this moment.

When his fist connected with William's face, Ren never felt the pain. Only a fleeting pleasure. Then he was out the door in search of Jess.

Entering his apartment, he saw no lights on, no sign of Jess. He ripped into the bedroom and immediately saw her backpack was gone.

She'd left him. She'd gone home. Without even giving

him a chance. He knew she had, and the darkness of the room permeated his mind, his heart, and his soul.

Chapter Twenty-Six

"Thanks, Gus," Jess said as she climbed out of the long-hauler's cab. "Tell Rocky your food's on the house."

"Anytime, kiddo," the gray-haired trucker said. "And thanks. You know I love the grub here."

Jess smiled, already distracted as she checked out Last Chance Camp. Nothing seemed amiss. There was snow on the ground, but it was obvious it hadn't snowed since she'd left, which felt like weeks ago. The camp had settled into the slower mode of winter, preparing for the long, hushed quiet broken only by truckers hauling gear to the oil fields.

Home.

In the late afternoon dusk, Jess closed her eyes and let the smells and sounds of home soothe her soul and close the jagged wounds crisscrossing her heart. She'd tried to make sense of everything during the long flights. Tried even harder when she stayed overnight in Anchorage. Somewhere on the ride from there to here, she'd given up and prayed for numbness to bury the ache. Rubbing her chest, she knew there was no salve for Ren's betrayal. How could she have been so wrong about him?

Jess pulled her coat tighter against the cold and headed for her trailer, knowing she wasn't ready to face Mary, John, and Rocky. She stepped inside, kicking the lights on and the heater up in quick succession. Dropping her backpack on the floor, she slumped into a chair and looked around. This place, painstakingly decorated by hand, had always been her solace. Yet the edge of her bed peeking through the half open doorway mocked her, reminded her what she'd done in that bed...and how good it had felt.

Crud.

Jess stood, yanking coat, shirt, and the rest of her layers off and headed for her shower. A shower that turned out to be way less than satisfying, since the water was only lukewarm at best. They'd apparently put her trailer in winter mode for the few days she'd been gone.

Dressing, she still couldn't erase the chill that permeated her body, so she grabbed her coat and headed to the restaurant. A hot cup of coffee would do the trick. It was early evening, but Jess figured she wouldn't be sleeping anyhow.

Molding her hands around the warm mug, she wandered into the kitchen, immediately thankful that only Mary was there.

"Hey, Auntie."

"Jess! What are you doing here? How did you *get* here? Where's Owen, his wife, that man of yours? Have you forgiven me? I sure hope so. I feel awful about it all." Mary didn't wait for answers, but just kept popping questions as she engulfed Jess into her signature hug.

God, it felt good. Like being enveloped in a quilt filled with down feathers and love.

Too soon, Mary set her back and eyed her. "You look like you've been dragged behind a semi-truck for about ten miles, girl." Mary grabbed her cup and gestured to the stools. "You sit. Let me get some coffee and we'll talk. Want some more?"

"Yeah, thanks."

When Mary returned, she settled next to Jess and

waited. Jess wasn't sure where to begin.

"How about we start with how you got home," Mary nudged.

"Something happened and I...well, I went to the airport and caught the first flights home. Ran into Gus in Fairbanks and he gave me a ride up."

"Good man, Gus." Mary sipped her coffee. "So, what happened?"

Jess's eyes filled as the pain washed over her yet again. "Oh, Mary. He didn't want me. He was after the oil!" Jess let the tears fall, laying her head and arms on the counter. "How could I have misjudged this all so horribly?"

Mary huffed and rested her hand on Jess's back. "We all met Renzo Gallini. We all spent time with him. None of us thought, after a while, that he had any ulterior motive. Is it possible you could be wrong?"

"Hardly. I heard it from a woman who works at the firm. His friend, one of the attorneys for the company, hatched the plan with him to—to try and figure out a way to speed up the decision-making and get drilling started in the ANWR." She looked at Mary, let her see the misery graying her face. "He *knew* how important the issue was to me, and still he used me."

Mary nodded, sipping again. "So, a woman who works with Ren told you this."

"Yes."

"Was she a nice woman? Did she know Ren well?"

Even feeling the way she did, green hit her smack in the face at the memory of Kathryn kissing Ren.

"You don't need to answer that," Mary said, chuckling. "I can see it written all over your face. So, a woman with obvious designs on your man told you the one thing that would get your hackles up."

"Well, yes, but—"

"How did Ren explain himself?"

Warmth infused Jess's cheeks. "I-I—"

"You didn't give him a chance to answer, did you?"

Jess slumped back down to the counter. "No."

Mary got up and set both their cups in the sink. "Then I think, young lady, you owe that man an apology."

Jess jumped up. "I will not apologize. He's the one who needs to apologize to me."

"That's not how I see it. You've never skirted issues before. Always took them on front and center. So why are you being so evasive now? Could it be you're scared? Maybe because you love this man?"

She opened her mouth three times to answer, but couldn't find the words.

Mary nodded. "I see. Well, it's late, and everything's done for tonight. I suggest you go get some sleep, or try, and see how you feel about everything tomorrow."

Mary hugged her tight. "Just so you know, I love you no matter what."

Jess hung on to Mary for several long moments, letting tears that had dried up fall again. "I love you so much, Auntie," she whispered. "And yes, I forgive you. I'm so glad to be home."

"Being glad to be home is fine, as long as it's not running away you're doin'."

With that, Mary turned the lights to night mode and left Jess to herself. Jess sat there, unaware of how much time passed, trying to figure things out. She hadn't let Ren defend himself. She'd tried him without giving him a chance, and after he'd asked her to trust him.

Had she just been looking for an excuse? Life would be so complicated if she stayed with Ren. Would they live here? She couldn't see him agreeing to that. And how would she do living full time in New York? Everything that was important to her would slowly fade away, and what would she be left with?

No. It was better this way. Let it go. She could stay here where she wanted to be, and Ren could resume the life he loved. *With Kathryn.* Jess's heart clenched at the thought. She tried to bury it deep, but that kiss just kept coming back to her.

Pulling on her coat, she wandered outside, realizing it was much later than she thought. The ribbons of a bright auroral showing already danced across the sky.

Tonight, not even this could make her smile. Jess crumpled to the ground and put her head in her hands. "Oh, mother, I'm so lost. I wish you were here. I don't know what to do."

The only answer she got was silence. No whisper on the wind. No whistle. The spirits gave her only the hush of night.

Jess pulled herself up and to her trailer. Inside, she peeled off her coat and shoes, crawled onto her bed and pounded her fists into the pillow.

Early the next morning, Jess opened her eyes and glared at a clock she'd seen way too much of overnight. She climbed out of bed, every muscle sore from tossing and turning. Washing the grit out of her eyes, the solution to her predicament still eluded her. She knew, deep down, she should give Ren a chance to explain. But the spike of hurt in her heart just wouldn't dissipate, and nothing else could fill that space until she found a way to make it disappear.

Jess dressed and went to help with breakfast, although they made a very limited menu this time of year. Just enough for the layovers and themselves. Mary was already in the kitchen and raised an eyebrow when Jess walked in, but Jess shook her head, not ready for another heart-to-heart. Mary grunted something about stubbornness and they both went to work.

Rocky plowed into the kitchen about fifteen minutes later and skidded to a stop. "What the hell are you doing here?"

Jess glared at him. "What? I can't come home?"

"Well, uh, sure. You can come home. We just didn't expect you. Figured you and—"

Jess cut him off. "Don't say it. I don't want to hear that man's name."

Rocky's eyes widened, and he glanced at Mary. Jess saw her shake her head, and Rocky clamped his mouth shut, but not by much. It seemed mumbling about stubborn was the theme of the day.

Jess worked doggedly through breakfast and cleanup, went to her office and checked the weather, even tried to finish an overdue assignment for her masters' program. Nothing interested her. Nothing distracted her from the pain. Nothing eased the ache in her heart. It wasn't sharp anymore, wasn't the sting of deceit. It surprised her to realize a melancholy had replaced the hurt. She searched for her anger. It was righteous, and she needed it. But it had disappeared.

And inactivity wasn't helping. Throwing on her coat, Jess trudged across to the combination museum and State Trooper detachment. As expected, the place was empty. Tourists didn't head this far north this time of year unless they were crazy. Jess wandered around the familiar exhibits, feeling at home with the history surrounding her. Cocooned. Safe.

Except safe no longer meant happy.

"Jess!"

Before she had time to answer, Meg was in front of her, pulling Jess in for a hug.

"How are you home? *Why* are you home? Is that hunky man of yours with you?"

"He's not my man," Jess mumbled, extricating herself from the hug.

"Uh oh. What's up?" Meg leaned against the counter.

"Nothing. It just...didn't work out."

"Hmmm. There's more there than you're telling me."

"Honestly, I will explain. Just not now. I'm tired of thinking about it."

Meg watched her for a long moment, making Jess fidget. Then, with some sort of decision made, she grinned. "Then I guess it's not the best time to tell you my news."

"If it's good news, it's the perfect time. I could use some of that."

"Rod and I are an item."

"What?" Jess's heart swelled with joy for her friend. She'd been pining for Rod for so long. "Spill, my friend. How in the heck did you crack that hard line he stood by?"

Meg laughed. "All it took was an ultimatum. I told him

I loved him, had for a long time. And that it was obvious
he was not able to return that feeling, so I was taking leave
for a while and after that would be putting in for a transfer.
It probably helped that I had my packed suitcase right
beside me."

"Oh, my God. How did he react?"

"Stunned is too light a word for the look on his face.
But he didn't wait. Just blurted out 'I love you, too' before I
had a chance to pick up that suitcase." She shrugged. "The
rest, as they say, is history."

Jess hugged her friend, then twined her arm through
hers. "I'm so happy for you. So, are you going to both stay
here? God, please tell me you're not leaving."

"We don't know yet. Neither of us is getting any
younger, and I know it's only been a few days. But we've
pretty much lived together for a year, just without the sex."
She blushed. "Well, up until now."

Jess laughed.

"We've decided to come clean, tell our boss we're
getting married."

"Married?" Jess just about shrieked.

"Yep. Rod doesn't mess around once he sets his mind
to something. That's one of the things I love about him. He
proposed right after our first...well, that night, anyhow. I
said yes, of course."

"Ah, Meg, I can't describe how happy I am for you
both."

Her friend nodded. "Rod's in on the phone with the
man now. That will determine our fate. If they'll allow us to
be a married detachment, we'll stay. Or maybe I'll quit, and
we'll stay anyhow. We're not sure yet."

"Yes, we are," Rod said, coming up behind Meg and wrapping his arms around her. "They said the only way we can stay in the same place is to be married...and quick." He grinned at Jess. "Sorry, babe. I hope your feelings aren't hurt that I picked Meg here."

Jess laughed. "Not at all, my friend. I'm so happy for you both."

"Did he seriously say we needed to get married quick?" Meg craned her neck to look at him.

"Yep. And he's making arrangements for coverage so we can fly to Anchorage, get the license and do the deed."

"What the heck?"

"Turns out, everyone's had bets going on how long they thought it would take us. He gave it the longest, a year, and wins. Hence the good mood."

"Wow, wow, wow." Meg turned to Jess. "Umm, I know it's quick notice, but would you come with us? Be my maid of honor?"

Jess felt her melancholy amp up a notch, but tightened the lid on it. "I'd be honored to."

"Great," Rod said. "We'll get all the arrangements made and let you know what's up. Should be in less than a month."

Jess headed back to camp trying to let the happiness for her friends override her own issues. Rod had finally seen the light and acted on it. Good for him.

She watched a plane circle for a landing behind the station, then trudged back to camp thinking about how much Rod and Meg were made for each other.

Not like her and Ren, who were complete opposites. No, that wasn't true. The only opposite was the place they called home. Beyond that, they were both driven, hard-working, strong-feeling people who loved their parents, loved what they did, and were honest to a fault.

Oh, God. He was honest. If Kathryn, who had motives, was lying, then Ren had never lied to her once. And she'd leapt at the first excuse that came along to drive a wedge between them.

Wedge? More like a continent.

What had she done? She'd screwed up big time. Jess almost tripped as an overwhelming fear turned her legs to jelly. She loved Ren, and she'd pushed him so far away, she probably had no chance of getting him back. Jess needed to explain to Ren, to beg his forgiveness. Urgency quickened her pace. Maybe she could call him. No. She couldn't do this over the phone. Crap. That meant getting on another plane—planes, really—and going back to New York.

She rushed through the restaurant, past a startled Rocky, straight to her office to look at flight information and see how she could get back to Anchorage. It didn't take her long to figure out it would take her two days minimum to get to New York. By then, Kathryn could have sunk her claws deep into Ren, especially if he was nursing some lingering hurt over her betrayal.

Crap, crap, crap.

"Um, boss?"

"Not now, Rocky. I've got to make plane reservations. I'm going back to New York to beg Ren to forgive me."

"I'm very glad to hear you say that." The voice, deep timbered with a hint of reserve, was so very familiar to her.

"Ren," Jess said, looking up into dark, clouded eyes. "You're here."

"I came to make you listen to me, give me a chance to explain. I think I like your idea better. Now, about that begging thing you were mentioning?"

Chapter Twenty-Seven

The deep circles underneath Jess's eyes about unmanned Ren. He wanted to step around her desk, pull her into his arms and take her to her trailer, then hold her while she slept long and hard. After that, they could sort this all out.

Jess stood. "Ren, I—"

"Hold that thought," he said, turning her chin to see her face better. "You look like you haven't slept in days."

A thin chuckle trickled out of Jess. "I don't think I have. You don't look much better than I do, I'm afraid."

"In an interesting turn of events, I now find it's impossible to sleep without you next to me."

"I know the feeling," she said with a nod. "I'm so sorry I doubted you, Ren."

"I know. And I should have told you my suspicions about William's plans long ago. Yes, he mentioned the oil drilling. But I knew we were selling that company, or thought we were, so it was a non-issue for me. I had no plans to do any sort of reconnoitering. At all."

"I should have trusted you." She stepped around the desk until she was right in front of him.

Ren pulled Jess into his arms and breathed in her scent. Just breathed. In and out.

"I'm so sorry," she whispered into his chest.

Her voice infiltrated him, filled him with a peace that had evaded him for the past few days. Everything would be okay now. They were together. He kept breathing.

"Ren?" She pulled away, looked up at him. He could see the sorrow in her eyes.

"I know you're sorry. So am I." He kissed her, keeping it light because if he deepened it, there would be no sleeping. "Right now, though, I think we both need some sleep."

"It's the middle of the day."

"I don't care. We've been on planes since forever."

"And I didn't sleep any better here," Jess said.

"So what do you say we just shelve anything until later."

"Good plan. Hey, what do you mean, 'we've been on planes'?"

They walked into the restaurant, where her father and his wife were chatting with Mary, John, and Rocky.

"Dad!" Jess said, hurrying over to hug him. "You came home."

"We met up with Ren and flew in together," Owen said. "Wanted to make certain our part in this deception wasn't causing a problem between you two. And I wanted to show Amelie Last Chance Camp."

Amelie's lilting laughter rang through the group like a fairy's magic. "Yes, dear," she said, patting Owen's arm. "We flew all this way just so you could show me where you've lived."

Ren put his arm around Jess's shoulders and addressed the group. "We're going to get some much needed time alone."

When Owen and Amelie grinned, and Jess stiffened, he amended his statement. "Sleep. Something neither of us have had much of lately. We—" he nudged Jess toward the door, "will see you all much, much later."

In Jess's trailer, they peeled most of their clothes off and climbed under the covers. Jess snuggled into his side like they'd never been apart, and Ren drifted into a much needed sleep listening to the peaceful, rhythmic sound of her breathing.

Jess dragged herself from sleep slowly. It smelled like home. Sounded like home. It felt like her bed. She smiled as she came fully awake, recognizing Ren's body tucked up against her back, his arm securely around her waist as if unable to let go even in sleep. She glanced at the clock. 8 p.m. Six hours they'd slept. Six blissful hours. And she could easily slip back into dreamland for another few, especially in Ren's arms.

Her stomach growled, a long, rolling, ungainly sound.

Ren's chuckle vibrated through her. "Sounds like we need to feed you," he said sleepily.

"You're probably hungry yourself."

His hand toyed with her bra, then covered her breast, making her shiver as need threaded through her. "I am hungry," he said. "But for more than food."

She turned in his arms, into his kiss, and all thought of food fled.

A long time later, they dressed and went to raid the kitchen for something to eat. Sitting on stools at the counter, they munched on leftover chicken and salad, washing it down with juice. Ravenous, Jess stuffed herself, then sat back to watch Ren, who ate at a more sedate pace. She palmed her chin, knowing she could watch him for hours, no matter what he was doing.

"I want to state it plainly again," Ren said. "I never came here with the intention of nudging this oil thing. I know you know that now, but I want you to understand. William leveraged our resources to purchase an oil company when he'd been instructed to sell it off for the owners, in pieces if necessary. We weren't supposed to be in the oil business at all. He's gone, by the way. Had him clear out his office that night. I've set in motion plans to sell that oil company and the proceeds will go into a foundation to help local Alaskans sort all this out and make the best decision for them, and for this land."

Jess nodded, started to speak, but Ren held up a hand.

"Kathryn."

"Yes," Jess said. "Kathryn."

"I definitely should have told you about her before we ever got on the plane to New York. Yes, she works for the company. Or did. She's gone, effective the same night as William. Yes, she's a friend, or was. But there's never been anything more between us."

"She said your mother wanted you two to be together."

"That might have been true at one time, but Mother is extremely happy with how things have turned out. And Kathryn assumed a relationship that just wasn't there."

"Why not? She's perfect for you." Jess felt a twinge as she said that, but tossed it aside.

Ren shrugged. "On paper, she probably is. But she's not what I want."

"What do you want?"

"I want fire, and fighting, and making up, and a partner who will listen without ulterior motives. I want someone who pushes me to be more than I am, whose passion shines through. Someone with hair the color of midnight splashed with starlight. I want you, Jess Jenkins. For forever."

Jess's eyes widened. Did he mean what she thought he meant? She couldn't catch her breath. Everything was happening so fast.

Ren waited, although his drumming fingers showed his impatience.

"I think I'd like forever, too," she answered. "But can we just work on today, this week, maybe even the rest of winter, then go from there?"

His grin was the widest she'd ever seen. "We can do that."

Her smile joined his.

"At least, until I can convince you about the forever part."

Jess laughed and hugged him. "I love you, City Boy."

He buried his face in her neck. "I love you just as much, beautiful."

The whoops and hollers they heard didn't come from either one of them, but from the menagerie that pushed through the door into the kitchen. Jess's father, Ren's mother, Mary, John, and Rocky were all clapping and hollering congratulations.

And Jess wouldn't have had it any other way. Family was everything, and they had a right to share this moment.

Epilogue

Winter's hush had given way to the early birds of spring. Yes, there was still snow on the ground in the New York country, but the night sky had cleared. After a few months here in the home she and Ren had picked out together, Jess was happy to see a plethora of stars out tonight. It was late. They'd been at a fundraiser for yet another cause of his mother's.

Still unused to a life spent more indoors than out, Jess liked to come out here to the backyard each night before bedtime and look up. She missed seeing the spirits, but they'd been back to Last Chance a couple times to oversea the new manager, Mack's, training. An ex-trucker who'd left the business to stay in Alaska, he was quiet and perfectly suited to camp life. Jess felt good leaving the place in his capable hands. Mary and John would stay on for a couple more years, but no longer. Owen and Amelie had given them a retirement gift of their choosing, and they'd decided on a home of their own in Anchorage.

Jess stared up at the starlit night. They'd thought about staying at Ren's condo in The City tonight, but Jess had wanted to be home. So they'd made the drive, and she was glad they had.

"It's still pretty chilly out," her husband said, wrapping a blanket, and his arms, around her. Jess smiled. She'd managed to hold him off for an entire month on the marriage thing, but he'd worn her down, and they'd had a quick civil ceremony a shy week after she'd finally said yes.

They'd flown everyone in from Alaska, including Rod and Meg, who'd stood up for them as they had stood up for them only a few weeks earlier.

Life had turned in a direction Jess could have never considered possible. She never imagined that she would leave Alaska. Now, she couldn't imagine living anywhere else than here, with Ren. Especially now.

And now, they were about to embark on the next phase of their life together. Jess took a deep breath. "I'm pregnant."

"I know."

"How could you?"

"Honey, don't take this the wrong way, but you eat...a lot. I don't know how you manage to stay so slender. But lately, you've been eating less. And no alcohol at all."

"Why didn't you say something?"

"I was waiting for you to tell me first."

"I didn't know. Well, I suspected, but I didn't know for sure until earlier today, when I did the test."

"You happy?" Ren asked.

"So much I feel ready to burst."

"Me, too."

Jess turned her face to his kiss, filled with gentle excitement for their future. When they parted and looked up, ribbons of green had begun to color the sky.

"I think your mother approves," Ren said, his voice catching as he hugged her to him.

Jess watched the green brighten, then other colors joined them. Reds and whites and oranges. "I think all the spirits approve," she said. "Just as much as I do."

The End

Thank you for reading *Northern Lights*. If you enjoyed this book, please consider leaving a review on Amazon, Goodreads, or wherever you prefer, and know that it would be greatly appreciated.

For new release information and news about Laurie Ryan, please sign up for her newsletter at:
Newsletter Sign-Up

AUTHOR'S NOTE/ACKNOWLEDGEMENTS

QUALITY CONTROL:

We strive to produce error-free books, but even with all the eyes that see the story during the production process, slips get by. So please, if you find a typo or any formatting issues, please let us know at laurieryanauthor@gmail.com so that we may correct it.

Thank you!

A NOTE FROM THE AUTHOR:

On a road trip to Prudhoe Bay, Alaska, via the Dalton Highway, I crossed an item off my personal bucket list. I saw the northern lights. That experience stuck with me to the point that I ended up writing a story around it. As well, the little community where we spent that night found a permanent place in my heart. Anyone who's driven the Haul Road might recognize bits and pieces of this place I've created, but it's not a mirror image. I only spent one night there and so there is a lot of literary license used in my design of the grounds and operations of the fictitious Last Chance Camp.

However, I do encourage anyone who hasn't yet seen the Aurora Borealis to make the trip anywhere there's a chance to see them. They are an amazing sight to view and a wondrous rendition of Mother Nature's beauty.

So I thank the people of Alaska for some of my favorite memories. Because of them, this story became reality for me. I'd also like to thank, well, so many people, for helping this story find its way to publication. First and foremost, to my critique partner, Lavada Dee, for keeping me focused and on the right track. And to my editor, Chantilly White. Both these women are superb authors in their own right and I strongly suggest you check them out at **lavadadee.com** and **chantillywhite.com** .

I'd also like to thank my prolific OlyRWA group. No matter how much I said stop, you all said Go! Go! Go! And I went...all the way to the end of this story.

Lastly, to my readers. I appreciate you more than I can say. I never thought anyone would read my stories, other than the odd relative or two. And now, here I am, with multiple books available and being sold. So thank you, thank you, thank you, for your support.

Laurie Ryan

BOOKLIST

HOLIDAY MAGIC - THE GIFT OF LOVE

A two story, emotion-wrapped Christmas anthology.
Available at Amazon, Barnes and Noble, and Smashwords.
Additional information is available at laurieryanauthor.com

ABOUT THE AUTHOR

Born and raised in the Pacific Northwest, Laurie Ryan writes contemporary romance and women's fiction with enough spice to be fun and endings that satisfy her need to believe this world is a happy place. When not writing, Ms. Ryan does contract editing for publishers, as well as freelance editing work.

A devoted reader, she has immersed herself in the diverse works of authors like Tolkien and Woodiwiss. She is passionate about every aspect of a book: beginning, middle, and end. She can't arrive to a movie five minutes late, has never been able to read the end of a book before the beginning, and is a strong believer in reading the book before seeing the movie.

Stay in touch with the author via her newsletter **or find out more at laurieryanauthor.com**